DELIVER US FROM EVIL

DELIVER US FROM EVIL

DELIVER US FROM EVIL

BOOK III

International Bestselling Author

MONICA JAMES

DELIVER US FROM EVIL

This book is a work of fiction. Names, characters, places and incidents are the product of the author's imagination, or are used fictitiously. Any resemblance to actual events, locales, or persons living or dead, is coincidental. Any trademarks, service marks, product names or named features are assumed to be the property of their respective owners and are used only for reference.

Copyright © 2021 by Monica James

Cover Design: Perfect Pear Creative Covers
Photographer: Michelle Lancaster
Cover Model: Lochie Carey
Editing: Editing 4 Indies
Formatting: E.M. Tippetts Book Designs

Follow me on:
authormonicajames.com

OTHER BOOKS BY
MONICA JAMES

THE I SURRENDER SERIES

I Surrender

Surrender to Me

Surrendered

White

SOMETHING LIKE NORMAL SERIES

Something like Normal

Something like Redemption

Something like Love

A HARD LOVE ROMANCE

Dirty Dix

Wicked Dix

The Hunt

MEMORIES FROM YESTERDAY DUET

Forgetting You, Forgetting Me

Forgetting You, Remembering Me

SINS OF THE HEART DUET

Absinthe of the Heart

Defiance of the Heart

ALL THE PRETTY THINGS TRILOGY

Bad Saint

Fallen Saint

Forever My Saint

The Devil's Crown-Part One (Spin-Off)

The Devil's Crown-Part Two (Spin-Off)

THE MONSTERS WITHIN DUET

Bullseye

Blowback

DELIVER US FROM EVIL TRILOGY

Thy Kingdom Come

Into Temptation

Deliver Us From Evil

STANDALONE

Mr. Write

Chase the Butterflies

Beyond the Roses

AUTHOR'S NOTE

CONTENT WARNING: Although I've consulted with many locals, please be mindful, this is a work of fiction. Places, events, and incidents are either the product of my imagination or used in a fictitious manner.

DELIVER US FROM EVIL is a DARK ROMANCE. It contains mature themes that might make some readers uncomfortable.

Godspeed…

ONE

PUNKY

"**I**'m sorry. I don't have it. But I can pay ye—"

Punch to the jaw.

Kick to the ribs.

Nothing hurts anymore. My mind, as well as my body, is numb to the pain.

This is how I felt ten years ago. However, this is so much worse. Back then, I had hope, but now, I have none. Hope was lost a week ago when Babydoll was taken from me and I killed my best friend in cold blood.

"Puck, I fucked up, so I did. I'm s-sorry. Please don't kill me."

Those were Rory's last words—begging for his life.

But it didn't make a difference. He'd made his choice as I did mine, and now, I must live with those choices.

It's because I once cared that I'm here, beating up a kid because he's hooked on the shite the Kellys sold him. He curls himself into a ball, begging for mercy, but I don't have any. I am dead inside.

Dropping to one knee, I yank him up by the collar of his shirt, pressing us nose to nose. "I'm not interested in yer excuses. You have twenty-four hours to get the money you owe. If not, I will kill yer family and make ya watch."

"O-okay," he whimpers, tears streaming down his face.

I toss him onto the ground and turn away. Bystanders watch on, too afraid to intervene because word on the street is that Puck Kelly is back; and he is out for blood.

Jumping into my truck, I calmly light a cigarette and drive away from the mess I made. It's just one of many. That's the consequence of being Sean Kelly's errand boy.

Clenching the steering wheel, I think how a week can change the course of everything. When I entered Connor's old factory, I thought I had things sorted. The plan was far from perfect, but I thought if anyone would suffer the consequences, it would be me—I suppose in more ways than one, I have.

I've lost my friends—one I murdered; the others see me as nothing but a monster. I've pushed my family aside in fear of them getting hurt. And I let down the only person who ever believed in me. Babydoll trusted me, and in return, she paid with her freedom.

I don't know where she is. I don't even know if she's alive.

All I know is that my father, Sean Kelly, has the answer, which is why I'm forced to live this way—his prisoner. Until I get those answers, I'm at his mercy, which is why I refuse to show any.

A week ago, I surrendered, something I promised to never do. But never before have I been placed into a position where my hands are tied. There is no compromise. No way out of this because I will do anything to protect Babydoll—even if that means selling my soul to the monster I call father.

I can't sleep.

I can't eat.

I feel so hollow inside.

Prison was nothing compared to the imprisonment I feel because being without Babydoll is a life sentence.

I can't even begin to think about what's been done to her. My hope is Sean is holding her ransom, knowing I will do anything to keep her safe, knowing I will happily sacrifice my life for hers. But I don't know anything anymore.

Blind faith is what led me here, and it's what leads me now as I drive to Sean's house. I was right. He's been in Belfast this entire time, watching and waiting like the predator he is.

He was waiting for the perfect opportunity to strike; and that time was when I was released from prison. He set the trap, and I played straight into his hands.

I thought I outsmarted him—but I did everything to benefit him. I killed Brody. I weeded out the traitors. I did everything thinking it would benefit me, but in the end, all it did was make his empire stronger.

Our associates believe the Kellys are back—that Sean and I are working together. They don't know he holds a loaded gun to my head.

When his modest home comes into view, I swallow down my disgust. I expected he lived somewhere fancy. But that would draw too much attention to him. He wanted to blend in. No one would suspect a vile monster living next door to them in this neighborhood.

The bright red roses he has growing in his front garden have me inhaling sharply. It's like he planted them as a fuck you to me. Peering down at the rose tattoo on the back of my hand, I'm hit with so many emotions that leave me nostalgic for something that'll never be again.

My ma is gone. And her rose brooch, the one I gave to Babydoll, that too is now gone. Everyone I've ever loved has been taken away, thanks to the bastard who stands on his front lawn, watering the roses like he doesn't have a care in the world.

I park my truck and exit, clenching my fists when I see Sean. He smiles.

"Bout ye, son? Are ye hungry? I've left ya some tea."

It takes all my willpower not to wrap the hose around his fucking neck and choke the life from him. But I can't. Until I know where Babydoll is, I'm his fucking dog.

"Don't call me son," I firmly reply, walking past him into his gaff. "And I don't want any fucking dinner."

When I smell the unmistakable fragrance of a beef stew, I shrug out of my jacket, unbelieving he was actually serious about tea. I shouldn't be, however. This is all a big game to him. As he sees it, this is his time for payback. I fucked up his plans, and now he intends on returning the favor by fucking up my life.

I reach for the bottle of whiskey and pour myself a large glass. But it'll never be enough to fill this void.

When Sean enters and sees me drinking, he shakes his head. "I'm worried 'bout yer drinkin'."

Throwing back the contents, I pour myself another glass. "We're not doin' this," I state, shaking my head, incredulous.

"Doin' what?" He has the gall to ask.

"Doin' this concerned father act. In case y've forgotten, I'm here 'cause I have no other choice."

"No one is holdin' ya prisoner," he counters, washing his hands in the sink. "Ya can leave any time ya want."

Gripping the glass in my hand, I measure my breaths before I impale it into his jugular. "I do that and what happens to Cami? Where is she? What have ya done with her?"

Sean continues lathering his hands with soap, ignoring me.

"I've done what ya wanted. I promised my loyalty to ya. What else do ya want me to fucking do?" I exclaim, my temper intensifying.

Sean calmly turns off the taps and dries his hands on a tea towel. It's a floral pattern, for fuck's sake. This would be laughable if not for the fact he is holding the woman I love prisoner. Or, so I hope.

"Yer word means nothin' to me, cub. Ya proved that when ya tried to double-cross me. But in time, if you prove yer loyalty, y'll get what ya want."

What I want is his head.

"I've done ya a favor. In time, y'll see Rory—"

Slamming my glass onto the kitchen counter, I shatter it in my hand. "Don'tcha ever speak his name. Don't ever," I warn dangerously low.

The hot sensation and the *drip…drip…drip* onto the counter confirms I've cut my hand, but the blood is a reminder I'm still alive.

"He was a traitor, Puck," he says, not knowing when to shut his mouth. "He was the one who betrayed ye. He was given a choice. I never forced his hand. Just how no one forced yours when ya shot him right between the eyes."

"Please don't kill me."

Rory's words haunt me every single day. When I try to sleep, those words rob me of any comfort because I don't deserve any. I killed my best friend in cold blood. He was unarmed, and I fucking shot him like a dog.

I am a fucking murderer. Aye, I've killed before, but Rory's death is the only one for which I have any remorse.

"Y'll see I'm not the enemy here," he says, which has a crazed laugh leaving me.

"That's all I fucking see," I reply, reaching for the tea towel and wrapping it around my hand. "What the fuck is wrong with ya? We are not friends. We are enemies. And I would happily use yer wee spatula over there to carve out yer tongue."

I understand he wants to appear like every Joe Bloggs, but his kitchen looks like something out of an Ulster Tatler Interiors magazine. It sickens me.

His mouth twitches. He finds this fucking hilarious. "I understand yer mad. But we wouldn't be here if ya didn't try to kill me every chance ya got."

"You killed my ma," I snarl, eyeing him fiercely. "And Connor. Ya wanted to steal my legacy. I spent ten years in prison because of ye. Ya got Ethan hooked on drugs. Ya beat up Hannah. Ya kidnapped Eva and Ethan. And y've got my fucking girl.

"Of course, I want to kill ya. Are ye fucking thick?"

Sean nods, accepting my slurs because he can't deny them. "In time—"

"Say in time once more, I fucking dare ya," I interrupt, jaw clenched.

"In time, ye will—"

However, he doesn't get a chance to finish his sentence because I elbow him in the face swiftly. His nose cracks, and the noise, it sings to my debauchery, and I can't stop. Reaching for a silver corkscrew on the bench, I don't think twice before I jam it into his thigh.

Just as I reach for a pair of scissors, Sean laughs sharply. "She'll pay for yer temper, Punky. I promise ya that."

Does this mean she *is* alive?

All it would take is imbedding these scissors into the side of this throat. Like a warm knife slicing through butter, they would enter easily, and I could end this all. But as we stand in his kitchen in the ultimate standoff, I know he's not bluffing.

I kill him, and I will never find Babydoll.

With a pained breath, I drop the scissors by my feet, defeated—in every sense of the word.

Sean rips out the corkscrew, tossing it into the sink. He'll live, sadly. "I want ya to do somethin' for me," he says, and I know this isn't optional. "Seein' as yer so eager to kill someone. I want ya to kill Liam Doyle."

I knew it would always come to this.

Sean doesn't need him anymore. He got what he wanted from him, and as usual, he's sending someone to do his dirty work. But this work I do not mind.

"I was plannin' on doin' that anyway."

"Grand." He leans against the counter as his beige pant leg begins to stain red. "But not before the wee party he's throwin.'"

"What party?"

"With Brody dead, he is desperately tryin' to get as many men on his side. Powerful men. I want those men on our team. It's a VIP event, but I'll make the arrangements to get ya in."

"This didn't work for either Brody or you last time, aul' lad,"

I remind him. "This is why we're here."

Sean smirks, once again proving he's thought this through. "Last time, I didn't have my son on my team. What ya did to Brody…it's made ye a celebrity. Yer public execution of Ireland and Northern Ireland's bossman has made you notorious.

"No one will want to fuck with us. They're afraid of us, and we will use that fear to our advantage."

If I could take it back, I would.

Killing Brody was supposed to be a calling to Sean, and it was. But it also called to the hundreds of other psychopaths Ireland and Northern Ireland have bred.

"I do this, and I want to see Cami," I demand, tired of his games.

Sean mulls over my order but shakes his head. "I can't trust ye, Puck. I'm sorry, lad. The fact I have a hole in my leg 'cause ya stabbed me proves this."

My anger is so close to boiling point, it's getting harder and harder to control. "How do I know she's even alive?"

"I give ya my word that she is," he affirms, which is the first time he's done so.

"Yer word means nothin' to me," I spit. "I want to see her. I promised I would do what ya wanted. Just let her go. I have nothin' left. What can I offer her? Ye don't need her anymore."

Sean mulls over my comment, watching for any signs of deceit. "Kill Liam, and I'll give ye what ya want."

This time, I'm the one who looks at him with watchful eyes.

"Y'll let her go?"

Sean tongues his cheek as he has chosen his words wisely for a reason. "Do what I ask, and I'll deliver. I promise ya that."

The way he is avoiding the question makes me nervous. I need to anticipate everything when it comes to Sean, and I wish I could believe he would deliver her alive, but I can't. He's given me nothing to tip the scales either way.

"All right. I'll do what ya want. But if any harm comes to Cami, all bets are off. I will destroy ye. I will find who or what ya love most in this world and make them pay for yer sins."

He smirks, the sight a diabolical display. "Ya can try, Puck, but I have no ties. I've lived a lonely existence for a reason… that's why I'm stronger than ye. The only person I care for is you…so if yer going to destroy anyone, it's going to be yerself."

I always wondered why Sean never got married. Or even had a girlfriend for that fact. Now I know why. He knew emotions are the downfall of any leader. He has been plotting this for years.

"I'm already defeated, *Father*," I state, leveling him. "Ya made sure of that when ya destroyed everything, everyone I've ever loved."

"One day, when ya want to listen, I'll tell ya about yer past. It's what y've fought so hard for, is it not? Ya wanted to know who yer ma was and how she could love a monster like me. By telling ya this, Puck, it'll help ye understand who *ye* are."

I don't bother replying because he's baiting me.

Turning my back, I take the whiskey bottle with me as I walk out the door. Once in my truck, I commence the drive home on autopilot. I am so lost right now, I don't think I'll ever be found. In the past, I would have spoken to Rory and Cian, who would have helped me see reason.

But I'm truly alone in this.

The castle stands unfinished; a visualization of what could be. As I ascend the drive and park in front of my gaff, I notice the kitchen light is on.

Someone is in my home.

Reaching for my gun from the console, I exit the truck with caution. I doubt an enemy would announce their presence, but stranger things have happened, like Rory betraying me right in this very spot. I open the front door, which is unlocked, and with my gun raised, I enter.

Who I see has me lowering my gun with a sigh. "What are ya doing here?"

Hannah stands from the couch, wringing her hands in front of her. "If I'd called, would ya have let me in?"

She has a point.

Closing the door, I ignore her and walk into the kitchen. Empty whiskey bottles are scattered on the counter, and I finished the one I snared from Sean's on the drive here, so I open the freezer and retrieve a bottle of vodka.

"You shouldn't be here. Go home."

The bluntness to my tone has Hannah flinching, but she

doesn't back down. "Please don't shut me out, Punky. We're all hurtin' too. It was Rory's funeral today."

Her admission has me opening the vodka bottle and drawing it to my lips.

"It was a lovely service. Lots of people paid their respects."

"Closed casket, I presume?" I say, savoring the burn of the vodka as it hits my empty stomach.

Cian is the only one who knows what really happened to Rory. Sean wasn't lying when he said the peelers are on his side. Constable Shane Moore is just as crooked as his father was. He was the one who labeled Rory's death as a robbery gone wrong.

The reporters bought it because of the ransacked state of Rory's flat.

But those closest to Rory know the truth. As do those who are, or *were*, closest to me. They know I murdered my best friend in cold blood.

"Don't be like that," Hannah scolds, horrified I would be making jokes. "Yer best mate is dead. Y've got to be feelin' somethin.'"

"The only thing I'm feelin' is annoyed that yer here, Hannah. Don't ya have friends ye can annoy?"

"Puck," she gasps, taking a step back. "Why are ye being so mean?"

"If ya don't like it here, then ye can always leave," I say, wiping the spilled vodka from my lips with the back of my hand. "I'd prefer it."

"I don't know what's wrong, but I know this is not you. What happened to Cami? We have a right to know."

No one knows that Rory was the one who betrayed us. All they know is that he took Babydoll away, saying he was coming to meet me, but neither returned.

No one questioned him, and why would they? They trusted him. We all did.

"Eva wants to know what happened to her sister," Hannah says, never giving up. Her tenacity is what set me free. I wish she'd left me to rot. "Stop treatin' us like wee kids!"

"Ya are wee kids," I correct, angered they got involved in the first place. "Go home, Hannah. I want to be alone."

She stands her ground. "That's all y'll be Puck if ya continue pushin' us away. Yer being a martyr, and I know that's because ye think we're in danger. I'll call on ye tomorrow."

There's no point arguing because Hannah is as stubborn as me.

The moment she leaves, I brace the bench and inhale sharply. Hannah won't give up, which is why I reach into my pocket for my mobile. I dial Fiona.

"What do you want?"

"I want ya to keep yer daughter away from me," I state bluntly. The sharp intake of breath hints I've caught Fiona off guard. "She isn't welcome here anymore."

"All right then. I'll let her know," Fiona finally says when she can find her voice.

"Cheers, thanks for that." I hang up, not interested in small talk.

It's a long shot, but I have to try something. I won't be responsible for yet another person being hurt. So many people have been brought into this mess, trusting that I knew what the fuck I was doing. But I didn't. I still don't.

My mobile chimes, and when I see a text message from Ron Brady, I sigh.

Ron proved to be a loyal ally. He, Logan, and Ronan did. But I have nothing to offer them. They were fighting for a new Belfast, but I don't even know what that is anymore. I'm not the leader for them.

I don't read the message. Instead, I decide to shower and attempt to sleep.

The moment I walk into my bedroom, I'm hit with a flood of memories. This place was a home because of the people inside it. But alone, it's just an empty shell of what it once was.

With Cami in my bed, I believed I was capable of anything. She was my reason to go on. Without her, the fight in me is slowly dying. I know those looking on want me to fight, but I've been fighting my entire life.

I am so fucking tired.

There is only so much a man can take before he reaches his breaking point. And this is what Sean wanted.

He's pushed me time and time again, building me up and giving me hope, only to tear me back down. He knew taking Cami would be my tipping point, and by using Rory to implement his plan…I'm broken.

Turning the taps on in the shower, I strip off and step under the spray, not bothering to adjust the temperature. Bracing my hands to the tiles, I bow my head, hoping the scorching water will wash away my sins.

It doesn't, and I know that's because the worst is yet to come.

TWO

PUNKY

Thanks to yet another sleepless night, I'm drinking my third coffee, and it's not even eight o'clock. This is my life now, however.

I simply function on autopilot.

The knock on the door puts me on edge because lately, I don't know who to expect on my doorstep. With a gun concealed in the small of my back, I open the door, but I won't need it because it's Darcy.

She smiles, but it's strained because, just like everyone else, she too is in the dark about what happened that night, the night she was here and oblivious to Rory's plans.

"Morning, Puck," she says. "I'm sorry to just pop round without calling first, but I have the new will for ye to sign."

Opening the door wider, I step aside, granting her permission to enter.

She enters, casually looking around my gaff, which is a shambles, but doesn't comment on its boggin' state. She places her leather briefcase on the kitchen bench and opens it, retrieving a document.

"I just need ye to sign here," she instructs, her hands shaking as she places the paperwork in front of me.

I hate that she's frightened of me, but I'm the one who's shut everyone out. No one knows what to expect anymore.

"I changed everything, as per yer instructions. By signing this, yer giving everything to Sean." She looks at me, ensuring this is what I really want. There is no turning back once I sign on the dotted line.

This was another one of Sean's power play moves. Everything Connor left me, he wants. The money, the castle, the factory—all of it. He wants to ensure I know he owns me. But I can never forget.

Taking the pen from her, I'm about to sign without delay, because I'll happily give Sean my possessions if it brings me one step closer to finding Babydoll, but Darcy slams her hand over the page.

"Puck, don't do this," she pleads, surprising me. "There's got to be another way. I don't know what he's done, but please don't sign this."

"Are ye speaking as my lawyer or as my friend?"

"I'm yer friend first and foremost," she says. "Let me help ya. My father can—"

But I shake my head. "Enough people have stuck their necks out for me, Darcy. I won't allow it. This is what I want."

"I doubt that," she argues stubbornly. "Yer always lookin' after others. What about you? It's one of the many things I like about ye, Puck Kelly. Yer noble, even if ya don't believe it."

I appreciate her words, but nobility has fucked me royally. I won't make the same mistake again.

Removing her hand, she watches with tears in her eyes as I sign my life away. "Thank you, Darcy. I'll talk to ye soon."

It's a not-so-subtle hint that I'm not interested in speaking about this further.

She sighs, realizing I'm a lost cause.

After gathering all the paperwork, she files it into her briefcase. I walk to the door and open it. With nothing left to say, she leaves and doesn't turn back.

Closing the door, I lean my forehead against it, utter fatigue rocking me. I don't know what to do anymore. I have no direction.

My mobile rings, a loud shrill which alerts me that I'm being summoned. I answer without looking who the caller is.

"Mornin', son. I need ye to come down to the factory. I'm callin' a meeting."

Gritting my teeth at his continuous use of the word son, I reply, "Why?"

"'Cause it's time everyone knew of our plans."

"And what plans are those?"

"I want the men to see we're unified. That we're a team now."

With a scoff, I say, "I don't think they're expectin' a public family reunion." But I know this isn't optional.

For this to work, Sean needs everyone on our side. The split between the Doyles and the Kellys took a toll on the men. They don't know who to trust. Sean wants them to believe he and I are in an equal partnership to ensure another uprising doesn't occur.

This means the men who remain loyal to the Doyles are a threat. Now I understand why killing Liam is so important to Sean. He wants all competition eliminated and done with haste.

"All right then. I'll be there."

"Grand. I need ye to do something for me first."

Of course, he does.

"I will text ya the address." And he hangs up.

When a text comes through a second later with an address in a shady neighborhood, I know I'll be expected to spill blood. Gathering my supplies, I peer at the face paints on my coffee table. I remember how brutal Babydoll looked, wearing a face that matched mine.

I've always found solace in the painted mask I wear. It's been a part of me since I was five years old. I always felt split right down the middle, like it was just as much a part of me as my natural face. But I don't see it that way any longer.

That mask and the horror it reflects is who I now am. I've never felt more connected to it than I do now, and I know that's because sooner or later, that face will replace my own—I will be the monster that mask represents.

Once I have everything I need, I lock my door and get into my truck. This once belonged to Cian. He offered it to me without thought because that's what best friends do. And I thanked him by killing our best friend.

Starting the engine, I reach into the console for a cigarette. I wasn't much for smoking, but now, it's the only thing that calms me down. I don't need the GPS and commence my drive to the derelict neighborhood Sean wants me to visit.

I can't help but feel like every day is Groundhog Day. I've lived this life before. Being the muscle for Connor, and then for myself when I thought I could beat Sean. I believed it would be different the second time around.

I was wrong.

Peering at the vacant gaff ahead, I sigh as I kill the engine. Literally anything awaits me.

Grabbing my things, I throw on my hood and lower my chin. The last thing I need is eyewitnesses. The house has been abandoned long ago if the dated graffiti is anything to go by. The door is unlocked. The moment I step inside, the smell of piss and stale cigarettes hit me.

I don't draw a weapon. I carefully search each room, but the gaff is small, and when I reach the last bedroom at the end of the hallway, I brace myself for who's inside. Opening the door slowly, I gasp when I see who the person tied to a chair in the middle of the boggin' room is.

I haven't braced for shite.

"Orla?"

Beneath that shaggy brown hair, I know it's her.

I'm transported back in time, when I was in her home and using her for my own personal gain. She had no idea I was there because Connor sent me. She has no idea I know what happened to her dad.

I haven't thought about Orla or her father, Nolen Ryan, who Sean murdered in fear of him telling me the truth in a long time. At the time, I thought Sean was looking out for me, but I know now Sean only looks out for one person, and that's himself.

Her chin is drooped, but when she hears my voice, she slowly meets my eyes. "Puck?" she asks, as if she's seen a ghost.

In some ways, she has, as we are clearly not the same people we were all those years ago.

Orla is thin, sickly thin, and that's 'cause she's hooked on whatever shite she's put into her body. If Sean has her here, it's because she hasn't paid up. She has a debt to pay. But these kinds of situations are reserved for those who have been given more than one chance.

Orla is on her last leg.

"Are ye here to help me?"

When I lower my eyes, she nods, biting her cracked lips.

"Please don't kill me. I promise. I'm good for it. I just need m-more time."

This would be the time I roll up my sleeves and reach for my brass knuckles. But as I look at Orla, a shell of the person I once knew, I know that I cannot.

"How'd ye get messed up in this shite, Orla?" I question, remembering the good girl she once was.

She snivels, her bony body shuddering. "My da left us. Without a word. My ma thought he found another woman, but I knew he wouldn't do that. He would have never left without a goodbye."

My heart clenches in my chest because she's right.

"I just wanted to numb the p-pain," she sobs, pleading I believe her. "But I didn't know when to stop. I promised myself just one more time. It's been that way for ten years. Please… help me, Puck. Please don't kill me."

"Please don't kill me."

Rory's plea echoes loudly, and I shake my head, hoping to expel these voices for good. But it seems to be a common occurrence—people pleading for their lives when I'm involved.

"I'm not gonna kill ye, Orla."

"Yer not?" she sniffs, eyes wide.

"Naw." Hunting through my bag, I retrieve my knife.

Orla's relief soon turns to panic as she doesn't know if I'm telling her the truth or not. Walking around her, I gently cut through the cable ties that bind her hands. The moment it snaps free, she sighs in relief.

She shakes out her arms as she was bound tight. Her feet are untied, but she remains seated.

"How much do you owe Sean?"

She sucks her bottom lip. "Two thousand."

"Orla," I scold, shaking my head. "Catch yerself on!"

No wonder he sent me here.

"I don't have it, but I can get it to ya next week."

I know what that means—she'll likely whore herself out. I don't want that.

"Ach, don'tcha be concernin' yerself with that. I'll sort it."

"Thank you, Punky. Ye were always a good man."

She wouldn't think that if she knew what I did to her father.

She stands, but I grip her bony arm—hard. "This is yer only warning, Orla. I don't give second chances. Understood?"

Her head bobbles as she nods jerkily.

"Get off that shite. It'll kill ya."

It pains me to see that it already has.

Orla is just a walking zombie with her emaciated face covered in scabs and sunken eyes which lost their spark long ago. All she cares about is her next fix.

There are different types of addicts—functioning addicts you'd never guess were hooked, and addicts like Orla, who society discarded long ago. These people exist because of Sean. He doesn't care who he sells to, or how often. They are just walking pound signs to him.

"I'm gonna check on ye, and so help me God, if y've gone back on yer word, I promise ya, A'll do what I came here for."

My threat isn't empty, and Orla knows it.

Digging into my pocket for my wallet, I pull out a wad of twenties. Orla eyes the money like a hungry wolf.

"This is to get ye home. Not to waste on smack."

She nods and snatches the money from my hand.

In case she's in doubt, I warn, "I'll know if yer lyin' 'cause who do ya think yer buyin' the gear off? The Kellys. Don'tcha be forgettin' it."

"Ye wouldn't hurt me, Punky," she says, and her confidence reveals she doesn't know me at all.

I lunge forward, and a cry leaves her when I twist her arm behind her back. "Don't mistake me for the hero, Orla," I warn, leveling her with a scowl. "'Cause I'm not. Fuck with me, and I swear, y'll be just as dead as yer da."

Her eyes widen when she realizes what I mean by that comment. I won't elaborate, but she can guess.

I let her go, shoving her away. "Away now, before I change my mind."

She doesn't need to be told twice and runs from the room, not turning back. I can only hope my warning wasn't in vain, because I meant what I said—if I see her again, I'll kill her. That's why I needed to be harsh.

The money she owes, I'll pay it. If I come up empty-handed,

Sean will know I let her go.

Grabbing my bag, I peer around at the boggin' surroundings, wondering how many of these shitholes Sean uses. Darcy gave me a list of houses such as this. I could always check them out. I don't want to think Babydoll calls a place such as this home, but she's got to be somewhere.

My heart sinks at the thought.

Walking to my truck, I jump in and drive to the factory. This pretense of playing happy families is an insult to anyone with half a brain. But Sean needs this public display to fortify his position and to warn off any potential rivals.

I'm not sure who's left. I've killed them all. Liam isn't a worthy opponent because if he steps foot into Northern Ireland, I'm going to kill him. I'm going to kill him regardless, and broadcast it for all to see—just like I did with his dad, Brody.

It's the one thing that makes me feel anything.

When I arrive at the factory and see the number of cars parked, I shake my head in disgust. These men are the reason Sean thrives. If he had no one supporting him, things would be so much easier. I could overthrow him, just as I'd planned on doing. And just how he knew I would, which is why he has Babydoll.

Parking the truck, I make my way toward the factory, comparing it to better times when Connor was alive. I didn't know it then, but that time in my life was one which I actually now miss. I miss Connor. If he were alive, he'd know what to do.

Me, however? I am so fucking lost.

When I enter the factory and see the faces of men willing to sacrifice everything for me, I am hit with guilt and shame. I failed them. I promised them change, but instead, I've condemned them to a life serving the devil.

Ronan Murray is here with men who sacrificed their lives for me. They look at me with hope in their eyes, like I'm the magical potion that will better all our lives. But I'm not. I feel guilty for dragging them into my personal vendetta, only to end up here.

Ronan pulled through in the end, and as I see it, he owes me nothing. His debt is paid. He tried to save Northern Ireland. We all did.

Ron Brady and his men aren't here, which is no surprise. They'd rather die than help Sean succeed. We were almost there. Victory was within reach, but the plot twist came out of nowhere and proved what a cruel, fucked-up bitch life really is.

Sean stands with men I know; Logan Doherty, Flynn, and Grady—they were all Brody's men. But now, it seems, they're Sean's.

Flynn and Grady were the arseholes who thought they could intimidate me, and in return, I broke one's nose and the other, I almost choked to death with my bare hands. I can't help but snicker when I see them.

"I almost didn't recognize ye…standin' on yer feet," I taunt the brown-haired cunt who I forced to crawl on his knees. "Did ya crawl here?"

When he advances, Sean grips his arm. "Flynn, enough. I'm sure yer not keen for another beatin.'"

He almost sounds proud of the fact.

Flynn settles down—for now.

Grady, the ballbag whose nose I broke, offers me his hand. I peer down at it, making clear I'm not here to make friends. He retreats quickly.

"I wanted to apologize for bein' disrespectful to ye when we first met. I didn't know who ye were."

"That's a grand yarn, but why the fuck are ye tellin' me this?"

He recoils, as he clearly believed waving the white flag would make everything okay. All it's done is make me think he's nothing but a lickarse.

He doesn't reply.

Logan Doherty, like Ronan, came to my aid when I needed them the most. The ironic thing was that I put my entire trust in Rory, not them, when in fact, they were the men who I should have trusted. They pledged their loyalty because of Connor and because I am his son—blood or not, that's who I am.

Now, however, they wonder what went wrong. Why am I working with the man who I fought so hard against? I wish I could tell them, but I refuse to jeopardize any more lives.

There are other faces I recognize, but there are some I don't. There are more men than I anticipated, meaning Sean's army grows.

"Did ya get it sorted?" he asks me discreetly as I stand beside him.

I nod in response, hoping Orla is a long way from here.

He smirks before clearing his throat. The room falls quiet. "This sight," he starts proudly. "This is one I've been dreamin' of for years. My men are here, in their rightful place, standin' before the Kellys."

This wee inspirational speech is already testing my patience.

"I know there have been rumors, but I called ye here today to put them to rest. Puck stands *with* me. Not against me, as most of ya have heard. But ye can see with yer own eyes that there is no feud between us. He is here, where he should be… where a son should be."

This comes as a surprise to most as they believed that Connor was my father.

"Puck is my son, not Connor's. I've wanted to tell you for so many years, but I couldn't do that to Connor. I wouldn't embarrass him in front of his men."

I clench my jaw because this load of shite is about to make me sick.

"I know I've let a lot of youse down," he says calmly. "And I'm sorry for that. But I'm here to make amends. I'm here to make Northern Ireland what she once was. I couldn't do that before because some of ye lost yer way. Ye forgot where yer loyalties laid.

"But I'm not here to dwell on the past. I want to look to the future, our future where the Kellys rule once more. Some of ye here used to work for Brody Doyle, and that's all right. I make no judgements."

That's rich, as he too used to be in cahoots with Brody, and everyone knows it. But no one dares speak it in fear of their life.

"But Puck made the choice easy for you when he ripped that arsehole's head from his shoulder. All that's left standing is Liam Doyle—a soft pussy who lives in his father's shadow. Unlike Puck, who is his own man.

"He's eradicated most of the Doyle bloodline. He is lethal, and with him on our side, we cannot lose."

The men look at me with nothing but pride. I wish they didn't as I'd happily kill every single one of them if it meant Babydoll's return.

"So, I ask ya here, now, do ya pledge yer loyalty to me, to the Kellys? Are ya ready to be the kings of Belfast once more?"

A holler echoes amongst the men as they beat their fists against their chests, voicing their allegiance. Ronan and Logan, however, don't seem as enthused as the others. They merely lock eyes with me, begging I don't do this.

Begging I take down Sean, just how I promised I would.

But I can't.

All I can do is mimic the barbaric actions of the men, showing support for my father and hope that one day, my betrayal will be rewarded.

Logan curls his lip and turns around to leave, unable to

watch as I bow down to the man who destroyed my life. I don't blame him—if I had a choice, I would leave too.

Sean stands tall, relishing in the glory because this is what he always wanted but was never able to achieve. He's lied, cheated, and killed to be here, and he'll remain here because of me.

Once the applause ends, Sean turns his attention to me. "All I ask for is yer loyalty, and I will ensure y'll be rewarded. But double-cross me, lie to me, and ye will be punished…that goes for ye all."

It suddenly feels like he's speaking directly to me, and when there is a scuffle to my left, I realize that's because he is.

It seems Flynn and Grady have slipped into their lickarse roles with ease as they drag Orla into the room. She is skin and bone. There is no need for both of them to handle her, but it seems they're happy to jump to command like the good little dogs they are.

They hold onto Orla, who peers around the room with fear in her eyes.

"This woman stole from us," Sean says, ensuring he uses the word "us" so it'll make what he's about to do easier for the men to stomach. "When someone doesn't pay for the gear they use, they are stealing from me, from you, from yer families."

"Fuckin' slut," one of the men slurs under his breath.

"We can't let this go unpunished. What will it say for us if we did? How can we rule this kingdom if we show weakness?"

"Kill her!" another man shouts.

This is what Sean wanted. To rile these men up, to have them bond over bloodshed as it's something which will tie them together forevermore.

Sean returns his attention to me. "We can't show weakness. That's why we're here," he says, no longer talking about Orla.

This is my lesson for disobeying him. This was his test; one I failed.

He doesn't trust me, as he shouldn't. But now I realize what letting Orla go has done. Babydoll will pay the price for my clemency.

"Showin' mercy is nothin' but weakness, and I can't have cowardly men on my side. Show them what happens to weakness, son."

He reaches into the small of his back, producing a gun. I eye it viciously, as I do him. But I accept.

Orla whimpers. "Punky, please n-no. I did what ya asked, but they st-stopped me."

My chest rises and falls dangerously slow because she never stood a chance. He was always watching, as Orla was the test to see what I would do. She was always going to be made an example of.

"I know," I assure her as this isn't her fault. It's mine. "On yer knees."

She blinks once, unsure if she heard me correctly, but when I press the gun to the middle of her forehead, she realizes that she did. "Please, don't ki-kill me. I don't wa-want to d-die."

Flynn and Grady help her to her knees, their smirks revealing what sick fucks they are. I'm saddened I didn't end their lives when I had the chance.

"How should she be made an example of?" Sean asks the men, who eye Orla in a new fashion. "Should we kill her? 'Cause that's what she deserves."

Orla interlaces her hands and begins to pray—just as her father did when in a similar situation. It makes me sick that history is repeating itself. I don't know how much more I can take.

"Or maybe she can pay her debt another way?"

All I see are hungry wolves, licking their lips at the prospect of Orla being their whore. She will be shared around, abused and humiliated in ways that no person should ever endure. And once they are done with her, she'll be killed—and killed slowly.

I know what I have to do.

"Lead us not into temptation…" she prays softly, eyes closed, begging for salvation.

But she won't find any here.

"But deliver us from evil," I whisper under my breath, and just as Orla peers up at me with hope, I pull the trigger. She leaves this earth with my face being the last thing she sees.

Forgive me.

The loud bang shatters the bloodlust.

"Should I leave her head on her father's doorstep?" I goad

Sean, slamming the gun into his chest. I don't want it. "Oh, that's right. Her dad's dead."

Sean reads my sarcasm and doesn't push as he knows I'm close to my boiling point. I did what he wanted, so I push past the men and leave before I kill them all.

Once in my truck, I speed away, wishing I could escape this emptiness inside me, but it's only growing. I know sooner or later, it'll eat me whole.

The faces of the men and women I've killed flash before me, and I know they'll haunt me for the rest of my days.

Turning down a winding backroad that is scarcely used, I push down on the accelerator, close my eyes, and surrender. I don't want to be the callous man Sean wants me to be. But what choice do I have? Things would be so much easier if I just… stopped breathing. I can't save Babydoll.

For the first time in my life…I give up.

"I'm sorry, Ma. I failed ye. I failed youse all."

Taking my hands off the steering wheel, I know once I veer from the gravel road I will either hit a tree or fall down the steep embankment. Either possibility I'm fine with.

I lose myself in Babydoll. Her smile, her laughter, the way a simple thing as her trademark scent could chase the monsters away. She is the last memory I want to have when I leave this world.

A tiny voice screams at me, demanding I don't give up. My mum never surrendered; she fought with the last breath she took. As did Babydoll; she fought for me when I didn't want her to. She never gave up. If I do this, then this is me, giving up on her.

"I love you too. I always have. Come back to me. Promise me?"

I made a promise, and I intend to keep it because I am Puck fucking Kelly, and I don't give up.

Opening my eyes, I frantically turn the wheel, but it's too late as I've careened off the road and am headed straight for a tree. I don't bother braking. Instead, I swerve and hope for the best. The airbag implodes the moment the bonnet connects with the trunk of the tree.

The engine dies with a splutter as I pat myself down, ensuring all my parts are still intact. I'm fine, just a gash to the forehead and some whiplash to the neck. The truck, however, is not.

Opening the door, I climb from the truck and exhale loudly when I see the damage. Swerving may have saved my life, but it didn't save Cian's truck. It's a write-off.

"Fuck!" I scream into the skies, threading my hands through my hair. "Fuck!"

Birds take flight, terrified of the madman screaming down their home.

With my heart racing, I do feel slightly better. I don't know if it was destroying something, or straddling the line of life and death which has woken me the fuck up because I clearly want to live. I'm no quitter. I never have been. I'm appalled at myself for even contemplating giving up.

I've been a miserable bastard, feeling nothing but sorry for myself, but that stops now.

Dialing a tow truck, I give them the address of where I am, but don't stick around because I don't want to be here in case the peelers arrive. I tell the driver to send me the bill and I'll take care of it tomorrow. He doesn't argue when I tell him my name.

Grabbing my things, I hobble up the embankment and commence my journey home. Up until now, I didn't realize how much I wanted to live, but I realize…I want to live for her. I'm going to find her, and when I do, I'll burn Sean's kingdom to the ground.

THREE

PUNKY

A ferocious banging on my door scares the shite out of me.

I reach for my gun in the couch cushions and jump from the couch, half-awake as I point the gun at the door. But when I see who barges in, I lower it.

"Yer not fucking dead," Cian says, slamming the door shut and storming over to me.

"Naw, I'm not, but bang any louder next time, and I will be. Ya near gave me a heart attack. Have ya not heard of a phone?"

He ignores my quip and shoves me in the chest. His arm is in a sling because when Rory shot him, bullet fragments ended up in his arm and shoulder, but he doesn't allow that to deter him and shoves me again. I allow him to push me because this is the first time I've seen him since that night.

This has been a long time coming.

"I got a call from the peelers. He says to me, yer truck is at the wreckers. Do I know anythin' 'bout that? He said the truck is banjaxed and that I was lucky to survive the crash. I told him I swerved to avoid hittin' a dog and that I'm fine," Cian says in a rushed breath. "But I'm not fucking fine, Punky!"

"I know that, Cian, and I'm sorry," I calmly state.

"I am so fucking angry with you! How could you do this? Why did you have to kill him?" he cries, beseeching I explain. "I want to hate you, but I just…why?"

Cian knows Rory turned, but this is the first time he's asked what happened.

"Because he betrayed me," I reply without pause. "He broke my trust 'cause Cami broke his heart. There is no way around it. Rory handed Cami over to Sean because if he couldn't have her, then no one could.

"He knew she wasn't my sister. He read Sean's journal before anyone else and then hid it, hopin' no one would find it. He didn't care. He wanted her for his own. But when I was released, he realized her love for me would never die.

"And then when she called off the engagement, and he saw us together…the boy we grew up with, Cian, he was long gone. Ten years is a long time. I never expected anyone to wait for me, but Rory fucking knew!

"He fucking knew what Sean did, and he let me rot. He

could have shown that journal to any of youse, but he knew what that would mean for Cami and him. He knew that if she uncovered the truth, she would have never agreed to be with him.

"I couldn't let him live. Not after what he did to Cami. His betrayal against me, I could forgive, but not for handin' Cami over to the man who has destroyed my entire life. He made his choices, and I made mine," I conclude with conviction.

"He told ya this?" Cian asks, clearly stunned.

"Aye. If he knew Cami wasn't my sister, he would have read about Sean being my dad. He knew everythin', and he didn't give a fuck. For ten years, I rotted alone, thinkin' I was doin' the right thing. Rory could have ended that. But he didn't. I couldn't let him live," I repeat, needing Cian to understand my actions.

"I don't know where Cami is, and once again, I'm a prisoner. Sean won't tell me where she is until I prove my loyalty to him. I don't even know if she's fucking alive!" I shout, shaking my head at this shitstorm.

"Thanks to Rory, I shot Orla Ryan dead. I let her go, only for Sean to outsmart me, yet again. She was hooked on the shite the Kellys dealt her because a Kelly took her father. That's all us Kellys do—we take!"

I toss the gun onto the couch as I don't need it. Cian is no threat.

He simply stares at me, void of emotion because there isn't

a single feeling which can sum this tragedy up. Even though everything I shared is the truth, that doesn't make it any easier to digest. I suspect Cian feels betrayed by Rory and me.

"I can't get my head around it," he says. "How could he have known and not said anythin' to us?"

I don't understand it either, and I like to think he only found out the truth not long before I was released. I don't want to believe he knew the truth for ten years and did nothing about it, because if that were true, then I really didn't know Rory after all.

"I don't know," I reply honestly. "He probably believed everyone was better off with me behind bars. And he wasn't wrong. The shit I've caused…I can never take back. The lives lost because of me; I'll never forgive myself for."

"What a fucking mess." Cian sighs, shaking his head. "Rory fucked up, but so did you, Puck. He didn't deserve to die like that."

I swallow past the lump in my throat because a part of me agrees with him. But Rory made his choice. "The man I shot was not the boy I knew. Given the choice, I'd kill him again."

The room falls silent.

"How do we get past this?"

"We don't," I reply. "I can't take back what I did, and I don't want to. I'm okay with that. But are you?"

Cian's cheeks billow as he exhales. "I don't know," he says honestly. "I can't get the image from my head. I've not seen ye like that before. It scared me."

"I've not been in a situation like that before, Cian. I saw no reason, no mercy. Rory took from me the only person I've ever loved and all because he was fucking jealous. It's somethin' y'd expect a chile or wee teenager to do, not a grown man, a man who y've known yer entire fucking life.

"I'm sick of these games. It's like every single day is the same fucking day. I've lived this life since I was five years old, and I'm sick of it. I want no part of it, but I've no choice. Until I find Babydoll, I'm forced to do Sean's biddin.'"

Cian's fight has simmered, and even though we're far from being okay, the fact he hasn't left means he hasn't given up on me—yet.

"What are ye goin' to do?"

This conversation is one we had in what feels like a lifetime ago, but the stakes are so much higher this time around. "It took crashing yer truck into a tree for me to realize that I refuse to surrender. I was feelin' sorry for myself, but that won't bring Babydoll back. I have to do what I've done my entire life."

"And what's that?"

Leveling Cian with nothing but honesty, I reply, "Fight."

The pity party for one is over. It's time I got my head out of my arse and go get my girl.

"And how do ye plan on doin' that?"

"Any way I need to. No one is off-limits. I *will* find her, Cian. Even if I have to tear this fucking country apart with my bare hands, I'll find her."

He nods, understanding that I will sacrifice anything, *anyone* to get her back, which is why no one is safe around me. If Sean asked me to prove my loyalty by killing everyone I loved to get her back…I would.

A knock on my door has both Cian and I looking at one another, ready to attack if we need to.

Reaching for the gun off the couch, I quietly walk to the front door. I don't ask who it is as I open it. Who I see standing in front of me has me exhaling in relief.

"Ethan."

"Can I come in?" he sheepishly asks, not knowing if I'll throw him out as I did to Hannah. But I don't.

Stepping aside, I open the door wider, allowing him entry.

This is the first time I've seen him since his return, and I'm happy he looks healthier than when I saw him last.

He and Cian shake hands as Cian was the one who rescued him and Eva while I was distracting Sean. How foolish I was to think that plan would work.

His chest is rising and falling rapidly, indicating he is nervous. I give him the time he needs.

Taking a closer look at him, I see he is the dead spit of Connor. He's tall with the same color brown hair and sharp blue eyes as his dad. He still needs to grow into his physique, but when he does, he'll be an unstoppable force.

The tattoo on his wrist, the same one as mine, has me

angered and saddened all in the same breath. I wonder what Sean made him do. I wonder who he made him kill.

"I know ye don't want to see any of us, but I needed to come here. It's been eatin' me up inside, Punky." He works his bottom lip between his teeth. "I wanted to thank ya for what ye did. Ya sacrificed everythin' to save Eva and me.

"I didn't deserve it. Not after what I did."

"Away ta fuck. I won't be hearin' that."

"Naw, I mean it," Ethan says stubbornly. "I tried to fucking kill ye. I'm ashamed of myself. Can ya forgive me?"

"There's nothin' to forgive, Ethan," I reply softly. "Sean is a manipulator. I don't blame ya for fallin' into his trap. I'm just sorry I couldn't stop him."

"Ya can't save the world, Punky," Ethan says, which is something I've been told before. "I made the choice. It was the wrong one, but I'll own that, and I will do everythin' I can to make amends for it.

"Sean has Cami?"

They all know that's the reason I've acted so reckless and pushed them away. I didn't want to involve them, but it seems I can't stop them, no matter how hard I try.

"Aye," I reply with regret. "Rory was the one who handed her over to Sean."

"Away on!"

"And that's why…I killed him."

Ethan's mouth hinges open.

I want to give full disclosure because if they want to be involved, they all need to know what they're getting themselves into.

"I don't know where she is, and if I don't do what Sean wants, I'll never find her."

"This is my fault," Ethan gasps, turning an awful shade of white.

"Naw, it is not," I counter, stepping forward. "This is my fault. And Sean's. But I'll make it right. How's Eva?"

I haven't been able to face her. I'm ashamed I allowed her sister to be taken when I promised to protect her.

"She's all right. She's tough, just like her sister," Ethan says with a smile; a smile I recognize. It seems my baby brother has fallen hard as well. "She's refusin' to go back to America."

"And she's just as stubborn as her sister too, it seems," I add, which gives me hope that Babydoll is still alive.

She wouldn't go down without a fight. She's also smart. Wherever she is, I have to believe she's okay and just biding her time until she's found.

"Sure, this is it," Ethan agrees, his smile widening. "I wanted to tell ya somethin'. I don't know if it'll help."

I wait for him to continue.

"Sean made me do some messed up things, but the weirdest was that once a month, I was to drop an envelope filled with cash into a lady's letterbox. It was never addressed. Just a white envelope stuffed full of money."

I arch a brow because this is news to me.

"How'd ya know it was a lady?"

"'Cause, one day, I waited and hid to see who it was. It was a lady. She has a baby. I didn't recognize her, but for Sean to give her money…she must be someone important?"

"Aye, she is, and yer goin' to take me to her."

Ethan nods, appearing pleased I've asked for his help. But we have one issue, as I'm certain Ethan rode his bike here.

I don't have a truck anymore, so I look at Cian, who sighs. "This is the last time, Punky. I can't be involving myself in yer shite anymore."

He tosses me his keys, and I'm impressed he drove here with his arm in a sling.

However, no matter what Cian says, we both know those famous last words mean nothing.

I don't know what to expect, which seems to be how I've lived my life since I was released from prison. But this feels different somehow.

This could be the missing piece I've been searching for. This could be Sean's collateral.

I keep to the speed limit as I don't want to rouse any suspicion. The cloak of darkness allows us to travel undetected, but I'm not naïve. For Sean to give this lady money means he values her for whatever reason. Therefore, I'm certain he has eyes on her house.

We have to be careful.

"It's just up the street," Ethan says, leaning forward from the back seat and pointing at a row of houses. There's nothing special or familiar about them, which just adds to the mystery.

I slow down and slip into a parking space.

"What do we do now? We can't just go knockin' on her front door."

Cian is right, but I'm not going to sit here either. I need a decoy…and I see one in the form of a young lady walking a fluffy dog with a pink diamond collar.

Before Cian can tell me what a bad idea this is, I open the door and step onto the footpath. The young lady has her headphones on, so she yelps in shock when she almost bumps into me.

"I'm so sorry," she says, removing the headphones. "I didn't see ya there."

"Oh, no bother," I say with a smile. "I love yer dog. What's its name?"

She brushes a blonde strand of hair behind her ear. "This is Coco."

Coco growls the moment I crouch low to get a better look at her. She must sense my ulterior motive.

"I was wonderin' if you and Coco would help me out?" I

ask, coming to a stand.

The young lady arches a brow.

"I've not spoken to my friend in a qaure long time. She lives just up the street there. We didn't part on good terms, and I'm awful sorry for that. I think she still lives there, but I can't be too sure. Do ya think ya could just knock on her door and ask for a drink for yer wee Coco?"

She tongues her cheek, clearly weighing up what to do.

"Please," I add, digging into my pocket for my wallet and offering two hundred quid. "Ya can buy Coco a new sparkly collar."

She eyes the money before accepting it. "All right. I can do that. What's her address?"

"Thank you. And thank you, Coco." I can't believe this worked.

The young lady changes direction and walks to the address I give her as I keep to the shadows and follow her. When I'm close enough to the house, I take cover behind a tree and watch the young lady and Coco walk up the front steps and knock on the door.

If Sean has eyes on the house, no one will think twice about a stranger knocking on the door and asking for a drink of water for her dog. I've done this as I hope to catch a glimpse of whoever opens that door. I can't act until I know what I'm up against.

When the young lady knocks on the door, and it opens, I'm

transported back in time.

"There's somethin' different about ya."

The ghosts of my past are here, in the flesh, threatening to drag me to hell with them.

I didn't know what to expect, but seeing Aoife is the last thing I *ever* expected. I am completely dumbfounded. Aoife was the nurse who helped tend to the many wounds I sustained when in Riverbend House. She was also one of the only people who showed me true kindness in a place which thrived on pain.

I watch as Aoife offers the young lady a bowl of water, still not believing my eyes. The last time I saw her was in prison. One day she was there, and the next, she simply wasn't. I never asked about her because I always thought she was too good for that vile place.

I was happy she got out. But now I wonder what exactly drove her to leave? Does it have something to do with the child Ethan saw her with?

The young lady and Coco leave, their job done, but Aoife doesn't close the door. She stands in the doorway, peering into the darkness. I shift farther behind the tree, suddenly paranoid she knows I'm here, watching her.

A moment later, she closes the door.

My legs feel like jelly because I am shook. Why is Aoife messed up with Sean? I need to speak with her, but I can't do that right now.

So, even though every muscle in my body is demanding I

stay, I turn and jog toward Cian's car. The moment I get in, he turns to look at me, instantly recognizing the look on my face.

"Fuck," he curses, shaking his head and pulling onto the road as he knows I'm in no state to drive. "Ya feelin' all right?"

Peering out the window, I numbly reply, "No, I'm not."

"Who was it?" Ethan asks. "Did ye recognize her?"

"Aye, I did."

He waits for me to elaborate, but I don't have the words right now. I can't explain why Aoife, the prison nurse who I had sex with on a few occasions, would have anything to do with Sean. I can't explain why he'd give her money. And I can't explain who the father of her child is.

She never mentioned a chile. Or the father of the child.

It can't be me. Aye, we had sex, but I never came inside her. I made sure of it—I think I did. This world doesn't need another Puck Kelly. So why can't I shift this heaviness pressing on my chest?

"What did ya do, Punky?" Cian sighs in defeat.

"I don't know, Cian, but the woman was the nurse in prison. She and I—" I don't need to explain any further. They understand.

"Why is she takin' money from Sean?"

"I don't know, but it can't be good."

We drive the rest of the way in silence as no words can describe the mess I find myself in.

FOUR

Cami

"**I**f ya don't eat, y'll starve 'cause I'm not bringin' ya any more food. This isn't a buffet."

Curling into a tighter ball, I close my eyes and wish for this to end. But it never does. I don't want to believe this is my punishment for breaking Rory's heart because he got his revenge when he tricked me.

He told me it was over; that Punky had defeated Sean. That's why I went with him. He said we were going to meet Punky, but he lied. When he took me to the flat, I knew that I had been tricked, and when Liam was waiting for me, I knew Punky had lost.

Liam was beaten, which proved Punky fought until the very end, just how I knew he would. Liam told me Punky was dead, but *they* weren't done with me yet, which is why I'm a prisoner in here; wherever here is.

Rory betrayed us because we betrayed him, and now, we're all paying the ultimate price.

"I'm sorry, Cami," he said with tears in his eyes.

"You fucking coward!" was my response before I was knocked out cold.

"I won't tell ya again. Eat. Y'll get sick otherwise."

Truth be told, I'm already sick. I can barely keep anything down. My nerves are shot because this waiting, this not knowing, it's the worst form of torture.

"Let me go, and then I'll eat," I stubbornly spit to my captor.

She doesn't reply.

With a sigh, she closes and locks the door.

The single mattress whines as I turn over as best I can with my hands cuffed to the bedhead and examine the bedroom where I'm kept hostage.

It's fitted nicely, and if I wasn't bound to the bed, I would say it has everything a bedroom requires. But all I see is a prison cell. The window doesn't have bars, but it's just a tease as the outside world is within grasp, but I can't fucking move.

My arms ache, as I've been bound since I arrived here eight or maybe ten days ago. I've lost count. Days and nights all mesh into one. But it doesn't matter. I don't want to live in a world where Punky does not exist.

My captor is a spiteful woman—a woman with a small

child. I was blindfolded when brought here, but when she's come to give me food, she doesn't conceal her face. And I hear her young child's happy shrills through the thin walls. His name is Shay.

I don't know who she is or why she would be involved with whoever *they* are. There must be a reason. I need to find out what that reason is because I need to see for myself that Punky is…

I refuse to even think it. He can't be. All of this can't have been for nothing. I need a plan. I need to think like Punky. I can't leave this room. I need someone to help me. And when I hear the happy cries of the young child, I realize he is the answer.

From his voice alone, I'm guessing the little boy is about five years old. I don't want to use him, but I don't have a choice. He is my key out of here.

I wait and listen, and when I hear him outside my door, bouncing a ball in the hallway, I strike.

"Hello!" I call out, almost crying in relief when the ball stops bouncing. "What's your name?"

Frantically twisting my body, I maneuver myself so I'll be able to see any movement from under the door. When I see his shadow walking toward the door, I quickly continue.

"If you come in, I can play ball with you. Would you like that?"

Silence.

His shadow is still outside the door, however.

"My name is Camilla."

"My mummy says I can't talk to strangers," he softly says.

"I'm not a stranger," I assure him calmly. "I know your name is Shay. Would a stranger know that?"

My eyes strain in the darkness, but the hallway light is all the light I need because it allows me to see Shay's shadow remains outside my door.

"Naw, I don't think they would," he replies, a little louder this time.

"Good boy," I say, the first smile I've smiled in days spreading across my cheeks. "Can you open the door for me?"

The handle rattles, but I know that it's locked.

"Your mommy has the key. Can you see it anywhere?" My desperation almost chokes me because I know I'm running out of time.

Shay's mom, wherever she is, will be back any moment.

"Shay?"

When I hear his little footsteps pound down the hallway, growing softer and softer, I tug at my restraints, crying out in anger. "Fuck!"

Arching my neck, I confirm these cuffs aren't budging by my raw red wrists. I've tried for days. Unless someone frees me, I'll be left here to rot. It's useless.

However, when I hear the lock click over and a sliver of light peek in from the open door, hope returns, and it returns thanks to a little boy whose curiosity will help me survive this. He cautiously enters, ensuring he keeps his distance. I can't see him because my room is almost pitch-black. The hallway is all the light I have.

"Hi, Shay," I say calmly, trying my best to conceal the cuffs, but he's seen them. "Please don't be afraid. I won't hurt you."

"Why are ye tied up?"

"I don't know," I reply honestly. "Do you think you can help untie me? I need a key to fit into this lock. It'll be a little silver one. Your mommy has the key."

She has uncuffed me to shower and use the bathroom, but that stopped a couple of days ago when I smashed a lamp over her head and made a run for the front door. It was locked, and she had the key. My punishment is the darkness I now reside in and soiling myself where I lay.

"I didn't see a little key, but A'll go look again," he says, wringing his hands out in front of him.

"Thank you, Shay. You're such a good boy."

"Did ya upset Mummy?"

"No, I didn't. I think someone is making your mommy do this. Maybe your daddy?"

"I don't have a daddy," he says, stepping closer.

The hallway light allows me to see his face a little clearer, and suddenly, I can't breathe.

"What's your mommy's name?"

Shay continues walking closer, and when he's a few feet

away, I gasp. His eyes—I've looked into them before.

"My mummy is—"

"Shay? Where are ye, my wee sweetie?"

His blue eyes widen, and he quickly runs from the room.

"Shay!" I cry, tears spilling down my cheeks.

"I'll look for the little key. I promise ya." He closes the door and locks it, trapping me in the darkness once more.

However, now, when I close my eyes, the darkness isn't the only thing that will haunt my dreams. Shay's familiar eyes will too.

Who the fuck is he? And why does he look like Punky?

FIVE

PUNKY

barely slept last night as I tried to recall every time Aoife and I had sex. I counted eight, maybe nine times. Some memories are fuzzier than others because when I was sent to the sickbay, it was because I was either concussed or bleeding on the cusp of passing out.

I never wanted any painkillers, but sometimes, I needed them to help shut out the pain. They've always messed with my head which is why I hate taking them. I now wonder if maybe one of those times when I was fucked up, I did something stupid—like getting Aoife pregnant.

"I'm not judgin', but how did ye get away with it?" Cian asks, sipping his coffee.

I, on the other hand, am on my third whiskey.

"Riverbend House wasn't yer average prison, Cian. There were no rules. But there's no way that could be my chile."

Cian doesn't look so convinced. "If ya rode her, and rode her numerous times, then it's very possible. It doesn't matter how careful ya thought ye were. Accidents happen."

He's right.

"I just don't understand why Sean was givin' her money?"

"Could *he* be the dad?" Cian asks, half-serious, but we soon both realize that isn't so far-fetched. "Getawaytafuck."

"Anythin' is possible," I state, throwing back my drink. "Until I speak with Aoife, then we're merely guessin'."

This would be the time I'd call on Rory to work his computer magic. But I'm on my own on this one.

"No one who knows me, no one associated with me can approach her. I need a total stranger to pass a message on to her. I don't want to send a letter or leave a note. It's too risky."

"Ach, yer right. But who?"

"Someone who knew her from work will look less suspicious, but I don't—" I never finish that sentence because I think I've figured out who.

Reaching for my phone off the bench, I do a quick search online for Officer Scott Grenham. He doesn't owe me a thing, but I need to try. He was the only officer who actually gave a fuck.

"Hello?" he answers on the third ring.

"Hi, um, I don't know if ye remember me, but it's Puck,

Puck Kelly."

"Puck Kelly," he says in surprise. "What's the craic?"

"I'm sorry to phone ya out of the blue, but I was wonderin' if I could ask for a favor?"

"That depends on what it is," he replies lightly.

"Remember Nurse Aoife?"

"Aye, I remember."

"Well, she and you were the only people who gave a fuck about me when I was locked up. Youse were the only ones who treated me like a human being. I wanted to reach out to her, but I didn't want it to be…weird. Do ya think ya could pass a message on from me?"

"Of course, Puck. I can do that." He almost sounds relieved.

"Could ya tell her to meet me tomorrow? For a coffee?"

"No bother. Just tell me the time and address, and I'll pass on the message."

I can hear him writing down the details as I recite the address. "I know this is silly, but do ya think ya could give this message to her in person?"

Cian nods, understanding why I've asked this.

The safest way to deliver a message is face to face. I can't assume Sean doesn't have access to her phone. I've learned that everything is possible when Sean Kelly is involved.

"Aoife doesn't live far from me. I can do that." He doesn't ask questions as he knows it's best this way.

I hang up, hopeful this will work.

Throwing back the rest of my whiskey, I decide to call another person—Ron Brady.

He wasn't at the meeting with Sean, but the fact he's called me numerous times means he still believes I can pull off what we agreed on before shit hit the fan.

"Punky?" he answers, his surprise evident.

"Hi, Ron. Thanks for answerin'."

"I thought we'd lost ye, lad," he says. "Can ya meet at Bull and Crow in an hour?"

I'd forgotten about the conversation I had with Ollie Molony, the pub owner. He made it clear he wanted nothing to do with the Doyles as they were exploiting him and many others. With Brody now gone and Sean back, I wonder if his stance is the same as Ron's.

"Aye. I'll be there."

With that organized, I decide to call a taxi, seeing as I don't have a truck anymore. But Cian shakes his head.

"I'm comin' with ya."

"Naw, Cian, y've done more than enough." I don't expect him to fight with me.

"I just want this done," he reveals, tossing me his car keys. "None of us are safe until this is sorted. Once and for all."

He's right.

I don't know how this will end, but I've got to try.

I nod, grabbing my gun and placing it in the small of my back. "I wish I could promise ye we're gonna win this, but I don't know that."

"Then we'll die tryin," Cian says. "This is it this time. This is our last chance."

"Aye, so it is."

With nothing left to say, Cian and I leave my gaff and make our way to Bull and Crow.

Sean hasn't summoned me—yet. So I want to make this quick. If anyone sees us, the cover of having a pint will be believable.

I park the car, unbelieving how quiet things are. This place used to thrive, but thanks to the closed down shopfronts which are bricked up, it's a shell of what it used to be. Cian and I enter the pub, and when we make eye contact with Ollie and Ron, Ollie gestures we're to take a seat in a booth.

There are ten patrons, drinking and playing pool, harmless enough. But I treat everyone as the enemy.

Ollie places four pints on the table and takes a seat near Cian. We reach for our glasses casually.

Ollie leans in close. "I'm happy to see ye, Puck. I heard what happened. What can we do to help?"

Ron takes a seat near me, examining our surroundings before speaking softly. "He has Camilla, does he not?"

Ron isn't stupid. He knows the only reason I would side with Sean is because he has something I want more than life itself.

"Aye," I reply, sipping my pint. "I don't know where she is.

Until I find her, I'm forced to do Sean's biddin.'"

"That bleedin' arsehole," Ron mumbles under his breath. "I knew it. I knew ya wouldn't do this without reason. Have ye any idea where she is?"

"None," I reply, gripping the glass. "I don't even know if she's alive. I want to believe she is, but I can't assume anythin' when Sean is involved."

"Fuck," Ollie says, leaning back in his seat. "How'd he get to her?"

Cian's jaw clenches as he turns to look away.

"Rory," I reply with regret. "He sold us out."

All men are silenced by my admission.

"What can we do?" Ron asks once he gets over the shock of Rory betraying us all.

"We can't let Sean know anythin' is wrong. Cami's life is at stake."

"Yer just expected to do his dirty work then, until he decides to tell ya where she is?"

I shrug because acting with violence is what got me here.

But as Ron peers around once again, I realize he may have the answers I need. "I might have an idea."

We wait for him to continue.

"Austin Bailey is a friend of mine. He used to be a little fish, but his dealings with a Russian drug lord have made him a feared enemy ya do not want to have.

"I believe he will want to help us."

"Why would a complete stranger want to help?" I ask, arching a brow.

"'Cause his boss doesn't take too kindly to men like Sean imprisoning women."

"What's the catch?"

There is always a catch.

Ron leans forward, eyeing us all sternly. "He'll want a cut. He'll help ya take out Sean, but at a price, of course."

"What's his boss's name?" I want to know who I'm dealing with before I sign my life away.

"Aleksei Popov, one of the most powerful men in all of Europe."

Never heard of him.

"I'll tell ya what," I state, running my finger around the rim of the glass, suddenly struck with an epiphany. "If he finds Cami, he can have the whole fucking thing. I am done with this life. I want no part of it anymore."

And I mean it. I want out.

Ron and Ollie are surprised by my admission, but they understand how this life has done nothing but take from me.

"I'll make some calls," Ron says. "In the meantime, yer to go on like normal. We *will* beat this cunt. I promise ya that."

We've learned from our mistakes, but I won't get my hopes up. Sean has his claws so deeply imbedded into this place, I have lost trust in everyone. But that doesn't mean I won't try anything at least once.

We've stayed here long enough, so Cian and I finish our drinks and shake Ollie's and Ron's hands. This is the first plan we've hatched. I can't help but feel apprehensive.

"Do ye know who this Aleksei mawn is?" Cian asks as we walk to the car.

I shake my head. "No, I do not. But if Ron thinks he can be trusted, that's good enough for me."

"And yer okay with givin' everythin' to him? Everythin' our fathers worked so hard for?"

"This life is what killed our dads, Cian," I bitterly spit. "He'd be doin' me a favor."

And I mean it.

As we get into the car and I drive away, I sense Cian's silence is filled with anything but.

"Spit it out, will ye?"

He turns to look at me, a heavy sigh leaving him. "I just want this over with," he confesses. "But on the other hand, I'm angry it's come to this. This was supposed to be *our* legacy, but now, I can't help but feel like I've let my dad down.

"There doesn't seem to be an outcome where we win."

"There are no winners," I state, clenching the steering wheel. "Merely survivors."

"That's right."

"Not everyone will survive this, though. Sean has asked I kill Liam. That was a given. But not after some party he's throwin'."

"Don't these buck eejits ever learn?"

"Doesn't seem like it. Sean wants any competition eliminated so the men have no other choice but to serve him."

"And what happens when you're the only competition left?"

"I can only hope I beat him before it comes to that," I reply, but my response lacks confidence.

"Whatever happens, I'm with ye."

Normally I would argue, but the truth is, I need him. I need all the allies I can get.

We ride the rest of the way in silence, and when I drop Cian home, I see the front curtain part. It's Amber.

She closes it a second later, clearly not interested in seeing her boyfriend being dragged into my shite once again.

Cian has lent me his car, but I plan on buying one as soon as I can because I can't keep imposing on him. I know he doesn't mind, but I do.

I drive away and am surprised I haven't heard from Sean. He would have usually called on me by now. The radio silence worries me because I am certain he is up to no good.

When I pull into the driveway and see he isn't waiting for me, I don't know whether to be worried or relieved. This paranoia is expected because of what I've done, but I can't let it get to me. I need my head in the game.

Parking the car, I decide to work on the castle as I wait for Sean to call, which I'm sure will be soon.

The castle is a work in progress with scaffolding holding the structure in place. Getting her back to what she once was has taken a back seat, but with Sean as the new owner, I wouldn't be surprised if he knocks it down.

So many ghosts haunt this place. I think he'll want a fresh start once he finally gets his throne.

Unlocking the front door, which has been replaced, I step inside, and like always, I'm hit with bittersweet memories. When she thrived, this castle was unmatched. Now, she barely stands. I can't help but draw the comparisons between it and me.

The construction crew has done a great job, but seeing as I'm no longer the owner, as I signed my life over to Sean, she sits waiting. We all do.

Peering upward, I see most of the ceiling has been replaced, but the inside is still gutted. Only a few walls remain. My mum and Connor would be disgusted to see the state of her, as they took pride in their home. So much has changed.

Lost in the past is a dangerous place to be because it's the present that has caused me the most harm, and now is no exception. I turn, but it's too late. This trip down memory lane has cost me when my world is shrouded in darkness; thanks to the pillowcase shoved over my head.

I kick out blindly, but it's in vain when someone sucker punches me straight in the guts.

Winded, I take a step back, only to be punched in the kidneys. And then the back.

Falling to my knees, I scramble to take off the pillowcase, but someone grips my arm and twists it back behind me, threatening to break it.

But I don't go out like this.

I stop struggling and study the sounds around me, and when I hear an intake of breath to the left, I strike out with my free hand and connect with something soft. The wheeze alerts me that the man will be singing soprano for a few minutes.

I ignore the pain in my arm, which is about to be broken, and twist, elbowing my attacker in the shin. He releases me, and just as I'm about to rip off the pillowcase, a pain in my thigh has me gasping for air.

"Stop fightin', or I swear to God, the next thing I stab will be your fucking throat."

I recognize that voice, and honestly, I'm surprised it's taken him this long.

"Hello, Cormac."

I knew Rory's father would find out the truth one day, and it seems that day is today.

Raising my hands in surrender, I don't remove the knife Cormac stabbed into my thigh. I'll allow him to avenge his son because we all want revenge on those who've wronged us. We deserve it.

"Yer joking me," he snarls, and I can imagine him shaking his head. "Y'll pretend everythin' is all right after what ye did?"

"Nothing's been all right in a long time. What's right about

Rory betrayin' us? Him using Cami like she meant nothin' to him."

"Shut yer lyin' mouth!" he snarls, ripping the pillowcase from my head.

Gathering my bearings, I see Cormac has two men I don't recognize as reinforcements. They are out for blood.

"It's true," I state, never breaking eye contact with Cormac. "He got what he deserved."

I won't disrespect Cormac by lying to him. I owe him more than that.

He paces back and forth, clearly trying to wrap his head around this. I don't know who told him, but it doesn't matter. What matters is what he plans on doing with the truth.

"Yer da would be disgusted with what we've become," he says, deep in thought. "When he died, he took a piece of us with him. Nothing's been the same since he's been gone."

"Aye, yer right. He was a bastard, but things were a lot simpler with him here."

"And it's 'cause of yer dad that I'm not going to kill ye…but I am goin' to hurt ye…awful bad."

Nodding, I remain on my knees. There's no point fighting— he won't stop until he gets his revenge.

"He didn't deserve to die that way," he cries, reaching into his back pocket for a flick knife. "He was yer best friend!"

"The man I killed was not the boy I knew 'cause the Rory I knew would never sell me out. He would never betray me the way he did."

Cormac inhales sharply, peering upward as if needing a moment to compose himself.

"Hold him up," he orders his two men as he rolls up the sleeves of his white shirt.

The men do as they're told and grip my arms—one on either side of me. My arms are out wide, akin to a crucifixion. I don't struggle. I dare Cormac to do his best because this is his only chance to get his revenge.

I won't be so complacent next time.

Cormac peers at me, no longer seeing the boy he knew but the man who killed his son. With a roar, he punches me in the jaw. My head snaps back with a sharp crack.

Cormac doesn't allow me to recover from his brutal blows. He punches me over and over again. Each hit is more frenzied than the one before it. His men ensure I stay upright, holding me tight.

"Ye were like a brother to him!" he screams, punching me in the stomach, then the ribs. "And ya fucking killed him because of a whore!"

Spitting out a mouthful of blood, I glare at him through one eye as the other has closed over. "I killed him because he was a fucking pussy. And call her a whore again; I dare ya."

Cormac launches forward, clenching my hair and arching my head backward. "Don't you dare say that 'bout my son!"

He presses the tip of the blade to my throat.

"Go on then," I dare with a smirk. "Do it."

"What's become of us?" he cries, shaking his head. "I treated ye like my own wain."

"We're not those people anymore, Cormac."

"Aye, yer right. Say yer sorry, and I'll let ye go."

"I'm not sorry," I counter, bracing for the repercussions of my confession. "He made his choice. I made mine. I won't insult either of ye by sayin' sorry 'cause given the chance, I would kill that fucker again."

He lets go of the past as he presses the blade to my face. He starts above my eye and then cuts downward, leaving a deep gash in its wake. Hot, sticky blood seeps from the wound, coating my face, but I don't cower. I don't scream.

Cormac's cries are guttural as he knows no matter how much blood he spills, it'll never fill the void. The knife drops to the ground with a hollow thud once he's sliced open the left side of my face. The men let me go, where I flop forward, gasping for air.

"I hope she suffers the same fate as my son. I curse ya both."

"Fuck you."

Those are my last words before he kicks me under the chin, knocking me out cold.

I fight with every ounce of strength I have to open my eyes because someone is here; wherever here is.

"Yer hurt," says a voice that transports me back in time. As does her tender touch. "Ye need to go to the hospital. Yer lucky it's just a flesh wound. Any deeper, he would have severed nerves."

I must be hallucinating. There is no way she is here.

But as I pry open my good eye, I see that she is.

"Aoife?" I croak, attempting to rise. But she gently stops me.

"Rest, Puck," she says, coaxing me to lie back down on the bed. "I would call an ambulance, but I'm guessin' ya don't want the peelers involved."

"What are ye doin' here?" I pant, not interested in resting.

She sits by my bedside, looking just how I remember, and tending to my wounds just how I remember too.

"We can talk later."

"No," I cut her off, struggling to sit upright as I lean against the bedhead. "Now."

She works her bottom lip, obviously nervous. Did she expect our reunion to go differently?

"Scott Grenham called on me. Said ya wanted to meet. But when ye didn't show, I knew somethin' was wrong."

I organized to meet Aoife tomorrow, but tomorrow is now today? So, it seems I've been out cold for a day. Cormac really did a number on me.

"We need to talk," I say, flinching as I try to get comfortable. Half my face is bandaged, so getting comfortable is a thing of the past.

She nods, averting her gaze. "I know. I never wanted this."

"Wanted what?"

She takes her time, her heavy sigh betraying her nerves. "I don't want ya to think I was…with anyone else in prison," she says, unable to fill in the blanks, but I understand. "It was only you. I liked ye, Puck. A lot."

"Who's the father of yer chile, Aoife?" I ask, not interested in a walk down memory lane. I need to know the truth once and for all.

"How'd ye know?" She pales, swallowing deeply.

"I know a lot of things. I know Sean Kelly has been givin' ya money. I want to know why."

She sniffs back her tears. "He approached me," she says quickly. "I want ye to know I didn't want anythin' from him. Or you. I still don't. But he knew we were…together. I don't know how, but he knew. And with you in prison, he offered to help.

"I had no one. I couldn't let anyone know who the father was. I would be ruined. And so would my son."

"Who *is* the father?" I ask again.

She covers her face with her hands, crying softly. "It's you,

Puck. He is yer son."

I suddenly feel like I've had the shite kicked out of me again because this is too much.

"I'm sorry I didn't tell ya. But if anyone found out the truth, I'd lose my job. I'd be known as the stupid slut who rode a kil—" She soon stops, as that sentence reveals the kind of people we both really are. "Sean said he wanted to help his…grandson. You couldn't, but he could, and I want Shay to know where he comes from."

Closing my eye, I welcome the darkness because I can't believe it. There must be some mistake.

"He's really helped us out. He's kind, Puck. He loves Shay."

"Yer away in the head if ya think he cares for anyone other than himself."

"Then why would he help us without askin' for anythin' in return?" she poses, which has me believing Sean needs Aoife on his side for a reason.

Opening my eye, I focus on her, and all I see is sincerity. She's been conned by Sean, just how we all have been.

"Don't mistake this act as one done out of the kindness of his heart," I spit, angered. "He'll come callin' when he needs ye."

Something passes over her, something I can't quite put my finger on.

I have no doubt Sean wants Aoife close as he plans to use them as collateral. He didn't want me knowing about them as this was another way for him to blindside me. But for once, I'm two steps ahead.

"Ye can't let him know that ya saw me. Yer both in danger if ya do."

She gasps, clutching at the gold crucifix around her throat. "He would never hurt us."

"Yes, Aoife, he would. Please, just trust me. Let me figure out what to do to keep you and…safe."

Shay, my son. I can't get my head around it.

"All right. I won't tell Sean. Did ya, did ya want to meet him?"

Inhaling deeply, I nod. "Of course, I do. Just not lookin' like this. And not if it puts yer lives in danger."

She smiles, appearing relieved I agreed. But if he is my son, I'll look after him. I'll look after them both. But I need to make sure he really is mine, as I've learned even a paternity test can be manipulated when Sean is involved.

"I know ye don't get along, but yer da has been good to us. I don't understand why he'd do that if he didn't care."

"Don't be fooled by him, Aoife. I was once, and look where I ended up," I state bluntly. "He uses people for his own gain and then disposes of them when he's done. Are ye sure he hasn't asked anythin' of you?"

She averts her gaze, revealing her guilt.

"What is it?"

"Nothin'," she's quick to reply, which merely cements her guilt. "It's nothin'."

"Please, it may seem trivial, but anythin' can help."

"Help what?" she asks, confused.

"Help me find…*her*," I reply softly.

Aoife has no idea what I'm talking about, but I'm at my wit's end. I don't know where to look. Cami could be anywhere. I need a fucking miracle.

"Who is she?" she questions, watching me closely.

"She is my everythin'," I reply, lowering my guard. "And without her, I am so fucking lost."

Aoife frowns and I know I've hurt her with the truth. But there is no one else for me. I will never love anyone as much as I love Babydoll. And I will never stop looking for her.

"She's a lucky woman then," Aoife says, but I sense her bitterness. "Did ya ever feel anythin' for me?"

"Aoife," I start, not wishing to wound her. "I—"

But she cuts me off as she jumps from the bed. "I have to pick up Shay."

I'm sorry to hurt her feelings, but what I had with her doesn't even come close to what I have with Babydoll. I used Aoife to help numb the pain I felt at missing Babydoll. I'm ashamed of my actions, but it's the truth.

"All right. Thank you for tendin' to my wounds—again."

"Old habits die hard," she replies with a strained smile. "When yer feelin' better, give me a call."

I nod because I plan on it. If Shay is my son, then he's in danger.

Aoife appears to want to say something but changes her mind at the last minute. "I'll see ya soon. And call on a doctor if ya can. Yer face—"

But I wave her off. I don't need her to tell me the cut is as bad as it feels. "Goodbye, Aoife. It was good seein' ya."

She smiles, and I can see it—hope. She hopes that when I meet Shay, my feelings for her will somehow change. But that will never happen.

"I'm happy yer out. Ye never belonged in there."

I remember her telling me that I was a good man, that I was different from the rest of my fellow inmates. I didn't believe her. I still don't.

When I'm alone, I exhale loudly, unbelieving how my life can change so drastically in the blink of an eye. I need to get to the bottom of this and find out if he is really my son. But before I do, I need to make sure I don't look like the monster that I am.

Reaching for my mobile off the bedside table, I dial Dr. Shannon, hoping he can help put me back together again.

SIX

Cami

I hear the lock click over, but I don't turn around.

My mind, body, and soul are spent. I've tried to fight. I've begged, but I'm no closer to escaping this nightmare. I don't know how many days, weeks have passed. All I know is that I'm losing hope.

Where is Punky? Could it be that he's really…dead?

I hold back my tears as my captor rushes into the room because she is usually a lot more composed. Her panic has me turning over my shoulder to look at her. She doesn't ask but simply opens my mouth and shoves a sock into it.

Before I can spit it out, she ties the belt of a velvet dressing gown around my face, securing the sock into my mouth.

A muffled "No!" leaves me, but she's done a good job at

gagging me.

This is new. I wonder why she wants me silenced.

Pure hatred is exchanged between us as I glare at her. I don't know what I did for her to hate me so much, but she will pay. They all will.

She's dressed quite nicely in a fitted green dress. Her hair and makeup are done too. I wonder what the occasion is. I would say she's stunning, if not for the fact she's holding me against my will.

"Don'tcha make a sound. I swear, y'll regret it if ye do."

My hands may be bound, but my fingers are free to show her what I think of her request when I flip her off.

She actually laughs before quickly closing and locking the door.

My interest is piqued, and I strain my hearing, hoping to get some clue to what's going on. When I hear a knock on the door, I hold my breath. Is this the reason she wanted me gagged?

"Hi," I hear her say. "Come in."

Heavy footsteps reveal the guest has accepted her invitation, and that it's likely a man. The front door closes, and the wooden hallway reveals the footsteps getting closer to the room I'm in.

"Shay!" I hear her call out.

The flat is small, so no matter where she and Shay are, I can usually hear them. Shay runs into the hallway, but comes to an abrupt stop when he greets whoever his mother has invited into their home.

"Hi," he says, his suspicion clear.

I've come to like him as when his mother is asleep, he often sneaks into my room. He promises he is still looking for the small key, and I believe him. Someone so small doesn't understand what a lie is.

I've learned where I'm being held—in a flat about an hour out of Belfast.

When he brought me his mother's phone, I thought it would be over, but without a password, I couldn't text or call anyone. I wanted to call the police, but I know they're dirty, so I can't take that risk. I will get out of here—one way or another—and I know Shay will be the key.

Being around him brings me a sense of…peace. I don't know why. He reminds me of…

"Hi, Shay."

Puck?

There's no way.

The world stops spinning, and I'm afraid I'll stop breathing, and that has nothing to do with being gagged. My mind is playing tricks on me, I'm sure of it, but time stands still when I hear the voice I've longed to hear wrap me in a warm embrace.

"My name is Puck. But ye can call me Punky if ye like."

My heart clenches. He's here. He's really here. It's finally over. A sob escapes me because he's alive. My world is whole again.

"Punky?" Shay questions, and I picture him curling his lip

in distaste. So this is the first time they've met? Is it also the first time he's met Shay's mom?

"Aye. I got called that when I was a wee lad. No older than you."

Shay's mother, whose name I still do not know, laughs.

Shay clearly doesn't share the sentiment. "That's a stupid name."

"Mind yer manners," she reprimands.

"Naw, don't scold the lad."

That voice, that voice has always been my salvation, but I don't understand why he's here. I want to believe he's here to save me, but he's not, and that's because…he doesn't even know I'm here.

That's about to change.

"Puck!" I scream, but it's merely a muffled cry thanks to the sock shoved down my throat.

But I can't give up.

Rattling the cuffs against the bedhead, I hope Puck can hear it. But the noise is muted as I have no slack with the cuffs. I am bound tightly.

"Puck! I'm in here!" I cry in vain because he can't hear me, but I can hear him.

"Can I go play now?" Shay asks, clearly not interested in talking to Punky.

"Maybe we can organize another time to meet?" she says.

But he isn't interested in that idea, it seems. "I don't want to."

"Shay! I'm so sorry," she says, horrified by Shay's outburst.

"It's all right," Punky assures her.

What's going on?

But Shay doesn't appreciate her speaking for him, and when I hear a thud, I guess someone just got kicked.

"Boys a dear!" she cries.

But a husky laugh, one which has set my soul on fire, slips free from Punky. "Good for you. Never let anyone force ye to do anythin' ya don't want to."

Shay's retreating footsteps reveal he's gone, but his mom and Punky still stand just outside my door. I'm running out of time.

"PUCK!" I scream, flailing madly on the bed.

I twist my body, hoping to make a sound, hoping to do anything which will alert Punky that I'm feet away. But what I hear next has the fight in me dying because I suddenly think that I am.

"I just need to get my head around it, so I do," Puck explains. "This is a lot to take in."

"I never wanted to bother ya with this, but Shay is stubborn…just like his dad."

I flinch at her words.

"Aoife, bring me proof that he's mine, then we'll talk."

Proof that he's mine plays on a loop while I try to come to terms with what I think is happening.

"He has a right to know who ya are. I don't want anythin' from ye."

"Aye, y've said that, but ye need to understand where I'm comin' from."

I do the math. Shay was conceived when Punky was in jail. Did he have conjugal visits? Did he see Aoife instead of me? I dedicated my life to him while he was getting his dick wet—nice.

"Yer quick to defend him, but do ya really know him?"

That's what Sean once said to me. I played it off as just another one of his mind games, but I now realize he's right. I don't know Punky at all. He failed to mention he had a son, which I can excuse as it's clear he hasn't met him until today.

But did he know he existed? Was he trying to keep him safe as he was with us? It's what Punky does best—protect the ones he loves.

I can't help but feel betrayed that he had no qualms seeing anyone bar me when in prison. I understand he was trying to protect us, but the fact he saw Aoife makes me feel sick inside.

I know I moved on with Rory, but Shay's age reveals Punky was with someone else way before Rory and I ever hooked up. I was pining for him, putting my life on hold while I tried to free him, all the while he was fucking some other woman.

I can't help but feel betrayed.

"I understand. You know all I've ever done was care about ya."

"I know that. And I don't deserve it. Yer a good woman, Aoife. Ya saved me in prison. Time and time again."

Each word is just another kick to the chest, and my heart shatters into a million irreparable pieces.

"I…love you, Puck, and I know ya feel somethin' for me too. What we went through, no one will understand it."

I wait for him to deny it. To tell Aoife that the only person who understands him is me. But he doesn't.

"Aye, yer right. No one will understand it. What we shared is between us, and I won't forget it."

Tears spill down my cheeks, wetting the gag his cherished Aoife bound me with. Each kind word he says to her just breaks me further.

"I've got to go. I'll phone ya later."

When I hear the unmistakable sound of someone's cheek being kissed, I curse the world. I've heard enough.

Seconds turn into minutes, hours as I lie on the bed, attempting to process that Puck was here. He was actually here. But he wasn't here to save me.

The door opens, and I can smell Aoife's perfume. She's here to gloat.

I allow her to remove the gag, moving my jaw from side to side. I don't say a word. But she knows I heard.

"Sorry 'bout that. I didn't want my boyfriend to hear." She is so elated at the fact, her grin almost blinds me.

She has no idea that I know Puck. But I also have no idea if she's lying or not. I don't want to believe he's her boyfriend, but my spirit is broken. I don't know anything anymore.

"Why am I here? What use am I to you?"

Aoife smiles broadly. "Yer goin' to bring my family together. They just don't know it—yet."

A shiver runs down my spine because her ominous words come with a warning. It's only a matter of time until my real use comes to fruition.

Aoife closes the door, once again locking me in my prison, but this time is different. No longer will I wait for someone to save me. It's time I saved myself, and when I do, every single person who betrayed me will pay.

Every single one…

SEVEN

PUNKY

It's been three days since I met Shay, and I still don't know how to process that he may be my son.

When Aoife left suddenly, I thought it was because she found a better job elsewhere, away from the depraved. But when I saw the little boy with blond hair and blue eyes, I realize she left for another reason.

For the first time in a long time, I was speechless. All I could do was stare at the wee lad who can be no more than five years old. He didn't cower. He stood tall, watching me just as curiously as I was him. I don't want to believe I could be his father, but I can see the similarities.

Aoife was right. We do share something only she and I can understand. I am grateful for everything she did for me. But I don't harbor the same feelings for her. I don't love her. I never did. I know that makes me a heartless bastard, but it's the truth.

I never asked about Aoife's life because honestly, I didn't care. I thought she was riding me because she was caught up in the hype of the Kelly name. We both made the other feel good, and I thought that was enough.

But I was stupid to think no deed goes unpunished.

I've asked Aoife for a paternity test, which she's agreed to, but I'm still waiting.

A car pulls up the drive, and I know by the engine's sound that it's Sean.

He's been keeping a low profile which worries me. What's he up to?

I can only hope Aoife keeps to her word and doesn't tell Sean I know about Shay because this is the first time I've got the upper hand.

When Sean enters the castle, he whistles, obviously not impressed with her state. "This place has seen better days," he says, and when he sees the state of me, he shakes his head. "The same can be said about you. What happened to yer face?"

He appears sincere as he examines the stitches in my face, but someone told Cormac I was responsible for Rory's death, and it wouldn't surprise me if that someone was Sean.

Dr. Shannon sewed up my face, but he said it'll leave a scar, which I already knew. As for my other injuries, they'll heal, as my body is used to the constant beatings.

"I fell down some stairs," I reply sarcastically. "What do ya want?"

Sean smirks as he peers around at the castle. "This place is a fucking mess."

"It's yer fucking mess now," I reply, seeing as I signed everything over to him.

"Aye, I suppose yer right. Connor would be ragin' if he were here."

Clenching my jaw and ignoring the pain shooting down my face, I snarl, "Well, he's not. Neither is my ma—thanks to you."

I've not forgotten that he's the final piece to this never-ending puzzle. He is the reason I started my quest for revenge. I just never anticipated it would end this way.

"Cara loved this castle. Even if she hated Connor, this place was always her home. She often wished it was *our* home—all three of us."

I exhale slowly, attempting to calm myself down because each time he mentions my mum, it feels like him spitting on her grave.

"I remember she spilled red wine on Connor's favorite chair." He laughs as if recalling the memory. "She was so clumsy. We searched all the shops to find a replacement, but it didn't matter. Connor knew and punished her for it."

I hate that he's the only one who can offer me insight into something I so desperately want to know about.

"She was full of life—"

"Before ya stole it from her," I interrupt, angered.

"I told ya why I had to do it. It was either her or me. I took no pleasure in it."

"Bullshit," I snarl, stepping forward. "I was there, remember? I saw what ya did."

"How much do ye really remember, Puck?" he questions firmly. "Ye were five. How much is actual memory, and how much is it yer mind filling in the gaps?"

I know what he's doing. He's trying to manipulate me.

"Aye, I killed Cara, but I didn't want to do it. She made her choice, and I made mine. Just how you did with Rory—ya eliminated someone who betrayed ya. We're not so different."

"We are worlds apart," I correct sternly.

"Whatever makes ya sleep easier at night," he counters, returning his attention to the castle. "But deep down, ya know you are yer father's son."

His words cut deep because I wonder if my son will turn out like me.

"At the end of this month, there is a shipment comin' into Dublin from the Netherlands."

I have no idea why he wants to announce this, as this is just another day in the office. He reveals why a moment later.

"It's worth—close to a million."

This haul is the biggest we've ever dealt with. The fact that it's coming into Dublin means it's not ours—it's Liam's. And

Sean wants to steal it.

"How do ya know about it?"

"Constable Shane Moore," he replies smugly.

I shouldn't be surprised.

"This is one of Brody's contracts, and the word is, he doesn't know he's dead. But we're goin' to send a message, and we're goin' to do that by publicly executing Liam and stealin' his haul."

"When you say we, you mean me," I correct, folding my arms across my chest.

"Aye, I thought ye'd be happy? Takin' out Liam after everythin' he's done."

"Don't disguise this as anythin' but for your gain."

"It's for both our gain," he replies, reaching into his pocket and producing something I thought was lost.

Babydoll's necklace.

"Do this, and I will tell ye where Cami is."

The rose brooch hanging off the chain is like a pendulum, hypnotizing me with everything that it represents because, for the first time in my life, I know Sean is telling me the truth.

We do this, and his reputation will be notorious. No one will dare challenge him because there will be no enemies left. He will be king—in Northern Ireland *and* Ireland. And this is why he'll let Cami go.

This is what he's been fighting for his entire life, and to achieve that, he needs me on his side. He will risk his life as he knows the moment I find her, his head is mine. I do this, and *both* our lives are at risk because he will hunt me, just as I will hunt him.

But I won't lose.

I will do what he wants. I will take great pleasure in killing Liam Doyle for he is merely an entrée to the main meal. Once I steal the haul and crown Sean, I will rip that crown *and* his head from his corpse. I may not have an army, but I will fight with the strength of a thousand men, for revenge fuels me.

"Sounds like good craic," I state, reaching for the necklace. "But if yer lyin' to me, it's the last thing y'll ever do."

Snatching the chain from his hand, I instantly feel like I can breathe again with it in my possession.

"I promise ye, you do this for me, and yer free to have yer happily ever after."

That's a lie because that will only happen with his death.

He's quite confident I won't kill him once I get what I want. I wonder if that has anything to do with Aoife? Or maybe he simply plans on killing me once I've served my purpose. He'll have hundreds of men, here and in Ireland, desperate to work for him. He believes I can't win against an army.

Time will tell.

"So, this party of Liam's is to celebrate one of the biggest drug hauls in history?" No wonder he's so eager for me to attend.

Sean nods with a smirk. "And it'll be one to remember when ye use Liam's entrails to paint the walls red. We kill him and then steal his drugs. If that doesn't send a message, I'm not sure what does."

"There is no *we*, just so we're clear," I correct. "No doubt, y'll be ensurin' others do the dirty work for ye."

"Yer my son, therefore, yer representin' the Kelly name. Everyone wins."

I can't help but scoff. "And what makes ye so sure I won't kill *you*? Once I do this, the power will be in *my* hands, not yers."

Sean grins. Not the response I was expecting. "'Cause I know ye never wanted this life, Punky. And for the first time ever, yer given a choice. I know what y'll choose."

I hate that he's right. I hate that he knows me better than I know myself.

"Y'll choose Cami. Y'll choose the safety of yer friends. I know this because that's the reason we're here. It's because ye care that I can do this and know that given the choice, y'll sacrifice it all for the people you love.

"If ye don't, ye know this cycle between us will never end. I know how ya think. And that's why I will always beat ya. Ye lead with yer heart, and that's yer biggest downfall, son. Ya want to be a leader, but leaders can't love.

"Love only leads to heartache. It's what'll get ye killed."

My breathing is measured, for I'm seconds away from showing him just what I'm prepared to do for love.

"Ye can try to kill me once I get what I want, but as long as ye have people in yer life ye'd do anythin' to protect, y'll lose. Do ya know how to make someone show ye what they hold most precious in this world?"

I don't want to hear it because I already know what he's going to say. It's what I've done time and time again.

"Set fire to their house, and it's the first thing they run for."

It's what I did with Cami, with Cian, with every single person I've tried to protect.

"So, do we have a deal?" He extends his hand as though this is a reciprocated transaction. But what choice do I have?

I've never had a choice, and when I shake Sean's hand, I realize this is the last deal we're to make because I just may lose this fight.

"Grand," he says, inhaling victory. "I'll let Shane know. Oh, Punky. As a sign of good faith, I want to give ye the castle. This was always more your home than it was mine. Cara would have wanted that."

I don't argue or thank him. I simply nod.

"I'll have Darcy draw up the paperwork."

This gesture is because Sean won't live in the house his brother ruled. The ghosts won't allow him to rest. He's going to start afresh. This is a new era—one no one has ever seen before.

My father is going to change history, and I'm going to help him.

"I need ye to take care of somethin' for me." He digs into his pocket and offers me a piece of paper with an address on it.

With a sigh, I nod. "Consider it done."

Sean doesn't stick around because his message has been received loud and clear.

Once he's gone, I tip my face to the ceiling and take three much-needed breaths. I'm one step closer to finding Babydoll. I wish it was different, that I could find her on my own and dispose of Sean, but I won't risk it.

I've tried to do this on my own, relying on good men for help, but I refuse to allow history to repeat itself.

I will kill Liam and take great pleasure in doing so. I will steal his drugs, and by doing so, I will make my father the most powerful man since Connor. I don't have a plan past that because truth be told, I don't know if I'll survive once I give Sean what he wants.

I'm not naïve. I don't trust him. But I do believe he will give me Babydoll because her exchange gives him everything he's ever wanted.

I don't know what our reunion will be like; I haven't thought that far ahead. I don't know how she's going to react to the news that Rory is dead, dead because I killed him. And I don't know how she's going to respond to Shay.

Even if he isn't my son, I can imagine she'll be hurt I had sex with Aoife when I didn't reply to her numerous attempts to see me.

This is beyond fucked up.

Everything I need is in my new truck, the one I bought with the last of my money, so I make my way toward the address

Sean gave me. Memories of when I was last sent on an errand come to mind, and I sigh, thinking of Orla.

When I pull up a couple of blocks away from the abandoned house, I can't help but think it's just another house in another neighborhood. This life has taken so much from me. I hope it'll stop because I don't know how much more I can take.

Shouldering my bag of supplies, I don't bother concealing my presence when I walk to the unlocked front door and enter. The house is a squatter's den. There are no doors on the rooms, so I peer into each one cautiously. When I look into the last bedroom and see a man with his back turned to me, staring out the window, I reach for the gun in the small of my back.

"Ya won't be needing that."

He turns slowly and smiles.

I have no idea who he is or why he isn't bound. I thought this was someone who owed Sean money. But it seems I was wrong.

"Nice to meet ya, Puck. I'm Austin Bailey. I'm a friend, so ya can put yer gun away."

I'm impressed he knew I was reaching for my gun.

Ron Brady came through. I don't know what Austin wants, but I'm here to listen.

"Why are ye here?" I ask, taking my hand off my gun—for now. "Sean Kelly sent me, so if yer a friend, start talkin'."

He chuckles, not at all bothered by my tone.

"Yer dad is an eejit. I can't believe he's in the position he's in. But that's not because of his doing, is it? It's because of you.

"I heard what ya did to Brody—good for you, lad. I never liked that ballbag. But the thing is, he was easy to control."

"So yer boss, this Aleksei, he was dealin' with the Doyles then?"

I wonder if maybe I was too quick to give him the benefit of the doubt.

Austin smirks, casually placing his hands into his pockets. "Aleksei Popov doesn't deal with anyone," he states proudly. "They deal with him. I handle his Irish affairs, and Brody Doyle was just an arsehole who did what he was told.

"But yer different, are ya not, Puck Kelly?"

"What d'you mean?"

"Yer not all bad," he states, watching me closely. "I think ya fight for honor. I think ya have morals, and I think yer the rightful leader, not yer dad. I've spoken to Alek about yer situation. Ron told me Sean is blackmailing ye. He has yer girl?"

I nod once.

"Alek doesn't appreciate men who have no balls, and from the sounds of it, Sean has none. Alek also doesn't take too kindly to men manhandling women. It's personal."

He doesn't elaborate.

"This is why he has a proposal for ya. He wants to deal with ye, only you, and in return, he'll help ya find yer girl."

Well, this changes everything.

"If you agree, y'll not only get back yer girl, but y'll also be a very wealthy and powerful man."

Clucking my tongue, I shake my head with a smirk. "I suppose I am different because I have no interest in that. Find Camilla, and Alek can have it all. But I do have one condition."

Austin waits for me to continue.

"I want Sean dead, and I want to be the one who kills him. I want him to suffer in ways unimaginable. I also want Liam Doyle dead."

Austin breaks into a loud burst of laughter. "No, lad, yer not that different after all. I'm sure Alek will be accommodating to yer terms."

I decide not to tell Austin about the haul I'm supposed to intercept. I need to have at least one ace up my sleeve in case Austin is dirty, even though Ron vouches for him. I've learned that the hard way.

"Let me discuss everything with Alek, and I'll get back to ye. Are ye sure ya want to give this up? It'll be different with Alek and me. I didn't know Connor Kelly, but he sounded like a good man. He sounds like ye.

"You went to prison to save the people ye love. Alek and I respect that. We could do with a man like you on our side. And Northern Ireland is rightfully yers."

"I appreciate that, but the only thing that matters to me is findin' my girl."

Austin nods, his respect for my honesty clear. "All right. I'll call on ye soon."

He reaches into his pocket and produces a wad of money. "You can't go back empty-handed."

I don't know how Austin managed to fool Sean and his goons, but I'm impressed.

I catch the money, bound with a gold money clip, and place it into my pocket. I go to turn, but Austin stops me.

"We want the same thing, Puck. For the good guys to win."

With a snicker, I reply, "Is there such a thing? Because the line becomes blurrier every single day."

Austin nods. "Alek is a good guy where it matters, as I'm guessin' you are too."

His comment resonates with me because I understand it completely.

With nothing further to say, I leave Austin with a new sense of hope. If he can find Cami, then Sean's days are numbered.

My phone rings. It's Aoife.

"Hello, can I call ya—"

But she doesn't let me finish.

"She has him!" she shrieks, her panic palpable.

"Has who?"

"Shay!"

"Who has Shay?" I ask calmly, as panicking won't solve a thing.

But what she says next changes everything.

"I'm sorry. I lied to ye. I thought I was doin' the right thing."

"Who has him?" I repeat, commencing a jog to my truck.

"Aoife!"

She begins to sob, but through her tears, I hear the only thing which matters. "Camilla. I'm so-sorry."

My tires leave skid marks as I tear down the street, heart in my throat as I speed toward the unknown.

EIGHT

Cami

Three Hours Earlier

My wrists are rubbed raw, but I persevere because I can feel the cuffs slipping free.

I am done being a prisoner, especially when I have no idea who holds me captive. Aoife is merely a puppet. Liam was the one who brought me here, but why?

What purpose do I serve?

No demands have been made. Not to me, anyway. But I am certain they have been to Punky. I'm being held as collateral, but for what? And for whom?

Whatever the reason…I refuse to sit around and wait.

As I'm twisting my wrist, ignoring the pain, I hear the front door open and Aoife enter with Shay. I assume she's picked him up from school. His excited footsteps pound down the hallway while she follows.

She doesn't bother to check on me, which is her error because I am getting out of this fucking house. Today.

"Oh feck, I forgot the milk. Mummy won't be long. Don't open the door for anyone. Okay, Shay?" I hear keys jingle, and then the door slams shut.

I don't know if this is a sign from the universe, but I'm going to exploit it.

"Shay!" I call out, listening for any movement. I hear it a second later when the door unlocks, and Shay enters my room.

"Hi, Cami," he says, extending his hand. "Do ya want some of my biscuit?"

I've grown to really like this kid. "Thank you, but I'm not hungry. But can I ask for a favor?"

Shay nods, biting into his chocolate chip cookie. "Sure."

"Do you think you can find some soap or cream and bring it to me?"

He looks at me like I've lost my mind, but when he realizes I'm serious, he quickly runs from the room. He returns a moment later with a bar of soap.

"Oh, good boy!" I praise, unable to contain my happiness.

He walks over to the bed and offers it to me. But I need his help.

"Do you think you could rub the soap around my right

wrist? I promise, it'll be okay."

I can sense his apprehension as he knows being in here is wrong, but when he stuffs the cookie into his mouth, I know his rebellion has won. Reminds me of someone else…

But I focus on the task at hand as Shay reaches overhead and commences rubbing around my wrist. I bite the inside of my cheek to stop my pained scream.

Arching my neck, I see the soap needs more lather. We're running out of time.

"Can you go into the bathroom and run the soap under some water? We need it to be really soapy. Can you do that?"

He must be able to sense the urgency to my tone as he runs for the bathroom where I hear the faucets being turned on. He returns, the suds covering his tiny hands and dripping onto the wooden floor.

"Thank you, Shay. You're such a brave little boy."

My encouragement spurs him on and determination overtakes him as he furiously commences rubbing the soap around my wrist and cuff. I move my wrist from side to side, begging it slips free. Each time I move it, I can feel it budge, bit by bit.

Shay continues lathering my skin, and with a sharp twist, I slide my wrist free.

"Oh, thank God!" I cry, reaching for Shay and pressing a kiss to the center of his forehead. "I can do it now."

He offers me the soap, smiling happily.

I come to a stand, ignoring my jelly legs, and frantically rub the soap around my cuffed wrist, yanking at the metal. It moves a little, but I'm still bound tight.

Just as I'm about to ask Shay to run the soap under some more water, I hear a car door slam outside and footsteps get closer and closer.

"Shay," I whisper, "can you see who's outside? I need you to be really careful, though. They can't see you."

He tiptoes to the window and cautiously peers out. The lace curtain thankfully offers him some protection against whoever is outside.

"It's the man."

"What man?" I ask, still working the soap around my wrist desperately.

"The man who brought you here."

My heart drops into my stomach because if Liam is here, then something is wrong. It means Shay is in danger. But I won't let anything happen to him. I will protect him with my life.

"I need you to hide. Can you do that for me? Please, don't make a sound," I plead, long forgetting using the soap to break free.

Tears leak from my eyes, and I curse the universe for allowing history to repeat itself, for another five-year-old was forced to hide when monsters knocked on his door.

"I won't leave ye," he stubbornly contests.

I want to argue, but I don't have time.

"Okay, turn your back and cover your ears," I order and exhale in relief when he complies.

As the footsteps get closer to the front door, I close my eyes and bite down my tongue. Gripping my wrist, I count to three, before thrusting it downward, breaking it sharply. I see stars and almost pass out from the pain, but as I guide my wrist out of the cuff, I forget everything but getting the fuck out of here.

"Let's go," I say, removing the pillowcase to make a sling.

Once I slip my arm through it, I offer my good hand to Shay and quietly walk through the room. My legs are weak, and I'm afraid I won't make it three steps, but when I see Liam through the curtain as he climbs the front steps, I forget everything because it doesn't end this way.

I gesture with my head that we're to walk down the hallway. The moment we step out, I put my finger over my lips. Shay nods.

Interlacing our hands once again, we tiptoe down the hallway, each step a gamble with our lives. I don't look back. I can't. The doorbell sounds, which has me quickening my steps as I desperately navigate my way around the house, looking for a back door.

I almost cry in relief when I see it.

Pulling a large knife from the wooden block, I tuck it into my sling and reach for the handle on the door. I turn it so slowly, I'm afraid it won't open, but when it unlocks, a small sob escapes me.

Shay and I exit through the back door, where I close it softly. The backyard is small but has a tall fence. We're going to have to climb it.

"Come here, baby," I say, not even realizing the nickname I use for him. "I need you to hold on tight."

I bend low and pick him up as best I can with one arm. He does as I asked and wraps his small arms around my neck.

Using my foot, I carefully move the trash can toward the fence and step on top of it, ensuring not to make a sound. Adrenaline courses through me, and I boost myself up, climbing over the fence with Shay holding me. The moment my bare feet connect with the ground, I take off into a mad sprint, not even sure where I'm running to.

I just need to get the fuck away from here.

My body is protesting I stop as I'm dehydrated, malnourished, and every muscle lacks strength. But I don't. I continue running, holding Shay tightly.

I don't have any shoes on, so when I step onto a broken bottle, I curse, hobbling to stop the broken glass from digging deeper into the sole of my foot. I know I can't keep running, but I don't know where to go. I don't know who I can trust.

Without a cell or money, I am at the mercy of a Good Samaritan. But I've come to learn there aren't too many of them around.

I see a park up ahead surrounded by some dense forestry. This will have to do until nightfall. Hobbling through the foliage, I walk and walk until my body threatens to collapse in fatigue.

"I think this is a good place for me to catch my breath," I say to Shay calmly, not wanting to freak him out any more than I already have.

I gently lower him to the ground, and once he's safe, I slump against the trunk of the tree, unable to stand any longer.

He peers down at me, nothing but worry reflected in his blue eyes.

"It'll be okay," I promise, gesturing with my hand that he's to come sit with me.

He snuggles into my lap, hugging me tight, and this is where we remain as I slip into a comatose slumber.

My eyes pop open as I have no idea where I am.

The last thing I remember was escaping hell and making a run for my life. The pain in my wrist confirms this wasn't a dream. We made it out alive.

Shifting into a sitting position, I strain my eyes to see in the darkness because night has fallen.

"Shay?" I call out, searching from left to right. Panic overcomes me because I can't see him. "Shay!"

The rustling of leaves has me reaching into my sling for the knife I tucked away, but when Shay appears, I sigh in relief.

"I thought ye'd be hungry and thirsty," he says, offering me a bottle of water and a picnic basket.

"Where'd you get that?"

He smiles. "I stole it, but they had two baskets. So we can share."

I can't help but smirk and think to myself that the apple doesn't fall far from the tree. The more I look at Shay, the more evident it becomes that he is Punky's son. His looks and mannerisms are the same, and I also feel an inexplicable connection to him.

Punky isn't here to protect his son, but I will do so until I can return him home.

Shay drops to his knees, opening the basket. He searches through it, offering me a wrapped sandwich.

"You eat what you want. My stomach is a little unsettled." That's because I haven't eaten in days. "But can I have some water?"

Shay nods and passes me the bottle. But when he notices me looking at the lid, he opens it for me.

"Thank you." I can't gulp down the water fast enough, but quickly stop as I don't know how long we'll be out here for.

I need a phone.

I can't trust the police. There is only one person I do trust, and I'm certain he's with Aoife, who is looking for her son.

"Shay, once you're finished eating, we need to go look for

help. Your mommy is going to be really worried."

He chews his sandwich happily. "Why did Mummy lock ya up?"

"I don't know," I reply honestly. "But I don't think she had a choice."

"Mummy's friend can help us. He'll have a phone we can use."

"Who's your mom's friend?"

"His name is Sean," he replies while I almost choke on the water I downed.

This can't be a coincidence. Sean has to be Sean Kelly, which means Aoife was doing Sean's bidding. I wanted to give her the benefit of the doubt, but there is no way I will forgive and forget. Once I return Shay, I'm going to return the favor and see how she likes being a prisoner.

I suddenly worry for Punky. He surely doesn't know Aoife is involved with Sean. If he did, I doubt he would be paying her a casual visit.

Once Shay has finished eating his sandwich, I come to a shaky stand because I hurt—all over. My feet still have broken glass imbedded into them, but I can't stop. I need to get to Punky, and I need to do so now.

Each second Shay and I are out here is putting his safety at risk.

"I can carry ya," he says, watching as I hobble a few steps.

"I have no doubt about that," I reply with a smile. "But I'll be okay."

I offer him my hand, which he accepts.

With the picnic basket in hand, we commence a slow walk toward where I'm hoping will lead us to safety. I have no idea where I am, but Shay does. He patiently waits as I limp through the dense woods, using the moon as our beacon of light.

It takes about half an hour, but when we get to a clearing that leads to a road, a shaky exhale leaves me. He did it.

This little kid is remarkable.

I don't recognize any landmarks or streets, but we continue walking, in hopes of finding something which will look familiar. A few cars pass us by, but no one stops, which is both a blessing and a curse. We need help, but I won't risk it in case the Good Samaritan works for Liam or Sean.

We continue for what feels like hours, and just when I'm about to give up, I see it—a fountain which isn't too far from Fiona's home. We're farther out than I thought, but now that I have some sense of direction, nothing can stop me.

We keep to the shadows, remaining undetected because there is no way I'm getting caught so close to freedom. A car sounds behind us, slowing down when its headlights shine our way.

"Shay, want to have a race?"

He peers up at me with a grin, clueless to why I've asked him to run.

"Ready, set, go!"

We break into a mad sprint, me holding his small hand and directing him to take a sharp right, which is an alleyway. No cars can fit down here. The moment our feet hit the uneven surface, I exhale in relief but don't stop running.

Shay stumbles, and I pick him up, ignoring the pain radiating through my body. Nothing else matters but getting him to safety. My breathing is labored, and my heart threatens to burst from my chest, so when my frantic footsteps are the only ones I hear, I almost collapse into a heap.

Coming to a stop, I turn over my shoulder, holding Shay tightly as I check to see if we're being followed.

We're not.

A sob escapes me. My paranoia may seem far-fetched to some, but that's how fucked up my life is. Every shadow is a potential monster lurking in the dark.

Once I catch my breath, I smile at Shay when he says, "You won."

"We both did," I correct, my heart melting when he kisses my cheek. "Let's go. A friend lives close by. We can call your mommy when we get there."

He nods, but doesn't make any attempts at getting down, and that's fine. I feel comforted with him in my arms.

I walk the two miles with him clinging to me, and when I see Fiona's house in the distance, I assure myself it's just a little farther because I know the moment I get there, everything I've been through and done will catch up with me, and it won't be pretty.

The rusted gate whines when I push it open, and as I stagger the short distance to her front door, I can't believe these final steps are the hardest ones I've ever taken. I bang my shoulder into the door—refusing to let Shay go—with the last ounce of energy I have left.

I have no idea of the time, but I assume everyone is tucked safely into their beds.

The world begins to sway; however, I refuse to surrender. "Hello!" I cry out, kicking the door with my bare foot.

My body is broken and bruised, and I barely feel the pain any more.

Just as I'm about to kick the door again, a light flickers on from inside, and I see movement through the lace curtain. When the door opens, and I see Ethan, gun in hand, I gently lower Shay onto his feet, not bothering to explain who he is.

Eva appears in the hallway behind Ethan, or I think she does because everything suddenly becomes murky. I welcome the darkness because I am so tired. Before succumbing to the silence, the last thought I have is, *we did it*.

I don't know what comes next, however.

NINE

Cami

I hear whispers, but I'm not ready to face them.

Every part of me hurts, and I know when I wake, I'll have to deal with that pain—both physically and emotionally. I don't know what awaits me, but being a coward isn't an option.

It feels like my eyelids weigh a thousand pounds, but I push past the anguish and slowly open my eyes. Everything is fuzzy, and when I attempt to rub my eyes, I realize my arm is heavier than my eyelids felt thanks to the plaster cast on it.

"She's awake!" I'd recognize that voice anywhere.

Eva.

"Don't ever do that to me again!" She throws herself onto me, hugging me tightly.

I try to hug her back, but it hurts to breathe.

"Why are you here?" I croak, and soon flinch because who knew even speaking would be painful?

"I wouldn't go back home when you were missing," she replies, thankfully loosening her grip a little. "I couldn't. I knew you'd come back. That's why I stayed."

"Is Mom okay?"

"Yes, she's fine. Stop worrying about everyone else. You're the one who looks like they got their ass beat in a UFC cage match."

Nice to know I look as shitty as I feel.

Ethan enters with a glass of water, and when Eva turns to look at him, her cheeks turning bright red, I see there is another reason she stayed.

Oh, boy.

"I brought ye some water," he says, placing the glass on the bedside table.

Eva smiles and gently untangles herself from me, coming to a stand. "You're so thoughtful."

And now my stomach hurts, and I want to puke from this PDA.

Hannah appears a moment later, standing in the doorway because the room is small and it's a tight squeeze. "Thank God yer okay. I knew ye would be."

Smiling, I shift against the pillows and lean against the wooden bedhead. "You should see the other guy," I quip, attempting to whistle, but it sounds like a balloon deflating.

Everyone laughs, but it's strained, and that's because no one wants to address the big fat elephant in the room—where is Punky?

However, when I hear a banshee scream and footsteps pounding against the hallway, it seems the elephant has come charging.

"How dare you take him!" screams Aoife, not bothered that the room is already full.

Eva, Ethan, and Hannah walk into the kitchen sheepishly, not interested in being a part of this shitshow.

"My wrist is broken, not my hearing. There's no need to scream," I taunt, which just infuriates her further.

"Don'tcha be smart with me! You took my son!"

"Well, Aoife," I smugly reply, wanting her to know I'm aware of who she is. "You handcuffed me to a bed. You fed me stale bread and water. And you let me rot in my own piss and shit. So, I'd say we're even."

The room becomes smaller, and my heart commences a deafening staccato.

She blanches, and that's because of the man who towers behind her—the man who has stolen my breath from the first moment we met.

"Is that true?" Punky asks smoothly, his poker face in play. "Did ye treat her like a…prisoner?"

She turns over her shoulder, her bravado soon dying as she tugs at the gold crucifix around her throat. "Puck, I—"

"Answer my question. Now," he interrupts, not interested in her excuses.

"Sean told me she was hurtin' ya," she cries, begging he shows mercy. "I did it for yer own good."

She reaches out to touch his cheek, and just as I'm about to throw off the blanket, ready to take this bitch down, Puck seizes her wrist in midair.

"Maybe I should break *your* wrist then?" he poses, jaw clenched as she whimpers.

"Yer hurtin' me."

"Oh, trust me, I'm not."

A shiver runs through me because there he is—my feral, vicious Punky who shows no mercy to anyone. And this bitch deserves none after everything she's done.

"I'm sorry. Please forgive me."

I curl my lip, disgusted by how easily she surrendered.

"I'm not the one ya should be apologizing to."

Her whimpers grow louder, and when she focuses on me, I see it—utter hatred. She wants Puck for herself, and no matter her story that she thought she was doing the right thing, I know she can't be trusted. She will do everything in her power to have her happy family without me in it.

Punky releases her, but stands close, sensing a fight brewing. "I'm sorry, Camilla. I did not know. Sean said you—"

"Save your breath," I snap, not interested in her bullshit. "You knew the difference between right and wrong, and what you did was wrong, very wrong. So I don't accept your apology."

Her eyes narrow while I dare her to say another word to me.

"I understand," she finally replies. "Shay told me you looked after him."

Punky's jaw clenches.

We have so much to talk about, but something is…wrong. I can't put my finger on it, but he's avoiding eye contact with me. I wasn't expecting a reunion filled with roses and rainbows, but I was at least expecting him to be able to look at me.

"He's a good kid," I reply, averting my eyes.

The silence is deafening and just adds to the pounding in my temples.

"I'll give ya some time alone," Aoife says as if she's doing us a favor, and I'm the intruder, not her.

I shift against the pillows, focusing on the floral bedspread instead of Punky as he enters the room. His footsteps are measured. He's nervous too.

This isn't the first time we've been reunited after tragic events, but it feels different.

He doesn't sit. He stands by my bedside, the silence continuing.

Tears prick my eyes, but I sniff them back because crying won't solve a thing. I want to ask him so many things, but I don't know where to start. We've been broken before, but this time, it hurts so much more.

With the gentlest of touches, Punky reaches out and lifts my chin. The moment we lock eyes, I feel whole again. But there is so much pain reflected behind his blue gaze.

He examines me slowly, tenderly rubbing his thumb over my chin. I remain perfectly still, caught under his spell. I've dreamed of this day.

His hair is tousled, his beard unkempt. A savage fresh scar on his face has me gasping.

"Wh-what happened?"

He jolts as though my voice shook him from a daydream. "Cormac," he replies, and I arch a brow, confused. Why would Rory's dad do something so cruel?

Unless…

"What did you do?" I whisper, almost afraid of the answer.

He rubs his thumb over my bottom lip, appearing transfixed by it. "I did everythin' ya think I did. Rory betrayed us…and he paid with his life."

I blink once, his blunt statement winding me. "You…ki-killed him?"

"Aye, I did," he confesses without remorse while my stomach drops.

I think I'm going to be sick.

Reaching for the glass of water Ethan left me, I gulp it down, Punky's words playing on a loop as my mind refuses to accept them as truth.

"How could you?" I cry, my voice uneven. "I know what he

did was wrong, but he was your friend. He meant something to both of us."

"And that's why I killed him," he counters without feeling.

The glass trembles in my hand. Now I know why things feel so different this time.

"Tell me what happened." It's not a request but rather a demand.

I lick my lips nervously. "Rory said we were going to meet you. But when we got to the flat, and I saw Liam, I knew he'd set us up. He didn't tell me why or what he got in return, but I can guess.

"He did this because we hurt him, Punky," I say with utter regret. "It's not an excuse, but it's an explanation. We're all as guilty as one another, but you and I are still alive. We can try to make amends. But Rory cannot."

Punky stands like stone. "I know ye hate me for it, but I did what I had to. I accept whatever the consequences are."

Just how he accepted Cormac's abuse.

He accepts the consequences because he isn't without feeling—I know Rory's death affects him. He wouldn't be human if it didn't. Puck knew the repercussions of killing Rory, but he accepts them because his need for revenge will always win.

For his whole life, he has searched for vengeance, and it just continues to grow.

"Is Shay your...son?" I ask, seeing as we're all about truths.

"I don't know, but he could be. I'm waitin' on paternity results."

"Fuck this vicious cycle," I whisper, shaking my head. "Just how you waited for paternity results about who your father really was? When will this end?"

Expressing my frustrations out loud just makes me feel worse. I don't know if Punky and I will ever live a "normal" life. We are stuck in an endless loop, always looking over our shoulders to defeat the bad guys. But I've come to realize, what if we are the villains?

"So you had conjugal visits then? You had no issues seeing other women, but not me?" I can't help myself because I need to know.

Rubbing the back of his neck, he sighs. "Aoife was a nurse. She—"

"Nice," I spit, tonguing my cheek. "She clearly takes her duty of care very seriously."

"I don't want to fight with ya."

"Who said anything about fighting? I was merely asking a question. I mean, it's nice to know you had time to stick your dick in anything that walks but couldn't see me."

"Cami," he says, defeated. "It wasn't like that."

"It's exactly like that," I argue, suddenly so mad. "Do you know what she did to me? She took pleasure in seeing me suffer. Her story about doing it to protect you is a load of shit. She did it because she wants a happy little family which I am no part of."

"If Shay is my son, then I will provide for him," he says, which I knew he would. "But that doesn't mean I want anythin' to do with Aoife."

"That's not what I heard," I dispute, remembering his words like they were spoken mere seconds ago. "No one will understand what you two shared. And you won't forget it. Isn't that right?"

His cheeks billow as he exhales loudly. "Y've misunderstood what I meant. Aoife was the only good in a place which almost broke me. Ya wouldn't understand because ya weren't there."

"Because you refused to see me," I counter. "Do you know how that makes me feel?"

"I understand that, but I've explained why. Just how you moved on with Rory. I lived the best life I could, considering the circumstances, but it was barely livin' most times. If I could take back what I did with Aoife, I would.

"I missed you…so fucking much. She was a distraction. I'm ashamed to admit it because all I wanted…all I *ever* want…is you!"

His confession has the fight in me simmering. But that doesn't change how fucked up this is.

"Why was I held prisoner?" I can't deal with anything but this right now.

"Ethan and Eva were just a diversion. You were always the end goal because Sean knows no one means more to me than you."

I clear my throat, his sentiment touching me.

"He tricked us into thinkin' we'd won because he knew Rory was on his side. Rory worked with Sean because he wanted out. He knew we weren't brother and sister. He read Sean's journal."

Time stands still. "*What?*"

"He confessed to me right before I—" He pauses as I can fill in the blanks. "He told me he wanted more time with ye but proposed when he found out I was gettin' out of prison."

"Oh my God," I gasp, cradling my wounded arm. "I don't know who anyone is anymore. And that includes myself."

I know my confession has hurt Puck, but everything is so fucked up. Rory is dead. Punky may be a father, and his baby's momma is a diabolical bitch. Sean and Liam are still out there, threatening our lives. And the list just continues to grow.

Rory's proposal was fast and unexpected, and now I know why. He knew I would have never accepted when Puck was out of prison because I would have eventually found out the truth. He lied to me. He knew I harbored feelings for Punky, ones I was ashamed of, yet he allowed me to suffer when he could have told me the truth.

I am so sick of the lies.

"Sean has held yer location over me, knowin' I would do anythin' to make sure ye were safe," he shares with me. "I didn't even know if ye were alive. I didn't know where to look. Each and every time I think I've beaten him, he proves me wrong.

"I wouldn't gamble with yer life. Therefore, I did what he

wanted. I would do anythin' if it meant bringin' ye back to me. I've done some deplorable things…and I'd do them again. All I wanted was to find ye, and now that I have, I fear yer still lost to me."

My lower lip trembles, but I bite the inside of my cheek to stop the tears. "So this was Sean's plan all along? To assert his dominance? He can't kill you because he needs you. But he can't trust you either. So he kidnapped me and held me as ransom, knowing you'd do anything he said?"

Punky nods.

"How does he know Aoife? Does he know Shay is your—"

"Yes, he does. Aoife told me he's been helpin' them out financially. She disappeared. I didn't know Shay existed until a few days ago. I suspect Sean had eyes inside of the prison, probably Constable Shane Moore, and figured out why Aoife quit her job.

"She and Shay are just another pawn for him to use against me. He knows I would never abandon my child. He doesn't know I know they exist, however. I've finally got one up on him."

"And you trust her?" I ask, because I sure as shit don't.

"I don't know," he replies honestly. "Which is why I need to keep her close."

"Or you could just kill her." My reply wasn't supposed to come out so harsh, but I can't help the way I feel.

Why aren't she, Sean, and Liam dead already? They are the

enemies.

"I would never do that to Shay," he says, his disappointment evident. "I know what it's like to grow up without a mum. I wouldn't wish that upon anyone, especially my son."

I'm ashamed of myself for even thinking it.

"Why did ye take him?"

Now I'm the one who's disappointed. "I didn't take him for ransom, if that's what you're thinking. Regardless of who his mother is, I actually really like Shay. He is the reason I was able to escape. When Aoife left me alone in the dark, he'd come visit me.

"He'd sneak me fresh food and water, and even though I couldn't eat because each second I was handcuffed to that bed made me sicker and sicker, I appreciated the gesture. If it wasn't for Shay, I would still be a prisoner."

I swallow down the memories as they threaten to make me sick.

"I always felt a sense of…calm around him. Like he was familiar to me, and now I know why that is. He saved me. His courage reminds me of someone else I know."

Punky's chest falls as he exhales heavily.

"There was an opportunity, and I took it. I wasn't going to wait around to be saved. I had to save myself and was prepared to do that at any cost." I wiggle my cast, proof that I mean every word. "Aoife left to get milk, and I knew it was now or never."

He flinches, and I wonder why.

"Shay brought me some soap and helped free me from the cuffs. But as I was working on the other wrist, I heard someone at the front door. It was Liam."

I rarely see Punky surprised, so when his lips part, and he's left speechless, I know I did the right thing in leaving.

"I broke my wrist because I was running out of time. And I took Shay because he was in danger. We escaped and hid in a forest. I passed out, and when I came to, we walked and walked until I realized where we were."

My exhaustion suddenly returns when I detail what we went through to get here.

I wait for Punky to speak, but he doesn't. He simply stands frozen, barely blinking.

As I shift to get comfortable, a sharp stinging shoots up my leg. I'd forgotten about my feet. Pulling back the bedspread, I see my feet are bandaged.

I wonder how long I've been asleep for.

But I ask the most important question. "Where's Shay?"

"He's watchin' TV," Punky replies blankly.

This stilted conversation is new. We've never been stuck for words. I want nothing more than for him to comfort me, but I need…space. A lot has happened, and I need time to digest it. I can't help but wonder about Rory.

Was it a merciful death? I suppose there is no such thing in our world.

It's hard for me to accept that he knew the truth the entire time we were together. I feel nothing but a fool. But I suppose I should have never accepted his proposal. I suppose I should have done a lot of things differently.

But when I look at Punky, I know that no matter our history, I would never change falling in love with him.

"I'm goin' to fucking *kill* him," he snarls under his breath, startling me with his fury.

"Who?"

He finally meets my eyes, and when he does, I realize this is the final chapter. Punky is done. Those who betrayed us are going to pay—once and for all.

"Liam."

"When?"

"Now. And once I am done with him, I will do the same to my father."

I open my mouth but soon close it because I want that as much as Puck. But there can be no room for error. If we do this, then we do it without fail.

"Do you have a plan?"

Punky shakes his head slowly. "No plan. I'm just goin' to find that fucker and blow his brains out."

Punky is known for his temper, but I've never seen him this angry before, which is why I have to be the one who sees reason for us both. "You do that, and then what? We continue to fight for the rest of our lives? I am done running, and I know you are too."

"Then what do ye propose we do? Just wait around for them to attack us? I've waited long enough. When ye were gone—" But he soon stops himself from continuing.

I never thought our reunion would be so fractured, and that's what Sean wanted. He knows Punky and I are stronger together, everyone does, and that's why they've tried to tear us apart.

"We kill them without a plan, a solid plan that is, then this will never end. There will always be another enemy who will want retribution. This feud will never end. I'm tired, Puck. I just want this over with."

He runs a hand through his hair, exhaling heavily. "I do too. But the thought of Liam and Sean still breathin'…I can't handle it. With them alive, yer always at risk. I won't lose ye again. I can't."

He's still standing, appearing not to want to touch me. We both need time.

"Maybe I should take away the prize they're all fighting for then," I state while Punky's jaw clenches.

"Yer not goin' anywhere." He steps forward, his dominance almost suffocating me…and I like it. "I'm not lettin' ya out of my sight."

A wave of heat washes over me because I like the thought of Punky being close by.

"So what do we do?"

Those astute blue eyes examine me closely while I feel

every part of me respond in ways that have my cheeks turning a bright shade of red.

"Let me think it over, but yer right, we need a plan. We've got an advantage now, somethin' we've never had. Sean has no more collateral over me, and that..." He inhales sharply, needing a moment before he continues. "And that's why I'm findin' it so hard to restrain myself.

"People fade, piece by piece. I barely remember my ma anymore. I don't know if the memories I have are real or if they're my mind making up recollections I desperately want to be real. But regardless, I still need to avenge her.

"Simply killin' Sean won't be enough. I need him to suffer and be humiliated after everythin' he's done. But this isn't just about my mum now. It's about all of us. His greed has destroyed all our lives, and his time has come."

"You're talking like a man who has an ace up his sleeve." I have no doubt Punky had a plan before I broke free. Things may have changed, but whatever Punky was planning, we can now carry it out together. "What can I do to help?"

A twitch touches his lips, and my stomach somersaults because seeing Punky smile is a sight that always steals my breath away.

"Ye can rest."

Before I can protest, he leans forward and gently presses a kiss to my forehead. The moment we touch, memories come flooding back, almost winding me with the force. When a low hum escapes him, I know he feels it too.

He quickly pulls away while I nervously tuck a piece of hair behind my ear. "Okay, I'll rest because I'm tired. But when I'm not, I want to know everything."

And I mean everything. For us to move forward, I need to know the good and the bad.

He nods, reading between the lines. "I'll call on ye later. Believe it or not, being here, at Fiona's, it's the safest place for ye at the moment. But ye can't stay here much longer as I'm sure Sean will find out soon enough."

I have no idea where Fiona is, and I doubt she would be so accommodating to house me here. I know we're on a tight deadline.

Punky looks at me, absentmindedly toying with the hoop in his bottom lip. The simple action shouldn't get me so hot, but it does. However, my attraction for Punky has never been the problem. It's all the other stuff in between that has been the issue.

And that other stuff now includes a maybe son.

"All right. I'll talk to you soon." It's all so formal, and I hate it. But I need to sort my head out and not act with my heart. And I think Punky feels the same way.

The pull between us leaves me breathless, and I almost throw caution to the wind—almost.

Shuffling under the covers, I turn my back to him and allow the tears to fall in time with his receding footsteps.

TEN

PUNKY

I can't focus on anything because this rage inside me threatens to eat me whole. All I can think about is Aoife holding Babydoll prisoner while I was feet away.

I failed her.

I promised to protect her, and I've failed in every sense of the word.

I can't imagine how she felt finding out about Shay the way that she did. I was just outside her door while she was handcuffed to a fucking bed. It kills me to know she was within reach, and I couldn't do a thing about it.

But I can now.

Those who hurt her will pay, and pay in ways unimaginable—Aoife included.

I'm pacing back and forth in my living room when the door opens. Cian, Ron, Ronan, Ollie, Logan, and Ethan enter. I called them because they are the only men I trust.

Some sit. Some stand. But I get down to business the moment I have their attention.

"Cami is back," I start, which comes as news to some of the men. "She escaped on her own. She's fucking braver than any of us."

"Aye," they say in unison.

"This means Sean and Liam no longer have the upper hand. I was doin' Sean's dirty work because of her, but now that she's free, it's time those fuckers pay. I called ya here because I can't trust anyone involved with Liam or Sean.

"That was one of the many mistakes I made last time. I won't make it again. Those men aren't loyal, and if anyone found out about Cami, they'd have collateral over me, and I refuse to allow that to happen again.

"Yer the only ones I trust because no one can know about this. I need ye to help me pull this off."

Cian sits taller in his seat. "Pull what off exactly?"

I haven't slept since leaving Fiona's because there is much to plan.

"I need to know if Liam or Sean are aware that Cami is no longer a prisoner," I say, hating that she ever was. "If they are, we lose the element of surprise. And we can't be havin' that.

"The woman who was holdin' Cami…was a nurse I met in

prison. Her son may be mine." I don't need to go into further detail. "As much as I want to punish her for what she's done, I cannot. Not yet. Sean has wormed his way into her world, knowin' she would be useful to him.

"If she tells him that Cami is gone…we're all dead. Cami was the only reason I was doin' his biddin'. If he finds out she's gone, he knows I'll be huntin' him. And he will do everythin' in his power to get to me first.

"He won't bother with games this time, which is why the stakes are so much higher."

The men nod, understanding my reasoning.

"I need him to believe he's still in control because that will make him complacent. That's what will make him weak…and that's when I will strike. If I could, I would go over to his gaff and kill him right now. But I cannot."

"Why not?" Ollie asks, his dark brows knitted together.

"'Cause this will never end. This feud will live on for generations. I don't want that for my son. For any of our sons. We need to be smart about this. I need to end it—once and for all. I need Liam and Sean to be slain at the same time, so there is no chance for escape or for retaliation."

"And then what?" Ron questions.

"And then, I give it all away."

The room falls silent as they were clearly not expecting that.

"Punky," Cian says, shaking his head.

His feelings have clearly changed from when we spoke the

other night. He now sees how serious I am about giving it all away and doesn't agree.

"Belfast is rightfully yours. It belongs to a Kelly. It's been that way for generations. What of Connor? Of my da? Of all the fallen men who fought wars they believed in?

"We just forget them, is that so?"

"No, Cian, I'm doin' this because of them. There is no victory. Only surrender."

Yes, we will win the war against Liam and Sean, but for that to happen, I must surrender my beloved Belfast. It's time she's ruled by another.

"I spoke to yer friend, Ron, Austin Bailey. Although things have changed, the deal is still on. If he and Alek help me defeat Liam and Sean, then they can have it all."

"Let's go over there and just kill that son of a bitch!" Cian spits, anger leading him. "We'll deal with the consequences. Y've got Cami back now. What's stoppin' us?"

"Losin' ten years of my life is what," I counter with reason. "We are in this mess because we continue to underestimate Sean's power. How do we know he doesn't have a backup plan where Amber, yer families"—I look at each man—"are the next best things for collateral?

"No one is off-limits. And both Liam's and Sean's men will retaliate if we don't assert our dominance. If we simply kill them and don't make an example out of them, then someone will take their places in a heartbeat, and we're just back to the beginnin'.

"No, we need them to see we cannot be fucked with. That there is new blood in town."

Ron sighs, and I know he understands why I've chosen this path. "Yer right, Puck. For Alek to assert his place in Northern Ireland and Ireland, he needs to earn the men's respect. Otherwise, they will simply see him as some Russian who doesn't belong here.

"They will challenge him, and that's hardly a deal Alek will want to agree to."

"Exactly," I agree, thankful he understands. "If Sean gets wind of this, he will run, but not before he kills everyone we love, ensurin' we suffer and forcin' us to chase ghosts our entire lives.

"I've lived that life, and I am done with it."

There are too many factors in this equation. Too many men who may rise up and challenge a place for the throne. We need to simplify it. There can only be one king. And I will offer that to Alek in place for my freedom. And for the freedom of those I love.

Cian stands, curling his lip in disgust. "If this is what surrender looks like, then count me out. I won't sit back and watch ye spit on my father's grave. This makes no sense. We could go over there, right now, and end it for both Sean and Liam.

"Yet yer choosin' to hide. Yer choosin' to give everythin' away! We could do this together, but yer choosin' the coward's way out!" The door slams shut as he storms outside.

It upsets me to see Cian this way, but this isn't negotiable. This is happening my way. "If anyone else feels the same way, then now is the time to leave," I calmly say. "I know it seems simpler to just kill them both.

"But that will mean we are constantly lookin' over our shoulders for the rest of our lives. I don't want that. Not anymore. I don't want to fear walkin' into a pub in case I get shot in retaliation by some cunt who thinks they are doin' it in the name of their fallen leader.

"We do this, we demonstrate our influence and the ties we have, then no one will fuck with us ever again. If ye choose to deal with Austin and Alek, that is yer choice. But me, I want out. But before I do that, Sean must pay, and pay in ways unimaginable for what he did to my ma. What he did to me."

I wait for them to process what I just shared because the easier option would be what Cian suggested. But that's not the smartest plan of attack. A smart predator waits for the perfect time to strike because a missed opportunity can mean the difference between life and death.

I look at Ethan and no longer see a boy. He is a man who has the right to choose what path he decides to take because rightfully, Belfast is his too. It was *his* father who ruled, not mine. I can't make that choice for him.

I wanted to protect him, but I can't do that anymore. This is as much his fight as it is mine. Sean took Connor away from

Ethan, used Ethan for his own gain, then disposed of him when he was done. So I understand Ethan wants his revenge too.

"Let's make that fucker pay for everythin' he's done. In the name of our father." Ethan's acknowledgment that Connor was *our* father has my heart swelling. "I know I'm in no position to fill Connor's shoes, but I think I would like to learn."

Nodding, I grant him the choice because it's his life and he has the right to choose which path he wants to take. I can't protect them all, but I can teach them how to protect themselves. "Then I will teach ye. Connor would be proud of the man y've become. And so am I."

Ethan's eyes, eyes so much like Connor's, fill with tears, but he quickly brushes them away. "When ye organize the meetin' with Alek and Austin, I want to be there. I want them to know who I am and that I want in."

"If that's what ye want, then of course."

Truth be told, it warms me knowing that Belfast will still be in the hands of a Kelly. Hannah won't be pleased with Ethan's choice, but they're both grown. I can't shelter them forever.

"Whatever ye need, I pledge my loyalty to ye, Puck," Ron says, bowing his head.

"Me too," Ollie agrees, as do the rest of the men.

And just like that, a plan, a solid plan is hatched, and I think we will win.

"Grand," I state firmly. "It's business as usual, yeah? We can't let anyone know what we've got planned. For this to work,

Sean, Liam, and their men need to think they're still in control. Sean wants me to intercept a shipment of drugs and kill Liam very publicly like I did with his father.

"This is to send a message to anyone who wants to fuck with Sean Kelly. He also knows the impact a public execution has. I do that for him, and he realizes no one will dare fuck with him ever again. But what he doesn't know is that I intend to kill him too.

"The deal was I do that for him, and he returns Cami to me. So he cannot know she's free."

"And ye trust this Aoife?" Ethan asks, eyes narrowed. He saw firsthand what she did to Babydoll.

"Naw, I do not. But I need her, Ethan. Let this be the first lesson I teach ye when it comes to takin' down yer enemy. Sometimes, ye have to do things ye don't want to get what ye want."

He nods, understanding that sleeping with the enemy is sometimes for the greater good.

"She has the ability to ruin this for us, and I won't allow it. Not this close to victory. I will be in touch once I speak to Austin. Until then, remember, it's business as usual. Whatever Sean and Liam want, we submit."

I know it's asking a lot, but it's not for long.

We shake hands, a new lease on life bouncing between us because we're finally at an advantage. The men leave, and it saddens me that it doesn't include Cian. I can only hope he sees reason as I understand his stance. This does feel like giving up, but I can't do this anymore.

I never wanted to live this life. It was forced on me because of the Kelly name. I now have a choice, something I've never had.

A knock sounds on the door. She's right on time.

Running a hand through my hair, I slip on my invisible mask, a reflection of the one I paint whenever I need strength, and open the door.

"Hi, Puck."

"Hey." I open the door so Aoife can enter my home.

It takes all my willpower not to throttle her.

She examines my house, smiling. "I always wondered about yer home. About who ye were before ye were thrown into prison. I like both."

"Thank you," I reply, her compliment making me uncomfortable. "Can I get ye a drink?"

"Thanks."

Walking past her, I enter the kitchen and pour us some whiskey. It's clear by the way she watches me that she doesn't fully trust me. Good, because she shouldn't.

Offering her a glass, I use the kitchen counter as a barricade between us. I need to put space between us because even though I'm forced to play nice with her, I can't guarantee my temper won't snap.

"We need to talk," I start, running my finger along the rim

of my glass.

Aoife nods, sipping her drink.

"I need ye to tell me if Sean ever called on ye to visit Cami."

A trickle of whiskey spills down her chin which she quickly wipes away with the back of her hand. "No," she replies. "He would usually ask how she was. He trusted me to tell him the truth. I have no reason to lie to him."

Her loyalty and faith in Sean concern me.

"We now have a problem," I calmly state. "Cami is no longer there. So I need to know what yer goin' to say to Sean if he asks about her."

"I promise ye, Puck, I thought she was hurtin' ye. That's the only reason I did what Sean asked. He said he was doin' it to protect ye. I mean, she was engaged to yer best friend. I would never betray ye like that."

I rein in my temper. "It's okay, Aoife. I'm not mad at ye. But now, by playin' along, *this* is what will really protect me. I need ye to pretend that all is well. That Cami is still with ya."

She swallows, the glass in her hand trembling. "I can do that. But what if he comes by?"

"Then ye need to stall him. He cannot know that Cami is free. If he does, it puts all our lives in danger. Cami took Shay because the son of the man I killed was at yer house. He was lookin' for her, which means ye need to be careful."

"What?" she gasps, paling. "I didn't know that. I thought she took him—"

"Ye don't know the half of it," I interrupt. "Which is why I'm offerin' ye protection. I'd offer ye a place to stay, but we can't do that. We can't do anythin' that will alert anyone that somethin' is different. It's only for a wee while because this will be over soon."

"What does that mean?"

"The less ye know, the better it is," I reply, meaning every word.

"I'm scared, Puck."

"I know."

"I'm not scared for me." She opens her bag and produces a piece of paper. Sliding it across the counter, she offers it to me. "But I'm scared for our son."

The floor almost folds out from under me as I reach for the paper and read over the paternity results.

"Shay is your son."

The results are clear as day, but deep down, I didn't need a test to recognize my kin. I knew he was my son. And I will do everything to protect him.

"Say somethin'," Aoife whispers, watching me closely for any clues to how I'm feeling.

"I mean no disrespect, but I need to do my own test as well. I've been lied to before, and I won't let it happen again."

I slide the piece of paper back to Aoife, who seems disappointed I need a second opinion. "Of course. But I wouldn't lie to ye." She places her hand over mine. "I know I did wrong with Cami. But I did think I was doin' the right thing.

"All I ever wanted to do was protect ye."

"How did Sean know we were together in prison?"

Her cheeks turn a bright red. "I don't know. He turned up on my doorstep one day and told me he was yer dad and wanted to help with Shay. I was so desperate for money. He was a godsend."

I can't help but snicker.

This goes to prove Sean's reach is wide. He knows things which he shouldn't. We need to be so careful with how we tread.

"I don't feel safe in my own home," she confesses, squeezing my hand.

Every part of me is demanding I yank my hand away, but I don't. "I know that, but ye never really were. By accepting Sean's money, he owns ye, and he came callin' when he needed ye. And he will continue to do so for the rest of yer life."

Aoife lowers her eyes, appearing ashamed.

"I don't want this life for Shay," I state, still finding it difficult to say he's my son. "The life I lived when I was a wee lad. It only ends one way."

Aoife nods with tears in her eyes.

"This is why I need ye to do what I say to protect him. I will do what I must to ensure he never lives the life I did."

"And what about me? My feelings for ye, Puck. They're real."

I need to answer this carefully. "You and I will always share somethin' special. Out of hate, we created somethin' fucking remarkable. And because of that, ye will always have my protection."

"But what about yer…love?"

"That is somethin' I'm still learning about," I reply honestly.

I know what Aoife wants. I know she wants the paternity results to change things, that we will be a happy family. I will do what's right, but I will never be with her how she wants. I fear if I tell her this, she'll use it against me, which is why I need to be careful.

"Can I trust ye will do what's right? What's best for our…son?"

"Yes, always," she says, her sincerity clear. "He is all that matters."

I'm glad we agree. Now, I can only hope Aoife doesn't betray me. I hope that this is enough for her because it's all I can offer.

Removing my hand from hers, I open the drawer and offer her a mobile phone. "I'm goin' to contact ye on this from now on. Please don't let anyone know ye have it. It's safer this way."

She accepts, placing the phone into her bag. "So what happens now?"

"Ye go about yer day like usual. I need to take care of some things."

She nods, reading between the lines. "When can we see ye again?"

"As soon as it's safe. I promise ye, I won't abandon ye both."

And I mean it.

"When I can, I want to do my own paternity test."

"Whatever ye need."

Tests have advanced since I last did mine, and apparently, DNA kits are available to do at home, which are then sent away for the results. "I need a mouth swab from Shay," I say. "And some hair."

"I can run it over to ye."

But I shake my head. "Naw, I want to do it myself."

The last time I trusted someone with these results, I believed I was a Doyle, so I am not taking any chances this time.

I've offended her, but this isn't about her. It's about something more important than she and I—it's about Shay.

"No bother. All right, A'll chat to ye soon then." She gathers all her things and makes her way to the door.

Before she leaves, I leave her with something which I hope will ensure she does the right thing. "Thank you, Aoife, for doin' the right thing, the right thing for Shay."

Her shoulders shudder as she walks out the door.

With a sigh, I pour another glass of whiskey because so many things can go wrong. I'm relying on Aoife to think of Shay and to trust me. But if she tells Sean, we are so fucked. I also need to get eyes on Liam. I need to know if he's going to pay Aoife another visit. I need to know why he was there in the first place.

Reaching for my phone, I text Ron, asking him to keep dick at Aoife's place. I then send another text. It's to Austin Bailey.

I want to meet your boss. Some things have changed, but the end game is still the same.

He replies a moment later.

He wants to meet you too. I'll organize it.

I don't ask when because I know how this works. I wait for the details.

When my phone chimes, and I see the message is from Sean, I can't help the paranoia which creeps in.

Tea at my house. 7pm. See you then.

I don't reply as this invitation isn't optional. I have no idea what he has planned, but I know it can't be good.

When I pull into Sean's drive, I prepare myself for anything. No one has called me to alert me that something is wrong, so I hope that means this is just another one of Sean's mind games.

I knock on the door, and when Sean opens it, a big smile slapped on his face, I remind myself his days are numbered.

"Son, so happy ye could make it."

I grunt in response and push past him.

I head for the kitchen as I need a drink to deal with this shitshow, but almost fall over my feet when I see who sits at the dining table.

"One big happy family," Sean says from behind me when I lock eyes with Ethan and Hannah.

"What are they doin' here?" I can't contain my anger.

"I thought it would be nice to have a family dinner together. We've not done that before."

Bull-fucking-shit.

Sean is onto us, and Ethan knows it too as he subtly nods. Hannah looks to be seconds away from stabbing Sean in the throat with her silver fork. But we're all waiting to see what he's playing at.

"Sit. I will get ye a drink. Whiskey?"

"Bring the bottle," I firmly demand as I don't trust him pouring me a drink.

When he's gone, I lean in close and whisper, "Why didn't ye call me?"

"'Cause a car came to pick us up," Hannah quickly replies. "Cami is fine. But we had to go because we didn't want the driver to come inside. We've not been alone since."

"Fuck," I curse under my breath. "Is she there alone?"

"Eva is with her," Ethan replies, his concern clear because they are sitting ducks.

"This is not good."

"What does it mean?"

"It means Sean isn't takin' any chances. Lesson number two: the bad guys are paranoid fucks."

Ethan's cheeks billow as he exhales while Hannah reaches for her glass of water.

Déjà vu hits me because the last time Babydoll was left alone, she was kidnapped. What if Sean has sent his men to Aoife's in search of her? I don't have time to send for help because Sean appears, bottle in hand.

"Your favorite," he says, offering me the bottle of whiskey.

Accepting it, I break the seal as he knows better than to offer me an opened bottle. "Cut the bullshit," I spit, reaching for a glass. "What do you want?"

Sean laughs. "What I want is for us to act like a family. We are Kellys, after all."

"Ye didn't think that way when ye got Ethan hooked on whatever shite he was pumpin' into his system," I counter, filling my glass to the brim with whiskey. "I am done playin' yer games. I agreed to yer terms on the proviso that once it was done, ye would give Cami back to me.

"I am not interested in yer fuckin' theatrics."

Hannah whimpers, afraid. But this is what Sean would expect. If I was to behave in any other way, it would rouse suspicion.

"Ye really are my son," he says, insulting me in the worst possible way. "I just thought, with everythin' so close to completion, it might be a good idea to keep youse close."

I was right. He is paranoid. He wants to watch us in case we're conspiring behind his back. This close to the end, he doesn't want to take any chances.

"I am not interested in being anywhere near you," I retort, throwing back my drink. "I told ye I would do what ya wanted, so let Ethan and Hannah go home. They're not a part of any of this."

"On the contrary, they are," Sean argues. "They are Kellys, after all."

But what Sean really means is that *Ethan* is a threat. This is why he took him under his wing. Not for protection, but control. He knows that Ethan could retaliate, and being a Kelly, being Connor's son, could mean competition.

He thought he could use Ethan to do his bidding and to be on his side, but now that Ethan has turned, he sees him as a danger to his throne.

He has me where he wants me, holding Cami over my head. And I know he now has something over Ethan's—Eva.

We watch as Sean walks over to the wooden coffee table and opens the drawer. What he retrieves has me shooting upright, standing in front of Ethan.

"Get that away from him." All plans are quickly thrown out the window when I look at the small leather case in his hand. I will kill him before he gets that shite near Ethan.

"Calm down," Sean flippantly orders. "It's nothin' he can't

handle. It's just something to take the edge off."

"Yer not shootin' him up with that shite ever again." In Sean's hand is an ex-addict's weakness. It is also the way for Sean to subdue Ethan until he can cement his position on his throne.

When Sean steps forward, I strike out and punch him in the jaw. "I won't tell ye again."

He wipes the blood from his lip, smirking as I've allowed him to see my weakness. "Ethan, what would ye like to do?"

I never take my eyes off Sean because I am ready to end this—consequences be damned.

Ethan comes to a stand by me. "It's all right, Puck," he assures me.

"Naw, it is not all right."

"Ethan, no," Hannah cries, also coming to a stand.

It's three against one. Sean is outnumbered, and I like those odds.

"Ye see, I have a lot at stake, and I can't take any chances."

He needs Ethan as a comatose zombie because any threat, no matter how small, is still a threat.

"Why would I do that? That shite ruined my life."

Sean mulls over his comment. "I don't remember it bein' all bad. In fact, I remember ye likin' it. A lot."

Ethan lowers his eyes, ashamed.

"But if ye don't want it, maybe I can offer it to yer girlfriend? She's still at Fiona's, am I right? I like what she's done with her hair."

Fuck.

He cannot go there. If he does and sees Cami, all of this would have been for nothing. But I can't allow Ethan to do this. This will destroy him.

Who do I choose?

Eva has recently cut her hair, which means Sean has eyes on the house or, at the very least, Eva. Does this mean he already knows Cami is free?

I am presented with two options. I do as Sean wants, or…I kill him.

I decide on the latter.

Shoving Ethan and Hannah aside, I launch for Sean, primed on killing him with my bare hands. I don't think about anything but crushing this fucker. Anger explodes from me, and I attack Sean from every angle. He doesn't stand a chance.

He stumbles backward as I punch him in the stomach, then the ribs. He crashes into a cabinet, whatever inside breaking with the force. Gripping him by the collar of his shirt, I headbutt him, relishing in the pained wheeze which escapes him.

I know this is wrong, that by doing this I put everyone at risk. But I can't stop.

Elbowing him in the face, I holler in happiness when blood pours from his nose. I don't know what happens when I kill him, but I don't care. The bloodshed rouses the bloodlust, and I won't be satisfied until he's dead.

"Puck!" Hannah screams, but I can't stop. This is all I've dreamt of.

Slamming his back against the wall, I press my forearm over his throat, choking the life from him as he turns a bright red. He doesn't fight, and again, déjà vu overcomes me. I'm about to kill him; he should be fighting for his life.

"Let him go."

When I hear a gun being cocked, I turn over my shoulder to see Hannah and Ethan being held at gunpoint by Flynn and Grady. I regret not killing them when I had the chance.

Sean wheezes a laugh. "Yer temper will be the death of ye, Punky."

"From where I stand, it looks like I'll be the death of *you*."

"Kill me now, and y'll never see yer Babydoll again." Suddenly, something flickers behind his eyes. "Or is it possible that ye already know where she is?"

I think of what that means. If I go through with this, then what does that mean for Shay? He will be at risk because I have no doubt if anything happens to Sean, he has ordered my son pays. I can't save them all. I've already witnessed that firsthand.

And with Hannah and Ethan at gunpoint, we won't make it out of this alive.

This is why I decided on the plan because there will always be someone waiting in the shadows. I can't risk it, but by losing my temper, I just may have done so already.

With no other choice, I let Sean go.

He gasps for air, clutching at his throat while I stand back, needing to get my shit together.

"Let them go."

"We don't take orders from you," Flynn spits, lingering too close to Hannah.

Sean takes a moment to catch his breath, but continues scrutinizing me, looking for any signs that will prove his theory.

"Grady." His voice is raspy, thanks to his windpipe being crushed. "I need ye to check on sweet Camilla for me."

Hannah's eyes widen because Cami isn't where she's supposed to be. If they find that out, then Aoife and Shay will pay for my mistake. I keep my cool, however, as I need to think fast.

Grady nods and is out the door. Flynn, however, stays.

Playtime is over as Sean orders for me to sit.

Instead, I stand near Hannah and Ethan. "It'll be all right," I promise them, but I don't know how.

Grady is on his way to Aoife's, and when she doesn't deliver a cuffed Cami, we're all going to pay. This is really it this time. I fucked up beyond repair. But I couldn't allow Ethan to sacrifice himself that way.

"What's wrong, Puck? Ye look nervous," Sean says, pulling up a seat.

"What would I have to be nervous about?" I question with my poker face firmly in play. "Y've just confirmed that Cami is alive. And she's somewhere in Belfast. And I'll be able to gauge where dependin' on the time it takes for Grady to call ye. So maybe yer the one who looks nervous now."

Sean exhales sharply because I've just played him at his own game.

He gets up and exits abruptly, leaving us alone with Flynn.

Looking at the clock on the mantel, I estimate it will take roughly thirty minutes to get to Aoife's from here. That's how long I have to save my son.

Looking around the room for a weapon, I come up empty. My knife is in my boot, but by the time I reach for it, Hannah will be dead. I didn't bring my gun because I didn't want Sean to think I was suspicious. I told myself to humor him for only a little while longer.

How I now regret that.

The silence is deafening. I need to act, and I need to act now.

"You do realize I'm going to kill ye," I say to Flynn who snickers.

"I'm pretty sure I'm the one holdin' the gun."

"Not for long," I reply with a shrug. "Ye think he gives a fuck about ye? Yer ten a penny."

"Ye don't know what yer talkin' about. Sean has looked after my family."

"Yeah, well, we are *his* family, and I can tell ye this, he doesn't care a thing about it. Y'll just be another arsehole who fell victim to Sean Kelly. Run while y've still got the chance because if Sean doesn't kill you…I promise ya this; I will."

My reverse psychology is working as I've planted the seed of doubt, and I can see it growing.

"I'm not here to offer ye an ultimatum. I'm givin' ye a choice to walk away while ye still can. You and Grady. Call him right now and let him know, if he comes back here, I'll kill him too. And ye know I'm not bluffin.'"

The gun trembles in Flynn's hand. "I do that, and who will look after my family?"

"I'll tell ya what, ya do that, and I'll look after you and yer family for the duration of yer miserable existence, and then some. All y've got to do is call Grady and tell him to keep drivin.'"

"I want half a million. And yer castle."

A bargaining man is a man who can be bought. I didn't expect it to be that easy, however.

"All right. It's yours."

"And Grady gets the same."

"I don't know how yer goin' to split the castle, but fine, consider it done." At this point, I'd give him my right kidney if he asked.

No surprise, greed is the motivator behind Flynn, and when he reaches into his pocket, I nod at Ethan. This will be okay. It has to be.

He presses the phone to his ear, gun still aimed at Hannah's temple. "Where are you?"

I can't hear what Grady has said but I am ready to take Flynn down if I have to. There is no way Grady can pass on to Sean that Cami isn't at Aoife's. But when Flynn appears surprised, I wonder if I'm too late.

Sean appears a few moments later, stopping when he notices something is amiss. Flynn quickly pockets his phone.

"Who was on the phone?"

"It was Grady. He was callin' to tell me the news."

"Is that so? And what did he tell ye?"

Ethan subtly gestures with his chin that he can take Flynn. I shake my head. Not yet.

"That she's where she's supposed to be."

I don't know if he's lying. I don't know if my proposal was enough to convince him to lie. What I do know is this has bought us some time.

"Aye, he phoned me too."

He did? What in the ever-living fuck is going on?

I can't show relief, however. "And where is she supposed to be exactly?"

Sean snickers, gesturing Flynn is to give Sean his gun. He does.

A relieved gasp escapes Hannah as she scampers away.

"What were ye talkin' 'bout?" Sean asks me.

"Ach, ya know, the weather, and who's hookin' up on *Love Island.*"

I need to hide under my sarcasm because I have no idea what's going on.

"Somethin' isn't right," Sean says, eyeing us closely.

"You can say that again," I reply, keeping my calm. "Things haven't been right in a very long time."

"What were ya really talkin' 'bout?"

I have no idea where he's going with this, but it's either my arse or Flynn's, and Flynn knows it.

"He tried to—"

Before Flynn has a chance to tell Sean the truth, I snatch the gun from Sean. "Yer men don't know the first thing about loyalty."

Ethan seizes Hannah and cradles her into his chest so she doesn't have to witness me shooting Flynn right between the eyes. He drops to the floor with a hollowed thud.

I casually pass the gun back to Sean. "Sorry, I think that's gonna stain yer rug."

I've caught Sean off guard, who simply stares at Flynn, bleeding out on the brown carpet.

"If yer done playin' happy families, I'm takin' Hannah and Ethan home."

Sean doesn't know how to react because, on the surface, nothing is amiss. But things are far from perfect—for him. He'll never know what Flynn was going to say, which appeared to be a lot. That's why I killed him.

I can't allow anyone to fuck this up for us—including me.

"Flynn propositioned me," I say, as Sean won't let us leave without an explanation. "He offered to do ye in…for a measly half a million. Didn't seem he valued yer life too much. I would have offered at least a million."

"Ye expect me to believe that?"

Laughing, I gesture to Hannah and Ethan we're leaving. "I don't care what ye believe. I just did ye a favor. I kept to my word of servin' ye like the good wee dog that I am. Killin' ye doesn't get me back Cami. So it looks like we're stuck with one another until we both get what we want."

Sean doesn't know what to believe because my reasoning makes sense. Babydoll is at Aoife's, and my behavior hasn't been any different. But he senses something is wrong.

"I'll be watchin' youse," he warns, annoyed he lost this fight.

"Seems ye should be watchin' yer boys, do ye not think?" I leave him with that psychological mind fuck because two can play this game.

We don't run to my truck. We calmly walk because we know Sean meant it. Until Liam is dead and his drugs are stolen, we will be under surveillance twenty-four-seven.

I start the engine, and the moment I pull out onto the road, a sigh of relief escapes all three of us.

"What's going on?" Ethan asks, turning to look at me from the passenger seat. "Is Cami really at Aoife's?"

"I don't know," I reply honestly. "But I'm not waitin' around to find out."

ELEVEN

PUNKY

I've never been on higher alert than I am right now. If this fails, we will all pay, which is why we cannot.

I'm sitting in my truck, parked down the street from Aoife's house. I remain hidden because no one can know we're here. Ethan and Eva are with me. Hannah is at Fiona's in case. She said she'd phone if anything seems out of place.

I'm thankful I gave Aoife the phone as it's a secure line. When I called her, she confirmed that Babydoll was there. What she didn't explain was how she knew to be there when we needed her to be. The issue I have is getting Babydoll out of there undetected because there is no chance in hell I am leaving her at Aoife's.

This is why Eva is here.

I hate this plan, but I've learned that you can't stop people from doing things they want to. Eva wants to go into Aoife's and have Babydoll come out in place of her. This will work because the sisters look alike, and also, I doubt whoever is watching Aoife's will know the difference.

I know Babydoll will hate me for allowing her sister to take her place, but I need to get her out of there.

Eva will eventually sneak out when we've scouted the place to make sure the coast is clear. But for now, I just need to make sure Cami is all right.

"Be careful," I say to Eva as she slips into a raincoat. It's raining, which helps with the disguise as she slips on the hood. "Y've got the gun?"

"I will. And yes, I do."

"If anything looks suspicious, ye get out of there, all right? We will find another way to get Cami out."

Eva's dogged expression reveals that option is one she does not accept. She reminds me of her sister—both are strong, determined women, which is why I know this won't fail.

Ethan looks over his shoulder at Eva, his concern clear.

Their love is new. It's young love. I've almost forgotten the innocence, but when I think back to when I met Babydoll and the feelings she stirred in me, I remember the unbreakable bond we formed and how I promised myself to never let any harm come of her.

Young love is really a beautiful thing.

"Don't put yerself at risk. Promise me that," Ethan pleads with her, and I suddenly feel like I'm encroaching on a private moment.

"I promise," she replies, leaning between the front seats and placing a kiss on Ethan's cheek.

She doesn't cower—another trait she and her sister share—and opens the back door, reaching for the huge floral arrangement on the back seat. She closes the door, and Ethan and I watch as she walks toward Aoife's house.

The tension spills from him, and all I can do is touch his shoulder in assurance. "She'll be okay. She's smart."

He nods, but that doesn't lessen the weight pressing against his heart.

We watch in silence as Eva knocks on Aoife's door. This plan will work. To onlookers, it appears that Eva is simply delivering flowers. The door opens, and I sigh in relief when Aoife answers with Shay in one arm and a box in the other.

I instructed her to answer the door with her hands full as this gives Eva an excuse to enter Aoife's home, which she does. The window is small because anything over two minutes will rouse suspicion. So I can only hope Babydoll goes along with the plan.

Aoife nudges the door wide with her shoulder, allowing Eva into her home. She doesn't close the door fully but subtly closes it enough to conceal what's going on inside. Ethan leans forward, his nose all but pressed to the windscreen as he waits for someone to re-emerge.

Two minutes soon become three, a sure sign something is wrong.

"Fuck," I curse, reaching into the glove compartment for my gun.

Ethan already has his in hand and just as he opens the door, someone steps out of Aoife's. We both pause in our tracks, barely breathing as we watch the woman, donned in the raincoat, leave Aoife's and make her way toward us.

"Calm down, cub." I gently grip Ethan's forearm to stop him from launching from the truck. The energy vibrating off him almost burns me.

The woman's head is bowed, so I can't see who it is. The closer she gets, the faster my heart beats. She quickly opens the back door, and when she gets in, both Ethan and I turn to look at her. With her chin still drooped, she slowly removes the hood.

Raindrops somersault into the air, and if this was some romantic movie, this would be the moment the couple lock eyes when caught in a rainstorm and everything fades to black. But it's not because all I can feel is Ethan's heart crushing.

"Drive," Babydoll orders.

I can't read what she's thinking, but I know she's pissed.

Turning back around, I start the truck and slip into the night.

The drive back to Fiona's is filled with nothing but

uncomfortable silence. Ethan's attention is focused out the window, and as I risk a glimpse at Babydoll in the rearview mirror, it seems she too would rather peer into the night skies than look at me.

As I pull up by the curb, Ethan opens the door, but Babydoll doesn't move.

"I'm not staying at Fiona's," she states blankly. "Take me to a hotel please."

Ethan doesn't bother to stay for this fight and closes the door, leaving us alone. I wait until he's inside before pulling away.

The silence continues.

"Babydoll—"

"I don't want to talk to you right now," she interrupts sharply. "I just want to sleep. I am so fucking tired. Of everything."

My heart sinks.

This is the first time she's admitted defeat. Is she tired of this? Of *us*?

I get why she gave me the cold shoulder when she returned. She was held captive by the woman who gave birth to my son. It's a lot to process. I thought giving her space would help. But have I pushed her away? I don't understand anything anymore.

I wish I could take her back to my house, but I simply cannot. Sean will be watching the castle more than ever now. We have to be so careful.

"What hotel?" I ask, flinching at how harsh I sound. But I

don't know how to approach this. I don't know how to speak to her without saying something wrong.

"Kavanagh's Bed and Breakfast." Before I can ask how she knows of this place, she adds, "It's where I used to stay when I came back to Belfast to try to help you."

There is no malice behind her words. Merely exhaustion. She's been fighting for almost eleven years. I can't blame her for being worn out.

I know the B&B well, so we drive there in silence.

Kavanagh's is an 1800s family home on five acres of gardens. The white two-story home has been preserved to accommodate guests, but I don't think Babydoll stayed here for the comforts. I guess the fact that it's in the middle of nowhere, surrounded by nothing but silence, is the reason.

It saddens me that she mourned me so much that she too lost ten years of her life.

A part of me was angry with her for moving on with Rory, but Kavanagh's is a sure sign she never really left. She was always hopeful something would change, that a miracle would unite us, but as years passed, she realized that was a fantasy.

Everything is so fucked up.

Although I'm out of prison, we're still shackled to the past. So much has happened, and I wonder if maybe it's too much to overcome. I thought our love could prevail everything—was I wrong?

The moment I put the truck into park, Babydoll opens the

door without looking at me. But I can't let her go. I switch off the engine and follow her as she walks toward the front door. She doesn't acknowledge me. But she doesn't send me away either.

When we step inside, an aul' doll hobbles out from the elegant dining room, hands filled with cutlery. "Sorry, we're—"

She soon stops when she sees Babydoll.

"Camilla." She smiles broadly, her happiness clear. "Grand to see ye again. Yer needin' a room?"

Babydoll nods. "Hi, Aine. I'm sorry I didn't call and make a reservation. I understand if you're booked out."

"Hush, chile," Aine says, shaking her head. "I told ye, yer always welcome here. Come."

Aine places the cutlery onto a table before leading us through the home. She takes the stairs, our footsteps echoing on the wooden staircase. We walk down the hallway where Aine leads us to the door at the end.

She opens the door, and when I peer inside, the sadness I felt earlier returns. This isn't a bedroom, but rather a small studio space fitted with a double bed, a small dresser, and a red leather recliner. The floor isn't carpeted, and one would be forgiven for thinking this was used for storage because it's hardly decked out with the luxuries one would expect to find in a bed and breakfast.

"I'll leave ya fresh towels and linens in the bathroom. Call out if ye need me. If yer hungry, there are some sandwiches in the kitchen."

Aine doesn't acknowledge me, which has me guessing she knows I'm the reason Babydoll stayed in less than comfortable conditions for years. She closes the door, sealing us in.

The single bulb barely emits any light, and I think of Babydoll cooped up in here, endless nights alone, straining her eyes as she scanned over paperwork to help set me free. She didn't want to stay anywhere lavish as I know she felt undeserving.

She wanted to suffer, knowing I was too.

"How'd ye know he was comin' for you?"

Babydoll's back is turned to me, but I don't need to look at her to know she is hurting.

"When someone came to pick up Hannah and Ethan, I took a wild guess Sean was behind it. I suspected something like this would happen eventually. I went to Aoife's, knowing the consequences. So why did you send Eva?"

I knew she would be mad at me.

"I needed to get ye out of there. It's too dangerous."

"And it's not for my sister?"

Finally, she turns around, locking eyes with me. I'm unsure how we got here, to this place where it's hard to breathe. "Of course, it is. But I've come to learn, I can't command the actions of anyone. I tried that, and people died."

She flinches. "Do you know how it felt, leaving her behind? Her taking my place and putting her life in danger for me?"

"Aye, I do," I reply solemnly. "That's what youse have done for me. That's what *you've* done for me, time and time again. I didn't want youse a part of this, but yer the one who told me ye wanted yer revenge too. I'm tryin', Cami. I'm really fucking tryin'."

My desperation bursts from me because I don't know what she wants me to say anymore.

"Trying what?" she questions, arms folded.

"I'm tryin' to do right by everyone! I'm tryin' not to be the bad guy. I'm tryin' to be the man my ma and Connor would be proud of. And I'm tryin' to be a man who is worthy of yer love!"

She pales, taken aback by my outburst. But I can't help it. I feel like I'm losing myself—piece by piece.

"When I didn't know where ye were," I confess, begging she believes me. "When I didn't know if you were dead or alive…I wanted to fucking end it. I wanted to give up. It was the first time in my life that I ever felt helpless…and that's what you make me—I am helpless without you.

"You own me, Camilla. I am nothin' without ye. I know everythin' is fucked up. I know you probably wish ye'd never met me. If I could change that, I would. I want ya to live a normal life—away from this. Away from me.

"I am so fucking sorry this has happened. I wish I could change it, but I can't, and I don't know how to fix it."

I've never felt more helpless in my entire life.

"I don't think it can ever be fixed," she says, wrapping her arms around herself.

My heart sinks because I don't know what she means. But what I do know is that I can't let her go without a fight. So much has happened, and this was bound to take a turn sooner or later.

I got out of prison. She was engaged, then she wasn't. She thought we were kin, only to find out that we weren't. I killed her father and her fiancé. She was kidnapped, held captive by the woman I fucked, and set free by my son.

We were running on fumes, but now, with the end almost in sight, we need to get this all out in the open because it's the only hope we have at surviving this.

She sighs, defeated. But I won't give up—not when she never gave up on me.

I storm toward her, her wide eyes confirming she can't read me either. But when I drop to my knees before her in surrender, there is no mistaking my feelings.

"Please forgive me for everythin' I've done. I should have told you we weren't kin. I shouldn't have tried to save you because ye can save yerself. I'm sorry for killin' yer dad. I'm sorry for killin' Rory."

It's the first time I've apologized for Rory's death, and it's because it's the first time I've meant it.

"If given the choice again…I would choose differently. But I'll live with that guilt for the rest of my life," I confess, watching as tears trickle down her cheek. "I'm sorry for every single time I made you cry. I am just so fucking sorry.

"I have no right to ask for yer forgiveness, but I need it. I need *you*."

A sob escapes her, which she mutes behind her hand.

"I love you, Babydoll. I always have. And I need you to love me back. I cannot survive this if ya don't. I know that's not what most would say, but I'm not most. I can't give ya a choice because I need you…so fucking much.

"I know I sound like a buck eejit. A desperate man who is beggin' for yer love, and that's 'cause I am. This started with revenge, but I want to end it with love—our love. It's why I'm givin' this all away. I just…I just want to grow aul' with you."

I can't stop the words that spill from me. I want Babydoll to know that she makes me vulnerable, and I'm okay with that.

She doesn't speak. She simply drops to her knees too.

This moment is unguarded—just Babydoll and me against the world. We're beaten and bruised, a sure sign we were stronger than whatever tried to beat us, but together, we are unstoppable.

"I love you too."

Those four words are a salve to my soul.

"Everything is just so fucked," she confesses, her lower lip trembling. "And I am so afraid. What if we don't win? What if this has been for nothing?"

"This"—with apprehension, I reach for her hand and press it over my heart—"this will never be for nothin'. This is *everything*."

Tears continue to fall down her cheeks, and I don't wipe them away. Each one carries her pain.

"I'm sorry for being so…angry with you. I thought coming back would make everything all right. But things are different now."

I know she means Shay.

"I still need to do my own test."

But she shakes her head. "He's yours. I have no doubt about it. Your strength, your courage run through his veins. He is a Kelly. Shay is an amazing kid, and you're going to be an amazing father."

The reality of what she says sinks in—I'm a father, to a son who saved the woman I love. I couldn't be prouder.

"I will never forgive Aoife for what she did, but Shay is…he is something special. A gift."

I don't deserve her. She has accepted Shay when some may not have been so forthcoming. This entire situation is far from ideal, but we will make it work because we haven't come this far to give up now.

Gripping the back of her neck, I draw us together, brow to brow. I don't speak. I simply allow this moment of peace to shield us from the world. Now that she's back in my arms, I'll never let her go again.

Her steady breaths lull me into a comfortable stupor, but when she nudges her nose with mine, I understand she wants more.

"Yer arm," I whisper against her lips as she comes in for a kiss. I don't want to hurt her.

"It's okay. We just need to be careful."

"I don't think that I can," I reply honestly because the moment I taste her, all I can think of is throwing her onto the bed and devouring every inch of her gorgeous flesh.

She doesn't seem to mind and kisses me softly.

Her lips mold to mine perfectly—they always have. We fit in every way that there is. We've shared many kisses, but this one feels different, like this is really it this time. We know the obstacles that face us, but we'll tackle them together.

For the first time in my life, I feel like I've found my home.

I walk her backward, guiding her toward the bed. When her knees hit the mattress, she lowers herself onto it, taking me with her. Her arm is still in a cast, but she maneuvers herself backward, laying her head onto the pillow.

I ensure my weight isn't pressed into her as we continue kissing sluggishly. When she cups my cheek, I recoil instinctively. But she doesn't let me turn away.

"I'm sorry I don't have anythin' nicer to offer you."

The scar on my face is forever, and although it doesn't bother me, I'm sure it's not something Babydoll wishes to glance upon for the rest of her life. It's a reminder of all the awful things I've done.

"Don't be silly," she whispers, stroking over the jagged line. The stitches are out, but the wound is far from healed. "I love you—every single part of you."

Each time she professes her love for me, I feel like a miracle has been performed.

"We're quite a pair," she says with a small smile, and her words, they incite something inside me, something I didn't even know I wanted until now.

"Aye, that we are. I—" I pause, suddenly unsure, but I don't second-guess myself. This was destined from the first moment we met.

"What?" Her hand trembles on my cheek, revealing her nerves.

I don't know how to do this. I don't know what the proper way is. But when I look into Babydoll's eyes and see nothing but love, I realize this is as natural as breathing.

"Camilla, I want you to…I want ye to be my wife. Will you marry me?" Utter shock rocks her, which has me wetting my lips and adding, "Please."

I give her a moment or two because this has caught us both unaware.

"I don't expect you to answer right away. But I—"

"Yes," she cries, tears filling her eyes. "Yes, I will marry you."

I never thought a simple word when strung together with others could make me the happiest man alive, but they have.

"Y'll marry me?" I ask in case we're lost in translation. But when she nods quickly, tears spilling down her cheeks, I know that we're both ready to cement our union—once and for all.

"Yes, I'll marry you." She half laughs, half sobs, and I think that's a good thing.

Happiness I've never felt before tackles me swiftly, and I sit up, suddenly light-headed. Babydoll sits up and straddles me, sensing my emotions. "I want to be your wife. I want to be a Kelly."

Her admission has pride filling my lungs, and I exhale a shaky breath.

If we do this, then she's a Doyle no more…and that thought gets me harder than a fucking rock.

"I promise to make ye the happiest woman alive. Well, I'll try."

"You already have."

I can't take it any longer. I need her, all of her, before I fucking explode.

I slam my mouth over hers, and she kisses me back with urgency. She wraps the arm that isn't in a cast around my nape, pressing us closer because she feels it too. No matter how close we are, it's never enough.

Being her husband will help close the void, but I will always want more; I'll never have my fill. She is a drug made solely for me, and I'm an addict, desperate for his next hit.

"Fuck me," she pants against my lips.

I appreciate that although this moment is filled with love, she still refers to our lovemaking this way. But that's who we are—our passion is carnal, brutal, and depraved. And that won't change.

I unsnap the button on her jeans and slide my hand inside her underwear. When I feel her hot, wet flesh, we both moan because it doesn't get any better than this. I commence fucking her with my fingers while she bounces against my touch.

I don't want to hurt her and the only way this will work with her arm in a cast is if she fucks me…and my face.

Removing my fingers, I quickly yank down her jeans and underwear, hinting I want her naked, and I want it now. I help her undress, and the moment her bottom half is bare, I flip us over and coax her to sit on my face.

She lowers herself onto my mouth, and the moment her pussy touches my lips, I fucking eat her alive. Her cunt is on fire, and when she rubs herself back and forth, back and forth, I'm certain we will both explode. I fuck her with my tongue and lips, latching onto her hips and encouraging her to ride me faster and harder.

She arches her back and begins to rotate her hips while I peer up at her. She can clearly see what I'm doing to her, which I know is why she changed position. I reach around and smack her arse—hard, which has her bouncing against me with a moan.

"More."

I do as she asks and strike her voluptuous arse once more.

"Oh, fuck, I'm going to come."

Those words are just as hot as her telling me she'll marry

me.

I suckle over her clit, which has her throwing her head back and screaming a guttural cry. Her body trembles as she chases her orgasm, but I don't stop. I continue fucking her with my mouth, milking every last tremor from her.

I'm in heaven as she is slathered all over me, but when she shifts off my face and frantically tears at my shirt, I know this has only just begun.

She tries to take off her T-shirt, but because of the cast, she can't.

"Is this yer favorite shirt?"

She looks at me confused but shakes her head.

"Grand." Before she can ask why, I grip the collar and tear it into two.

I want to be gentle as she is injured, but I don't know if that's possible with the frenzied state we're both in. Or if this will last as long as I'd like it to. Just her scent alone has me threatening to come.

With a grin, she removes the now ruined garment before reaching around to unsnap her bra. The moment her breasts are free, I lower my head and suckle her nipples as she straddles me. They melt on my tongue.

She frantically fumbles with the button on my jeans, moaning as I take her breast into my mouth. We are losing control, but I've never felt more alive than I do right now. Lifting my hips, I tug down my jeans. I'm already hard, and she's oh-so wet—the perfect combination. I lift her, only to slam her back down onto my cock.

"Fuck," I curse, almost losing my shit right here and now.

She doesn't move. She just sits still, clenching her muscles around my shaft.

"You keep doin' that, and this will be over before it even begins."

Her cheeky smirk reveals she doesn't seem to mind.

She begins to move, the slide of her hips a spectacular torture I never want to end. She fucks me long and hard, taking and giving pleasure all in the same breath. Knowing this is forever has me gripping her hips, coaxing her to ride me until we're both spent.

"I love you!" she cries, bouncing frantically on my cock.

I would speak, but the air is robbed from me when she reaches down and begins to play with herself. This openness between us is something I can only ever do with her. Our walls have been shattered, and I refuse for them to ever be erected again.

She rocks against me while rubbing over her clit, and the sight has me letting go. I come hard, a winded breath leaving me as I pump my hips, coming inside of Babydoll. I don't even have the strength to pull out, but when she whimpers and follows suit, I know she doesn't mind.

The moment she's spent, she slumps forward, and I take her with me as I lower my back onto the mattress.

We're breathless and sticky. Her heart pounds against mine. This moment is utter perfection and to know we have a lifetime ahead of us has me leaning up and kissing her lips softly.

She moans, kissing me back languidly.

I'm worried about her arm, so I gently pull out, missing her heat instantly. She rolls off me and settles against the pillows while I gather the strength to get up and find the bathroom to get her cleaned up.

"No," she says, gripping my bicep. "I just want to lie here with you—sticky and sated."

She'll get no complaints from me.

Tucking her into me, we snuggle closely, basking in the afterglow. Exhaustion tackles me, and for once in my life, I'm willing to surrender because I'll deal with everything tomorrow.

"What happens now?" she whispers, drawing patterns on my chest with her fingertip.

"It's time I organized a meeting with someone who can help end this."

"And what does he want in return?"

She can guess but wants to hear it from my mouth.

"He wants Belfast, and ye know what, he can have it."

Her silence has me worried she's not fond of the idea.

"Do you think you can do that? Do you think after everything, you're ready to give it all away?"

Cian's anger crashes into me as he doesn't think I should.

"I have everythin' I want right here," I affirm, bringing her closer into me.

She doesn't reply, and I know that's because she agrees with Cian. They both seem to think handing over my legacy isn't what I should do. But if I don't do that, we will just be back at square one.

I need someone bigger than this to help me, and if his terms are taking my kingdom in exchange for destroying the men who betrayed me, then that's a sacrifice I'm willing to make.

Belfast needs to be purged, expunged of the filth so she can be reborn.

As Cami and I succumb to sleep, a small voice whispers that doing that may be easier said than done.

TWELVE

PUNKY

I hate meetings—I especially hate meetings with men I've never met before. But to get what I want, I need to put my faith in a stranger.

If Austin is lying to me and this is another trap, I've come prepared.

"All right," I say to Ron as I conceal my gun into the small of my back. "Ya stay out here unless ye hear trouble. And in that case, you come in, and shoot first, ask questions later."

Ron nods firmly.

He has the pub, Lucky Leaf, where Austin organized for us to meet, surrounded. But we've come to learn that no matter how prepared we are, things can change in the blink of an eye… which is why Cami is here.

Bad things happen when we're apart, and as much as I don't want to put her in harm's way, being by my side is the safest place to be. Besides, this is as much her fight as it is mine.

Cian isn't here. I sent him a text with the details, but when I didn't get a reply, I figured he'd finally had enough. I know he sees this as surrendering, as me shitting on the memories of our fathers, but it's because of them that I've chosen to do this.

I won't end up in a hole in the ground beside them because that's where I'm headed if I don't give this life away. But a small part of me, one that hasn't kept quiet since I agreed to meet with Austin and Aleksei, has continued to nag me—*can* I give this life up?

Taking Cami's hand and walking toward Lucky Leaf, I will soon find out.

Cami and I are quiet, unsure what we're walking into. But knowing she's with me, that she's safe, I can handle anything.

The place is jammers, which is why Austin chose it, no doubt. He wants things to appear casual, but experience has proven that witnesses or not, it makes no difference to me. If someone pisses me off or does wrong by my girl or me, I will kill them all.

The owners have changed since the last time I was here. Ron said they're on our side. We will see.

Drunken eejits shout at their mates, not aware of how loud they are, thanks to the many pints they've had—how nice it must be to live a simple life. The atmosphere is light, which puts me at ease. But I don't let my guard down, and neither does Babydoll as she nestles closer into me.

The last time she was in a pub, she was almost blown to smithereens. The thought has me clenching my jaw. Sean's death can't come soon enough.

I make eye contact with Austin, who raises his pint in greeting. The man he's sitting with has his back turned, but he instantly looks out of place as he is wearing a crisp white shirt. His dark hair is groomed neatly, and I am immediately hit with the air of authority surrounding him.

We walk toward the booth, and when I lock eyes with the man sitting at the table, I subtly draw Cami closer to my side. He is a handsome devil, even for an aul' fella. He reeks of power and control. He is someone you do not want to fuck with.

He is someone you want on your side.

Cami enters the booth first while I slide in after her, never taking my eyes off Aleksei Popov. However, he surprises me when he bursts into a husky chuckle.

"I like you already, мой друг. You need not worry; she is safe with me. I have my own красавица at home."

I conceal the fact that I'm impressed he could read the most discreet of movements so well.

Cami sits tall, not cowering in the presence of this man who has the ability to change our lives forever.

"Hello, Aleksei. I'm Puck Kelly."

Aleksei leans back in his seat with a smile. "Please, call me

Alek. Aleksei is so…formal. And I know who you are, Puck Kelly. Your temper is just as notorious as mine."

I'm about to show him what my temper can do by ruining his spotless white shirt with the pint Austin holds. But refrain when he adds, "As is your honor, something I admire and respect in a man. I want you to know that."

"You seem to know a lot about me, but I hardly know a thing about you."

"Ask away," Alek says, gesturing the floor is mine.

Our eyes have never strayed, which shows a mutual respect between us. But before I agree to anything, I need to know just who I'm selling my soul to.

"How do I know my enemies didn't send ya? How do I know yer goin' to work with me, not against me?"

Alek nods, appearing to weigh over my questions carefully. "Your father, Sean Kelly, is not a man I would ever work with," he states with conviction. "He is a coward, and from what I understand, he kidnapped your girl, blackmailing you into doing his dirty work on the proviso he would return her to you once you did what he wanted?"

I nod slowly.

Alek's lip curls in disgust. "I can assure you, I would never do business with a мудак such as him. He is indiscreet, and he is almost, what it appears to be…rather stupid."

An amused chuckle gets caught in Babydoll's throat.

"Ten years is a long time, and the fact he needs you to regain his throne, well, I believe he should just stop embarrassing himself in his fruitless quest."

It takes me a long while to actually like anyone, but Alek is the first person I've liked in a very long time.

"But you see, his failure, his inadequacy to get things done shows me who the real leader is. That's you," he states in his composed Russian accent. "Sean is a Kelly, a name which is feared among many, yet he can't get his affairs in order without blackmailing, extorting, and hiding in the shadows like a little pussy while you run this country and beyond.

"He doesn't deserve to breathe. He is a disgrace to any man who calls himself a leader."

To hear this Russian kingpin speak this way about Sean has me basking in something I didn't have five seconds ago, and that is hope.

"As for Liam Doyle…" His voice trails off into an entertained chuckle. "He needs to stop walking in the shoes of his father, which are ten sizes too big. Brody was a little more intelligent than Sean, but he's not sitting at this table with me, is he?"

Austin sips his pint quietly, but it's clear he respects Alek immensely, and I can see why. Alek makes it his business to know who his friends and foes are, and I suspect he's had business in Northern Ireland and Ireland for a long time.

"So ye worked with Liam?" I ask, never breaking eye contact with Alek.

That arrogant grin returns. "He worked for me, Puck. They

all do. I never knew Connor Kelly, but he sounds to be a true leader, one which I believe you are too."

I don't sense any sarcasm behind his words.

"And by the way your красавица is sitting proudly by your side, I think she agrees. But this is not for me to decide. That decision is one you must come to on your own. I want to be honest with you, Puck. I'd rather work *with* you.

"You know this business better than anyone. And for it to succeed, I need someone like you. No offense, Austin."

Austin raises his half-empty pint in a mock salute.

"This world has taken so much from me," I explain, not wanting sympathy but rather wishing to express why I've chosen to opt out. "It started with revenge, and my vengeance will be had when I'm holdin' my father's severed head in my hands.

"That's all I want. It takes a monster to fight a monster, and I'm prepared to fight. Once it's done, I just want to live a life *I* choose. Not one forced onto me. Not one where I fear for my fiancée's or my son's lives."

It's the first time I've said those words aloud.

Alek breaks eye contact to look at Cami closely. I'm thankful I trust her with my life and know she doesn't look at Alek with stars in her eyes like the rest of the women and men in here.

"I have a son too," Alek shares. "And three young daughters."

I can't mask my grin. "God help their future boyfriends."

Alek opens his mouth, primed on saying something, but

instead, a laugh escapes him. "This is true. If they know what's good for them, they'll stay away."

And just like that, the mood settles—two villains speaking about wains.

"I understand your choice, and I respect it. But for this to work, I need to know you want to give it up, all of it. There are no second chances in our world—you know that. If this is what you want, then I will help you. You will get your revenge on those who wronged you, and then…you will get your freedom."

My breaths are measured because this is the first time in my life where I know I can win. Alek is the man I need to avenge my ma and to set me free.

It's everything I ever wanted; so why do I feel this heaviness press down onto my chest?

"But think very carefully because once you agree and we shake hands, there are no takebacks. You can't change your mind because I will not trust you. I do not trust men who go back on their word. And I will be forced to kill you."

Cami stiffens beside me while Austin nurses his pint. Me? I burst into laughter.

"Ye can try, aul' lad," I playfully tease, not intimidated by him in the slightest as I stand my ground.

A cane is propped up against the wall. I wonder why Alek needs it. He notices me looking at it and answers my silent question.

"Courtesy of my half-brother," he states, his anger lapping

at the calmness. "But it's a small price to pay for what I did to him."

"And what did ye do?"

"I cut off his cock and fed it to him."

I know he means this in the literal sense. I wonder what he did to deserve that. Whatever it was, it has me liking Alek all the more.

I understand his stance on this, on why he wants me to decide. He is giving me a choice, something which I shared was never given to me. If I go back on my word, I will be seen as untrustworthy. If I turn my back on Belfast, only to change my mind, Alek would see that as a challenge, and there is room for only one leader.

This is how our world works. It doesn't make sense to most, but if the roles were reversed, I would be doing the same thing.

"My brother, Ethan, he deserves to rule. Not me, for he is Connor's true son."

But Alek shakes his head as this seems personal to him. "Blood matters not when it comes to matters of the heart, and you, Puck Kelly, you wear your heart on your sleeve. Take your time to think about my offer."

"I don't need time," I firmly state. "Ye help me publicly shame my father before I kill him, and kill him slow, ensure killin' Liam Doyle goes down smoothly, and look after the men who were good to me and Connor…then y've got yerself a deal. The drugs, everythin'…it's yers."

Cami exhales slowly, a sign she wishes I would have at least given Alek's proposal some thought. But I don't need time. Sean's and Liam's death mean more to me than ruling a kingdom I never wanted.

Alek runs his thumb across his bottom lip, deep in thought. "Will you at least sleep on it?"

"Naw," I reply, offering my hand over the table. "That won't be necessary. So, we've got a deal? Y'll help me kill those who deserve it and rule with loyalty and respect to the men who stuck by me through thick and thin?"

Alek simply sits still, contemplating my offering. I'm afraid he's changed his mind.

"I don't like many people," he states frankly. "But I like you, which is why, yes, we have a deal."

The moment we shake, I know this is the beginning of the end.

Austin stands and makes his way to the bar.

"Grand. The plan still goes ahead then. We allow Liam and Sean to think they're in control. We don't intercept Liam's shipment until the last minute. I want him to be humiliated, and I need Sean to believe I've not gone rogue."

"It wouldn't be easier just to kill them now?" Alek asks, adjusting his gold cufflink.

"Easier, aye, but where's the fun in that? I've never chosen the easy option. I want them shamed and to suffer in unimaginable ways for all that they've done. Just how you did when you fed yer half-brother his cock."

Alek nods, a pleased smile spreading across his face.

"Sean killed my ma, knowin' I was watchin', trapped in a wardrobe, helpless to help her. I was five years old. Then for years, he pretended he had my back when, in reality, he was keepin' me close, tryin' to control me. He cared not for me. He only cares for himself."

"Fucker," Alek curses under his breath. "Now I understand your need for vengeance. This is very personal to me because my daughter, Irina…she didn't have the best start to life either. So, I ensured everyone who did wrong by her suffered, and I will do so for the rest of my life."

"Then ye know why I need to do this. I can't just kill him. It won't"—I pause, searching for the right word—"it won't satisfy this burnin' rage within me. He needs to suffer for what he's done. If I simply end his life swiftly, it won't be enough.

"To know I'm the last person he sees before I kill him, after I have humiliated and taken everythin' from him, will help me heal. It's the only way I can live this life without his ghost hauntin' me until I take my last breath."

"I understand all too well, мой друг. I admire your loyalty, no matter the cost."

Cami gently places her hand on my thigh, a comforting touch to assure me she's here until the very end.

"You will have everything you need, and rest assured, no harm will come to your loved ones ever again."

"That's all I want."

Austin returns with a tray filled with shots. I take a stab in the dark that they're vodka. He places them on the table, where Alek slides two across the table for Cami and me.

"Za tvajo zdarovje," he says, raising his glass in salute.

I raise my own glass. "Cheers."

We all throw back our shots, which are vodka, and slam them onto the table once they are drained dry. The alcohol is smooth as it's top-shelf. Nothing but the best for Aleksei Popov—the man who is now my partner.

An unspoken warning lingers between us—we will respect the other, as essentially, we want the same thing. But if either of us fucks the other over, there'll be hell to pay. I think I've met my match, and I know Alek feels the same way.

With nothing further to say, I stand and exit the booth. Alek remains seated, always watching me with those astute eyes. "My finest, most loyal men are at your disposal. Whatever you need."

"What I need is for one of them to get Cami's sister."

Eva is still at Aoife's, as is Ethan, who is scouting the place. Men are watching the gaff, so we can't get her out.

"It's done," Alek says with a nod. "What about your home? Do you need extra men there?"

At the moment, we're staying at Kavanagh's, which I think will be the safest place for Babydoll. "Naw, it's okay. That's my home turf. I can protect it. Anyone dares to challenge me…

they'll pay with their lives. But my siblings—"

"Whatever you need."

Alek is someone who gets shit done, and I instantly feel better having him on my team.

"All right then."

I turn to leave, but Alek stops me. "Will killing him be enough?"

The hair at the back of my neck stands on end, and I don't know why.

"I ask this because I think, like me, you too take comfort in the darkness. It's where your demons thrive. You're split right down the middle. Good versus evil. I wonder which side will win."

Turning to look at him, I deadpan him. "Fuck with me, and y'll find out."

My warning isn't empty, and Alek's smirk reveals he appreciates that I haven't submitted. Yes, I have given him my country, but that doesn't mean I've surrendered—I've won.

Taking hold of Babydoll's hand, I calmly walk through the pub, never feeling more victorious than I do right now. I don't fail to notice how quiet she was throughout the meeting, and that silence continues as we walk toward my truck.

I know she isn't happy with my decision.

As I drive us toward Kavanagh's, I'm struck with an idea, one which I hope will help Babydoll understand why I've chosen the path I have.

She doesn't say anything when I miss the turn for Kavanagh's and continue driving toward the castle. I don't take the usual route, however, as I want to remain undetected. The grounds are vast, and I take the backroad that leads to a dead end.

I switch off the engine and get out of the truck. When I hear Babydoll's car door open, I sigh in relief, thankful she's willing to hear me out.

Stepping over the barricade and onto my property, I walk through the long grass, the tall trees shielding us from prying eyes. I don't hover around Babydoll. I give her space. She's following, no doubt her curiosity getting the better of her.

When the castle comes into view in the distance, I stop near a large tree and take it all in.

"This is what I'm fightin' for," I say, never taking my eyes off the place which will always be my home. "I'm fightin' for our future, a future where we're not lookin' over our shoulders, afraid for our lives. I want this to be a home again. And I want that to be with you."

Cami sighs softly.

"I know you don't agree with my choice, but it feels right. I've only ever felt that way once before"—I turn to look at her as I take off my necklace—"and that was when I met you. I can't do this without you, Babydoll."

She works her bottom lip as I slip the necklace, *her* necklace over her head. "I was keepin' it safe for ye. Close to my heart. Just as you are."

I brought her here to show her that *this* is the future I want, one I want to build with her.

"And you never will have to do this without me," she finally says, clutching the rose around her neck. It pleases me so. "I just don't want you giving this up because of others. Because of me."

Before I can argue, she levels me sincerely.

"Answer me this, and answer me honestly. If I wasn't here, would your decision still be the same?"

"But ye are here," I counter, and she shakes her head.

"That's not what I asked. If we'd never met, would you still give everything up? Would you give away your rightful place on the throne?"

I want to argue because that's a world of fiction, but she did ask me to be honest.

"No," I reply, hating how she manages to know me better than I know myself at times. "I would not. But now, I have so much more at stake."

The more I speak, the more evident it becomes that it sounds like I'm feeding her excuses.

"I won't have Shay live the life I've lived. I want him as far away from this shite as possible."

"I understand that. But being your son, I don't know if that's what he wants. Your blood runs through his veins, and I fear that when he's old enough to make his choices, he won't agree with the choice you've made.

"If Ethan does want a part in Belfast, then the Kellys will

never really be out of the game, so to speak. You can't protect them forever."

"Aye, yer right. But I have to at least try. Ethan is almost an adult. I can't stop him, but I can try to offer him a life away from this."

I understand what she's saying because I agree with her. But they will be given options, something that was never offered to me. I have the chance to provide a home, away from this life of greed and violence, and I'm going to take it.

"You're a good man, Puck Kelly."

"I don't know about that," I counter lightly, thinking of all the ways I intend to torture Sean and Liam.

My phone rings, and when I see the caller is Aoife, I quickly answer. "Bout ye?"

"Hi. Someone is here, on behalf of Aleksei," she whispers. "Is it safe?"

Alek came through, but I didn't have any doubts that he wouldn't.

"Aye. They can be trusted."

"Okay. Eva will be happy to leave. I don't think she likes me very much."

"Can ye blame her?" I question blankly.

She sniffs, and I instantly feel like an arsehole for snapping. But she is the reason Cami has her arm in a plaster cast. She is also the reason, however, that we're all still alive. She hasn't run to Sean—yet.

"Can ye call past?"

"When?"

"Now."

I look at Cami who seems to know who's on the other end.

"I've a—"

"I want to discuss our son," she interrupts, knowing this is something she holds over my head.

I really need to get a hair sample from him so I can do my own test. I've been putting it off because I can only deal with one dilemma at a time. But now is as good a time as any.

"All right. Cami and I—"

"Can ye come alone? She doesn't like me, and she has every right not to. But I think this is somethin' we need to discuss alone. I'll text ye the address of where to meet."

Looking at Cami, I realize Aoife is the one thing that will always remind us of a past I wish to forget.

"No bother. I'll see ye soon."

I hang up, wondering how Cami is going to react.

"Alek's men have come for Eva." I start with the good news. "Aoife wants to talk about Shay."

"Of course, she does." She snickers, rolling her eyes. "Let me guess. She wants to do it alone?"

"Aye," I reply, rubbing the back of my neck. "I'm sorry. I know this is fucking awkward for ye."

She shakes her head. "Compared to how fucked up our lives are right now, this is nothing. You do what you have to.

Get your own tests done so we can confirm what we already know."

Reaching for her hand, I kiss the back of it, wanting her to know how much I appreciate and love her. And what she says next confirms she is the only one for me.

"But if she tries to make a move on you, I will fucking end her."

"I love it when ye talk dirty," I say, showing her just how much I really do when I smash my lips to hers.

She has nothing to worry about, though her jealousy gives me an idea. But first, I need to deal with Aoife.

Aoife's directions have led me to a park.

I dropped Cami off at Kavanagh's, promising to return as soon as I can. Although Aine dislikes me, she agreed to what I asked she do. The only reason she did is because she knows Cami deserves it. I made one stopover before coming here and chose something which now burns a hole in my pocket.

But when I see Shay playing on the swings, I focus on why I'm here.

Aoife sits on a bench, watching him closely. It's evident she's a good mother. The way Shay has been reared is proof of that. She waves when she sees me.

Walking over, I take a seat beside her. I have on my sunglasses and a baseball cap, but this disguise is far from perfect, which is why I need to make this quick.

"Hi, Aoife. What did ye want to talk about?"

My tone is sharp, hinting I don't have time for games.

She clears her throat. "I thought it was time ya did yer wee test," she says, and I sense a touch of animosity to her statement. "Shay is here, so ya can get what ya need, seein' as ye don't trust me."

"No, Aoife, I don't trust you," I affirm, not sugarcoating anything. "I don't trust anyone, especially after a paternity test I took was a load of bullshit."

"That's not true. You trust Camilla."

"We're not goin' to do this," I warn, not interested in fighting. "We have to co-exist because of Shay, but I'll never forgive you for what ya did to Cami."

Before she can reply, Shay comes running over, eyeing me suspiciously.

He hasn't warmed to me, and that's my fault because I've kept him at an arm's distance which isn't fair to him.

"Hey, wee lad," I say, hoping my tone sounds light.

"I'm not wee," he states, standing his ground. "Are ye all right, Mum? Why are ye frowning?"

I can see why Cami is so certain Shay is my son, but I can't get carried away.

Reaching into my backpack, I produce the swab that I

received from the DNA test company. There is also a small vial where I'm to collect a hair sample. I don't want to scare Shay, so I allow Aoife to take the lead.

"Come give yer mummy a hug," she says, opening her arms.

He narrows his eyes at me angrily, but does what she says. The moment he does, she subtly plucks two strands of hair from his head. I need it by the root, which she clearly knew because she did her own test.

I feel like an arsehole, but it needs to be done.

She gestures I'm to give her the swab. "Can ye put this in yer mouth?"

She gently puts him out at arm's length and offers him the swab.

He accepts and does as she asks. Once he's done, he gives it back to her. "Is this goin' to make ye happy now, Mummy?"

His question cuts deep because I remember when I was his age, all I wanted to do was please my mother as well.

"Aye, go play now. Mummy needs to talk to Puck."

I attempt a smile, and in return, I get a scowl. I don't blame him. I would be scowling at the man who was making my mum upset too.

Shay runs off, looking over his shoulder a few times to make sure Aoife is all right. Once he's playing happily on the slide, Aoife reveals why she wanted to meet.

"When yer test comes back, provin' Shay is yers, what are we goin' to do?" There is no if in the equation as she gives me the swab and hair sample. "I want ye to be a part of his life. But promise me ye won't do somethin' like ask for full custody."

"I can ya promise ya that," I affirm, putting the samples into my backpack. "I would never take a chile away from his ma."

"Thank you." She sniffs back her tears. "What about livin' arrangements? I mean, the castle is big. Maybe—"

"If yer suggestin' movin' in, then best ye get that idea out of yer head. That's not happenin'. Ever. I will look after you and Shay, but we will never be together as a family how you want us to be."

"I know you felt somethin' for me," she stubbornly argues, refusing to let this fantasy go.

"Aoife, for fuck's sake," I say, exhaling in frustration. "We've been over this. I love Cami. And that won't change."

"But why won't you try? In prison, the way ye touched me. I—"

I burst her bubble awful quick. "Everythin' looks appetizing to a starvin' man. That's all it was. I fucked you. And you liked it. You fucked me. And I liked it. It was just sex."

She slaps my cheek. "How dare you! Shay was born out of more than just sex."

"Aye, from somethin' awful, somethin' amazin' was born, and I'm prepared to do whatever it takes to look after my responsibilities. But that's what it was to me, Aoife. There was nothin' more to it. I'm sorry if ye thought different."

But my apology means nothing to her.

She comes to an abrupt stand. "I can't believe how stupid I've been. Yer dad has been kinder to me than you have. Tell me why I should believe you when all y've done is make me feel worthless? Maybe yer the one I should be watchin' out for and not Sean? Maybe I'll tell him what I know and then decide who's tellin' me the truth?"

"Choose yer words wisely," I warn, removing my sunglasses so she can see how serious I am. "I don't take to threats too kindly."

"Threats?" she mocks, folding her arms. "If I were to threaten ye, I would give you an ultimatum—me or Cami. If you choose her, then I will tell Sean she's not where she should be. *That's* a threat."

Before she can gloat in her smugness, I stand and grip her arm, subtly drawing her into me so our faces are inches apart. "You do that, and I promise ye, y'll never see Shay again."

"And ye said ye'd never take a wain away from his ma," she snarls, attempting to break free. But she's not going anywhere.

"I wouldn't," I affirm, "but Sean would. Once you tell him what ye know, once y've served yer purpose, he'd have ye killed and take Shay. That's it. There's no doubt about it. So, go ahead, tell Sean. I dare you."

I call her bluff because I won't be blackmailed. Not again.

"Maybe I will." But she's full of shite.

"Are ye so desperate for me to fuck ye again? Is that it? Ye'd settle for forced affection than somethin' that is real?"

Tears sting her blue eyes because I know how to hurt her. She believes in fairy tales. I do not.

"Take Shay home. We're done here." And only then do I let her go.

I need to leave before I do something I regret.

Quickly turning, I walk toward where Shay is playing. When I approach him, he shields the sun from his eyes as he peers up at me.

"Look after yer ma."

He nods, not asking questions why. I think he's glad to see me go.

Once I get into my truck, I don't drive away. I simply sit, staring out the windscreen. Aoife is now a problem; one I don't know what to do about. Everything is riding on her keeping our secret. If she tells Sean the truth…

"Fuck!" I curse, slamming my hands against the steering wheel, needing to hit something before I explode.

My hands tremble as I reach for my phone and send a text to Austin.

I need eyes on Aoife. She can't be trusted.

He replies a moment later.

On it. Is she going to be a problem?

I hate that I don't know the answer to that. So, I respond as honestly as I can.

I don't know.

Aoife has just put a target on her head. Just another victim in this endless war.

THIRTEEN

Cami

I've tried not to think about it because Aoife will always be a part of Punky's life, but I can't shift this heaviness in my chest. It's only been a few hours since he dropped me off, but it feels much longer than that.

I know it's because a small part of me continues whispering doubts into my ear; that Aoife and Punky will always share something I won't. They have a child together, an amazing child, and no matter what happens in the future for Punky and me, Shay will always be Punky's firstborn son.

I've tried to keep busy. I walked to a local store to buy some necessities as I only have the clothes on my back. I don't know how long I'm staying, so I bought the essentials. I'd hoped dressing up and applying some makeup would help me feel remotely better.

I no longer look like the living dead, but I still feel like shit.

The meeting with Alek, who oozed confidence and charisma, made me feel somewhat calmer because this time, I know we can win. But I don't think Punky will be able to give all of this up. He says that he will, and I love him even more for it. But walking away from this won't be easy.

This country, this life—it's a part of him and I accept that. I don't want him to give something up because he thinks it's the right thing for others. I wouldn't want him to expect that of me. But the deal is done. I believe Alek will kill him if Punky goes back on his word.

"You look lovely."

When his warm arms and words wrap around me, every insecurity I feel melts away. I lean into him, relishing in his touch as I didn't hear him enter.

"Thank you. How'd it go?"

Punky kisses my temple as he hugs me tighter. "I don't want to talk about that right now."

Panic overcomes me, and before I can ask why, his hungry whisper into my ear silences my worries.

"Close yer eyes."

I do as he says because, honestly, I want to shut out the light for a little while.

He is at my back and guides me out of the room. I don't open my eyes and trust him as he holds on tightly to walk me down the stairs. Curiosity gets the better of me when he takes a left to lead me into the gardens out back.

Even though I'm blinded, I know this place like the back of my hand. "Where are we going?"

"Trust me," he says, his husky tone setting me alight.

We continue walking, and when my bare feet touch the soft grass, I instantly feel a sense of freedom. Being outdoors helps remind me that I'm merely a speck in the grand scheme of things, and what I choose is my choice alone.

And I choose Punky—always.

We come to a stop, but I don't open my eyes. I wait for Punky's command. But he doesn't speak. We simply stand together, savoring the quiet.

I'm almost asleep on my feet when Punky kisses my cheek. "Ye can open yer eyes."

I don't straight away. I appreciate this moment because I sense I will remember this for the rest of my life. Being here with Punky just feels so right.

Opening my eyes slowly, I blink quickly, certain I'm seeing things, but when the view in front of me of twinkling fairy lights and a table filled with delicious food doesn't disappear, I know my eyesight isn't deceiving me.

Punky did this. He did it for me.

"It's beautiful," I whisper, unable to look away.

The table is set exquisitely, and the candle in the middle adds to the romantic vibe. I wonder when he did all this.

"I owe ye a date," he says, which touches me as he still remembers the promise he made to me all those nights ago. "I hope I did it right."

His concern is clear, and it actually makes me love him all the more as he rules with such confidence and no apologies, but when it comes to this, he is so unsure.

"It's perfect, Puck. I love it. I love you."

"Say it again." He nuzzles against my cheek, turning me into mush.

"I love you. So much…but I'd love you even more if you let me eat all that food."

His husky chuckle threatens to distract me from the spread in front of me and feast on something more delicious—him. But I manage to control myself for now.

He leads us to the table, where he pulls out the chair for me. I accept, smiling up at him. He sits across from me, reaching for the bottle of wine. He pours me a glass while I stare in awe, taking it all in.

"I can't take all the credit," he reveals. "Aine helped. Even though she hates my guts."

I can't help but laugh. "She's just protective. She saw what I went through when you were gone. It was my refuge from the real world."

The mood soon changes when I mention why I came here.

We don't speak and decide now is a good time to try all the appetizing foods in front of us.

I don't realize how hungry I am until I take my first bite of food. Eating has been the last thing on my mind, but the moment the Irish stew hits my mouth, it's the only thing I can focus on. I'm gulping down my third spoonful when I notice Punky looking at me with a huge grin.

"What?" I ask, my mouth full.

Punky shakes his head playfully. "Nothin'. I just like seein' ye eat."

"Well, give me food like this every day, and I will continue eating until I pop."

Something passes over Punky, and just when I'm about to tell him I'm only joking, well, not really, he stuns me into silence when he slides a small blue velvet box across the table. I peer down at it and then quickly back at him.

"Open it." He smirks when he takes in my stunned expression.

I don't want to make any assumptions, but my hand trembles as I reach for it.

"If ya don't like it—"

But I don't hear another word because the moment I open the box, there is no way I cannot like what I see because it is the most beautiful thing I've ever seen.

Settled amongst the white silk is a white gold engagement ring. It's simple—a thin white gold band with a round diamond.

I know Punky is waiting for me to say something, but I am literally rendered speechless because this is too much.

"I know we didn't discuss the ring ye wanted, but when I saw this, I knew it was perfect for ye. My ma's ring was similar. I remember that. And when I asked the jeweler about that ring…" He pauses, needing a moment, and when he continues, I understand why. "He told me it was called Cara."

Tears sting my eyes because this means so much more than merely a beautiful piece of jewelry. This signifies our future—forever.

"I can take it back, though, if ya don't—"

"I love it," I interrupt softly, fingering over the sparkling diamond. "It's perfect."

A sigh of relief leaves Punky.

He comes to a stand and gently removes the ring from the box. He reaches for my left ring finger and drops to his knee. He then slides the ring on. It's a perfect fit.

We both stare at the ring, marveling at what it represents, at what we've overcome to be here. I never thought I would ever find happiness in this sometimes-cruel world, but right now, I'm the happiest woman alive.

I can't help but wriggle my finger, the dim lighting catching the sparkle of the impressive diamond. "Forever yours," I whisper, those words pleasing me in ways I never thought possible.

"Always," he replies, tonguing over his bottom lip. He's taken out his lip ring but still wears his nose ring. A heat spreads from head to toe.

I want him. And I want him now.

My arm is still in a cast, but I don't care if I have to break it again to touch him, to have him touch me in the depraved, wicked ways that I want him to.

"Babydoll," he warns, reading me like a book.

I know he's treading with caution because he doesn't want to hurt me, but I am hurting right now with him being so far away.

Fisting his T-shirt, I pull him toward me, and I slam my lips to his. He kisses me back just as hungrily, revealing he wants this as much as me. When we made love last, he was cautious, worried because I was wounded, but not tonight.

I want him to lose control.

We can't keep up with the ferocity of our kisses, and when he bites my bottom lip, I almost beg he takes me right here, right now.

However, not wanting to disrespect Aine that way, I stand, taking Punky with me. Our lips never lose contact. We continue kissing under this serene glow.

Pulling away, I pant, "Come with me."

He nods, and I know he would follow me into the depths of hell if I asked him to.

Taking his hand, I lead him toward an isolated place where I found peace when things became too much. That was often. But now, I can replace sadness with contentment as I lead him toward an unused shed. I push open the door, and we are on one another before it closes.

I'm tearing at Punky's T-shirt, desperate to feel his warmth against my tongue. The moment his chest is bare, I bite over his throat, leading downward. I lick his pectorals, relishing in the animalistic growls leaving him.

When I get to his taut abs and run my tongue over each hardened bump, I almost come right here and now because his body is muscled, lean, and drives me fucking wild. My fingers caress as my mouth kisses and licks, and when I get to his belt, I grin.

His V muscle is carved from granite, and I intend to devour every inch of him because he is mine…mine…mine.

Unbuckling his belt, I unfasten his jeans, and the moment I lower them and his heavy cock springs free, an untamed growl escapes me.

"Baby—" But he doesn't get to finish because now, it's my turn to drop to my knees.

I peer up at him from under my lashes, licking my lips before I take his length into my mouth.

"Oh, fuck," he curses with a breathless moan.

His profanity spurs me on as I deep-throat him.

Gagging, I pull away, only to go back to fucking him with my mouth hungrily. I can't get enough and continue working his shaft desperately, using my hand to stroke over him and work in unison with my mouth.

He pulsates in my mouth, and my needy center burns for

attention, but this is all for him.

I am sated, gorging on him as he thrusts his hips, sliding in and out of my mouth. Twirling my hair around his fist, he controls the depth and the speed, and he's not gentle about it. He fucks my face with a brutal swiftness, knowing I can take it.

I gag on him as he hits the back of my throat, and when he tries to pull out, I grip his muscular thighs, refusing to let go.

Doing this all one-handed is frustrating because I want to touch myself as I pleasure him. But the anticipation just adds to the desire I feel.

His cock grows even harder, and I know that's because he's going to come. "Babydoll," he pants, desperately trying to pry me away.

I only suck him faster and deeper.

He tastes musky and all man, and when I run my tongue along the underside of his length, before sucking the head of his cock, he throbs and growls low. A heat gushes into my mouth, and instead of pulling away, I take all of him into me.

I swallow deeply, his seed trickling down my chin because he's coming with a savagery that has me growing wetter. The carnal sounds spilling from him just adds to this untamed act, and I love it.

With two final pumps, he sighs, sated, while I finally let him go.

Reaching down, he wipes my lips with his thumb, smearing his seed off my mouth and chin. Tending to me this way is fucking hot. But I know things have just begun.

He strips bare and lifts me, spinning me around and shoving me against the wall. I don't have time to respond as he raises the hem of my dress and tears my underwear off. He coaxes me to spread my legs as he drops to his knees behind me.

"Give me that parful arse," he demands, pushing down on my lower back so I'm arched forward, bracing the wall as I offer him my ass.

Looking over my shoulder, I mewl when he buries his face between my legs, sucking over my back entrance. I didn't know I liked ass play until Punky, but the way he devours me without shame or disgust has me bucking back and forth onto his face.

He grips my legs and maneuvers himself low so he can alternate between my ass and pussy. He is everywhere, sucking, licking, setting me on fire. I can't believe I get to experience this for the rest of my life.

The ring on my finger feels perfect—like it belongs, and it does. This is my fate. Punky is my forever.

He takes my entire sex into his mouth, eating me out with such intensity that I gasp for air. I literally feel like he's eating me alive. As he devours my ass, he sinks two fingers into me, stuffing me full. He fucks me with his mouth and fingers, tipping me over the edge.

"Punky," I groan, grinding against him, needing to come and come now.

I bounce back onto him, desperate to be put out of my

misery, but his husky chuckle merely vibrates against me, hinting he's going to make me beg.

"Say it." His hot breath warms my slick skin.

"Please, make me come."

His low growl expresses his approval of my plea, and he gives me what I need as he twirls his tongue inside my pussy before circling my clit. Gripping my waist, he coerces me to ride his face, and the friction is just too much.

An explosion tackles me from within, and I come with a sated groan.

Punky milks every tremor from me, encouraging me to rock against his face as he licks, sucks, and bites over my sensitive flesh. He holds me up as my orgasm lasts for what feels like forever, but when I finally come back down to earth, I realize we both want more.

Standing, he spins me around, and the feral look upon his face has me lifting my dress over my head. I'm not wearing a bra, and Punky uses that to his advantage as he leans down and takes a pert nipple into his mouth.

Arching back, I enjoy the brush of his stubble against my sensitive skin because everything is heightened. Everywhere he touches feels so fucking good.

Lifting his face to mine, I kiss him, uncaring my scent is slathered all over him, and walk toward the small sofa. I shove him onto it, and he falls back against the cushions. Nothing but love is reflected on his face as he watches me climb on top of him.

He is hard again, and I'm still incredibly wet, so gripping his length, I guide him into me, inch by glorious inch. We both hiss at the connection because nothing, nothing compares to this.

I take my time, savoring our union, and when he's buried to the hilt, I hold my breath. I don't move. I simply feel this man owning me—mind, body, and soul.

I've seen him kill and kill brutally, but being with him this way has me appreciating our love even more because I know he doesn't love freely. He's chosen me to love and protect. Through ugliness, we've found this, and it's the most beautiful thing in the world.

"I love you," I say and commence to move.

He arches his head back as I ride him slow, wanting to savor this moment. Our passion has been filled, and now, I want to enjoy our love for hours, days.

Rocking back and forth, I torment us both with deliriously slow movements, but the anticipation only heightens the desire within.

Punky's blue eyes lock on where we join, watching the way we become one. "I love you too," he says, his smooth accent a punch to my center. "I can't believe yer mine."

I love that I belong to him, and he to me because I finally feel whole.

He interlocks our fingers, running his thumb over my ring.

I love that he too appreciates the importance of it on my finger as it means more than just marriage.

It signifies that we made it—we survived.

I continue rocking slowly, our passionate moans wrapping us tightly into a world where only we exist. He allows me to take control, trusting me as I trust him.

Our bodies are slick, warm, and when he places a hand to my hip, his fingers digging into my flesh, I increase the rhythm because I want him deeper. I lift my hips, only to lower myself slowly back onto him.

"Fuck, Baby," he moans, the veins in his neck corded. "Yer goin' to kill me."

"What a way to go," I counter, clenching my muscles around him.

We savor one another for what feels like hours, never breaking contact. I know if anything happened to Punky, the connection is so deep that I wouldn't survive it.

He leans forward, suckling my breasts as I run my fingers over his chest and his rock-hard abs. I can't remember a time when I've felt this close to him. I fuck him leisurely, rocking back and forth and side to side.

He grips my ass, encouraging me to take him deeper, and when I rearrange my position so I'm squatting over him, I know we're both ready to come.

Increasing the tempo, I bounce on his cock, using his slick chest as support as I ride him hard. He grips the back of the sofa, almost tearing it to shreds as he raises his hips, meeting me thrust for thrust.

Leaning down, I kiss him passionately while riding him hard. My legs are like Jell-O, but Punky grips my waist with both hands and milks the pleasure we both want. Before long, my body grows lax, and he's the puppeteer while I'm the marionette as he bends my body how he wants.

He is the one who is now fucking me hard, and when he strokes over my clit in just the right way, over and over again, I throw back my head and see stars as I come with a satisfied cry. My heart threatens to burst free as my body shudders uncontrollably.

With a guttural groan, Punky comes loud and hard and comes inside me. I don't think twice about the consequences because I want him inside me. I always do.

When my body is spent, I collapse forward, gulping in mouthfuls of air. I'm dizzy because holy shit, that was fucking incredible. Punky holds me tightly against his chest, breathing hard as we both catch our breaths.

We stay interlocked for minutes, simply enjoying the silence. I never want to leave.

Punky runs his fingertips up and down my back, spreading goosebumps from head to toe. I'm almost asleep when his cell rings. He makes no attempts to answer it, but when it rings again and again, he sighs.

"Sorry, Baby."

With a groan, I slowly lift myself off him, falling back onto the sofa and admiring his firm ass as he hunts for his phone. When he retrieves and answers it, our bliss has come to an end.

"Fuck!" he curses before ending the call.

As he frantically gets dressed, I jump up and follow suit. "What's wrong?"

Running a hand through his hair, he appears to need a moment before responding. This can't be good. "It's Aoife."

I wait for him to continue, but nothing can prepare me for what he says next.

"She's dead…and Liam has Shay. We have to go."

FOURTEEN

PUNKY

This has to stop.

I can't take any more.

When Alek phoned and told me what had happened, it was history repeating itself—again and again. But I won't allow another person to be used as collateral, especially my child.

Alek's men have followed Liam to his house in Dublin, which is where Cami and I are parked.

Alek's men didn't want to intervene, knowing this is my fight. There is no way anyone is taking this away from me. Alek said it was too late for Aoife, but he knew Liam wouldn't hurt Shay because he needs him; just how Sean needed Babydoll.

I don't know why Liam took Shay and killed Aoife, but I'm

guessing it's because he found out that Babydoll wasn't where she was supposed to be. However, I plan on getting to the bottom of this right now.

I can't construct a coherent sentence. All I can think about is killing Liam.

Babydoll and I exit my truck, both armed. Alek's men, as well as mine, are hiding, waiting for my command to storm this house and make those who betrayed me pay. I don't have a plan. I know I can't exactly walk up to the front door and knock.

I need a decoy, and that comes in the shape of one Russian drug lord.

Alek casually walks over to where we are, unruffled by what is about to transpire. I try my best to keep cool, but I need blood to be spilled to appease this rage within me.

"I'm sorry about the mother of your child," he says with a respectful nod. "It happened very quickly, not that that's any consolation. Before my men had a chance to help, she was already dead. She was strangled."

A whimper escapes Babydoll.

I don't make a sound because from what Alek has said, Aoife invited Liam into her home like she knew him. Could it be she was playing double agent? Was she willing to spill it all to get revenge on me? I don't know anything anymore.

"Thank you for doin' this," I say because Alek is the reason I'll be able to get into Liam's house.

"I don't appreciate men who involve innocent children in

their games. It's rather cowardly and displays weakness."

"Aye, so it is," I reply, clenching my jaw.

"I will get you inside his home, but the question is, what will happen once you're in?"

I know he means that if I kill Liam prematurely, I potentially risk fucking everything up. Sean will want to know why, and the shipment of drugs we're meant to intercept may be stopped. The dealers are expecting Liam, but word of his death will spread, giving his allies cold feet.

I need to keep my temper under control. Or at least, try.

"I can't make any promises, but I'll try not to rip off his head."

Alek chuckles, sensing my seriousness. He seems to love bloodshed too.

"Okay, I'll send word when it's safe for you to enter."

I don't know how, but I'm sure I'll know it when I see it.

Alek looks at Babydoll, smiling. "No harm will come of your beloved," he promises. "You remind me so much of my Ella—forever brave and never backing down from a fight."

"I think I'd like your Ella," she says lightly.

"I think she'd like you too."

I don't know why, but there is mutual respect between us. It was there from the first moment we met. Could it be because we're not that different?

Alek nods, and without making a fuss, he calmly walks toward Liam's home. He looks refined and in control with his cane, and this is the first time I've gone into a plan with the utmost confidence.

What I can't be too confident about is that I won't kill Liam. I know what it means for us if I do, but I am so fucking sick of this.

"It'll be all right," Babydoll says, gently touching my shoulder.

Her touch soothes me, as does the ring on her finger.

"I just want to get Shay out of there," I reply, my eyes never leaving Liam's front door.

There are men out front to greet Alek, who walks up the drive as though he belongs. After a few moments, they gesture he's to enter. It doesn't cross my mind once that Alek would betray me. I trust him, which is a rare thing for me.

It feels like hours as Babydoll and I wait for a signal, something to indicate it's safe for us to enter, and we see it when the front door opens, and Alek appears.

Babydoll turns to look at me, arching a confused brow. Surely, it can't be that simple?

But when Alek waves at us, it appears that it is.

I don't hesitate and march toward the house with Babydoll following by my side. I need to get Shay out as quickly as possible, and I need that to be with someone I, and also he, trusts. It was a no-brainer who that was.

The gate is open, so we sprint up the drive, keeping an eye out for Liam's men. I'm surprised the coast is clear. Alek is no longer here, but the front door is open, which is all the welcome I need. I charge inside, using Alek's voice as guidance.

Babydoll has her gun in hand as we mute our footsteps down the hall. I can't make out what Alek is saying, but without a doubt, he is in the last room at the end of the corridor. I don't know if this is supposed to be a surprise attack, so I slow my pace and gesture with my finger to Babydoll that we're to keep quiet.

She nods, ready for whatever the next few minutes hold.

When we get within feet of the door, I stop and listen to what is being said between Liam and Alek. "I'll make you a very rich man."

"I already am a very rich man," Alek counters while I can't help but smirk.

"Help me defeat the Kellys, and y'll be even richer. I need them gone. But if ye don't want to help, then I have other ways to make them submit."

I don't wait for Alek to reply. I've heard enough. Before Babydoll can advise me to wait, I shove open the door and storm into the room that appears to be Liam's office. When he sees me, his eyes widen.

"What the—"

I don't give him a chance to speak or lunge for the concealed weapon in his drawer. I round his desk and punch him straight in the face. A sharp crack hints I've broken his nose, but it's not enough.

I punch him once, twice more, relishing in him squirming in his leather seat, attempting to flee. But he's not going anywhere.

Gripping the collar of his now bloody shirt, I pick him up and shove his back into the wall. He tries to fight me but is rendered inept when I snap his wrist backward, breaking it.

"Where is he?" I snarl, pressing us nose to nose.

Liam spits in my face in response.

Laughing dangerously low, I snarl, "Have it yer way then."

Lifting his feet off the floor, I toss him onto the desk and use him to sweep the contents off the surface. Pressing my forearm over his throat, I push all my weight onto him as he writhes on his back, fighting to stay awake.

"Where is he?" I repeat, never breaking eye contact with him.

"Ye fucking cunt," he says, looking overhead at Alek who still sits serenely in his chair, despite the violence. "Ye played me."

Alek reaches into his pocket for a cigar. "It's not my fault you're an idiot and failed to realize needing to use the bathroom was code for fucking you up."

An amused chuckle escapes me because as far as insults go, Liam just got owned. "This doesn't have to end badly for ye. Just tell me where Shay is."

"I'm not tellin' ya a thing."

"Aye, ye will."

A silver letter opener catches my eye, which would be the

obvious torture choice. But I like to be creative, so I reach for a stapler. Without warning, I slam a staple into Liam's cheek. The sting of the staple as well as the force of my hand stuns him into submission.

"Oh, bravo," Alek commends happily, lighting his cigar.

Liam tongues his cheek, feeling the staple imbedded deeply into his flesh. "A'll fucking end ye all."

His empty threat is a sign he's scared and knows he's lost. He's all smoke and mirrors, which is why I intend to torture him painfully slow.

"You—"

His words die in a muffled mess as I take hold of his tongue and push the stapler into it once, twice, three times. The more violence I inflict, the more I want. I won't be able to stop. I know it.

"I can do this all day," I say with a smile as I hover over Liam, pressing my weight into him so he can't move.

"Shay."

When I hear Babydoll's voice, I'm ashamed that I only just remembered she is here.

With my arm still crushing Liam's windpipe, I peer up and see a beautiful woman holding Shay's hand.

"Samia, ye dirty whore," Liam wheezes, indicating someone else just betrayed him.

Alek clucks his tongue. "Come here, pet."

I watch as Babydoll gently gestures for Shay to come to her.

The trust between them is evident when Samia lets go of Shay's hand, and he runs toward Babydoll. She bends low and scoops him into her arms, hugging him.

"Shh, it's okay. I've got you."

Samia walks toward Alek, and I watch with interest as she drops to her knees before him. He reaches forward and rubs his thumb across her pouty lips. "Don't bow for any man, возлюбленная."

Alek can cast a spell on anyone he meets, and that's what makes him the powerful, feared leader he is.

She nods, her eyes fluttering as he caresses her cheek. "Thank you for returning the boy."

"Ye better stay on yer knees 'cause when I'm finished with ye—" Liam once again speaks as if he believes he is getting out of this with his head attached.

"Cami," I say, not wanting her and Shay to see this. "Go back to Belfast. I'll meet ye there."

Liam only realizes his sister is here and snickers. "Yer pathetic. Ye should be thankin' me for killin' his girlfriend. She gave ye up awful fast. Even her own wain."

That I don't believe as I know Aoife would have protected Shay with her last dying breath. I'll never know what happened—the truth died with Aoife.

"What were ye doin' at her house?"

"I was lookin' for my beloved sister. So ye can imagine my surprise when I found out she was gone. Sean trusted Aoife for a reason. I always wondered why, but when I saw the boy, I knew why."

"Why were ye lookin' for Cami? Ye were the one who brought her to Aoife's in the first place. Ye were more than happy to work with a Kelly to get whatcha wanted. Why the change of heart?"

I suspect Liam wanted to kidnap Cami and hold her as collateral against Sean. He knew she was the only thing he had over me. But if he took her, he could blackmail both of us. But something still doesn't make sense.

Something has changed for him to believe he can take us both on. He needed to work with Sean to get what he wanted, but to betray him this way means he's working with someone else. He knew Sean's and my weakness and was planning on exploiting that.

But I beat him to it.

Dread fills my stomach because we now have another player in the game, someone who's kept under the radar—until now.

"You couldn't have Cami, so ye took Shay, is that it?"

"One Kelly is better than none," he replies, snickering.

"Cami—" My voice is dripping with venom as I don't want Shay to hear another word. When he finds out the truth, it'll be from me, not some fucking sociopath. "Have one of our men take ye home."

"Let's go. Shay?"

Risking a glance overhead, I witness a look of utmost

violence reflected on Shay's face—it's a look I know all too well.

I promise myself here and now that I won't allow Shay to ever feel this way again. It's because I don't want him living the life I did, that I lock eyes with Babydoll, pleading she leaves. They've both seen too much.

She nods once, but I know leaving me is tearing her apart.

With Shay in her arms, the two most important people in my world leave, making room for the demons who demand vengeance and bloodshed. I trust they'll be okay as I know my men outside will die protecting them.

Samia stands, looking down at Liam with no remorse. "The men are in the kitchen, drinking. They'll be a while."

"Yer dead. You and yer family, they're all dead."

"Samia, I will come find you," Alek interjects. "You'll be rewarded for choosing the right side."

Her cheeks redden as she bows in gratitude.

She leaves the room and gently closes the door behind her, sealing us three in.

Liam wiggles, but he's not going anywhere.

"I want to know why ye'd betray Sean now. What's changed?"

Liam runs his front teeth over a staple and manages to pry it out. "I got in before he did. I'm no eejit. I know it's only a matter of time before he does to me what was done to my father. What *you* did."

Does Liam know that Sean and I were planning on intercepting his loot and making an example out of him? I suppose it doesn't take a genius to work it out. They once needed one another, but now, they're fighting for first prize.

"Yer father was weak, and he was also fucking stupid. Killin' him was far too easy."

"You fucking cunt!" Liam roars, fighting me desperately. But he's not going anywhere.

"So was killin' yer brother."

Alek stands and walks over to the radio. He turns it on, switching through the channels. When Bach comes on, I ask him to leave it on.

"Good choice," he says, walking over to me. "What are we going to do?"

Alek has clued on that someone else wants in, and the only way we will find out who is by forcing Liam to tell us. But as we both look at him, we know that probably won't happen.

However, I can always try…and I will take great pleasure in doing so.

"Who are ye workin' with?"

Liam laughs in response.

Reaching for the stapler, I slam it into his temple, the staple imbedding into his head.

"The Kellys are finally beaten. That's all that matters to me. So do what ya want to me 'cause I'm not tellin' ya a thing."

His resolve is firm, and I believe that Liam will take his secret to the grave, which means the plan has to change. By now, Sean would know that Aoife is dead or at least missing, as is Babydoll. He just lost his winning hand.

He'll either flee or fight, and knowing my father, he'll flee like the coward he is. This time, however, I have an army to help me hunt him down.

"He's not going to talk," Alek says, confirming what I know to be true.

His loyalty means he respects and loves this person. This is someone close to him and close to the Doyles. This isn't just about power. It's about honor.

He fights me, but I press his lips together and bring the stapler down, puncturing along his lips and sealing them shut. As he tries to scream, I punch him in the stomach, winding him, and continue stapling his mouth shut.

Over and over, I staple along the seam of his mouth, his pursed lips bleeding as he attempts to pry them apart. But each staple fastens them firmer, and before long, his mouth is no longer pink; it's silver. As Liam attempts to push me away, I reach for the silver letter opener and jam it into his shoulder, impaling him to the desk.

Jumping up, I stand back and watch Liam Doyle squirm like a bug, muffled screams trapped in his mouth as he fights for his life. But this is the end of the line for him.

So much has changed, and the truth is, the only way we'll ever be safe is if everyone is dead. I don't know who I'm fighting anymore. But what I do know is that Liam and Sean...they die...tonight.

With my decision made, a crystal paper weight in the shape of a pyramid catches my eye. Bending down to pick it up, the heavy weight in my hand comforts me. I wish I had more time to torture him, but the truth is, Liam Doyle isn't worth it.

He was Sean's puppet, so it seems fitting I cut his strings.

Tossing the paper weight in my hand, over and over, I look at Alek, hoping he understands that things have changed. I wanted this to run smoothly, to be discreet, but the gloves are off. I'm going to slaughter every last fucker who betrayed me—oh yes, there will be blood.

Liam's eyes watch my movements, wondering what fate is destined for him. "Really sorry, but you won't be makin' yer party," I say coolly because the festivities are off. "You kidnapped the woman I loved. And you took my son. You killed his ma. I know what that's like, thanks to yer dad. Yer rotten, all you Doyles are.

"So it's time I ended yer bloodline, once and for all."

Never breaking eye contact, I ram the tip of the paper weight into the side of Liam's throat. It breaks the skin with ease. A muted cry wheezes out of his stapled lips, but we're not done. Not yet.

Dragging the tip across his flesh, it rips away, hacking a jagged line across his throat. Blood squirts from the gash, covering my face and hands, but I continue sawing along his neck viciously. Liam is still alive, flailing weakly as he tries to break free, but these will be the last breaths he takes.

The gash is deep, but I make it deeper as I pry two fingers into the gaping incision and rummage through tendon and muscle. When I feel his tongue, I yank it out through the cut. His eyes bulge from his head, the realization of what I just did hitting him.

Smacking his cheek playfully, I grin. "Say hello to yer da for me."

I watch as Liam's rough breaths become shallower and shallower until eventually, they just stop. He's dead…and I don't feel a thing.

I drop the paperweight, and it bounces onto the carpet with a thud. Bach's serenity contrasts the grotesque scene before us, but as I look at Alek, I realize he appreciates the brutality as much as me.

"What a masterpiece," he says, sucking on his cigar calmly.

"Thank you. This is just a warm-up." I wipe my hands on Liam's shirt, leaving bloodied smears behind.

"I cannot wait for that. We must move quickly. So much has changed. Do you know who he was protecting?" Alek looks at a very dead and bloody Liam, his lips twitching. "Rather stupid move on his behalf revealing that piece of information."

"Aye, yer right." I begin to wonder…

"Ye don't think it's a trap? Him feeding us what we want to hear?"

"Would he sacrifice his life like that?"

I wouldn't think so. But I don't know for certain. "Someone

is definitely helpin' him out. I just don't know who because honestly, it could be anyone."

"This makes things very difficult for us. We need a new plan."

Nodding, I take one last look at a very dead Liam as it sets a bar to what I intend to do to Sean. "Aye, but first, I need to find my father…and fucking kill him."

Alek simply smokes his cigar, understanding my motives. "I'll be at your disposal. Once you're done, we will organize the next step."

"Thank you. I'll be in touch. But this may take a while."

Alek smirks. "I didn't suspect anything different."

Spitting on Liam's corpse, I leave the room, only half-sated. I want more.

Austin is waiting for me by the front door. I have no doubt Liam's men have fled, their loyalty piss-poor.

"Do you need help?" Austin asks.

I shake my head. "No, this is somethin' I need to do alone. I've dreamt of this day for ten years."

"Sure, this is it."

With vengeance fueling me, I march out the door, my bloody hands poised as I reach for my truck keys. Cami and Shay are safe as I know my men won't let anything happen to them. They have an army ready to fight and lay down their lives for them.

That gives me comfort and allows me to focus on one thing

only, and that's killing Sean. I don't know what I'm walking into, but I'm ready.

I jump into my truck and search the channels on the radio until Beethoven comes on. It was quite cathartic listening to Bach as I pulled Liam's tongue through the gaping hole in his throat. Beethoven, however, sets an entirely different mood.

It's time to fuck shit up.

I keep to the speed limits as I drive to Sean's house. I don't want to draw any attention to myself as I'm slathered in Liam's blood. The closer I get, the more excited I become. The analogy *I feel like a kid on Christmas morning* comes to mind, but I never got to experience those special milestones, thanks to my father killing my mother and robbing me of a normal life.

I turn down the road, and when I see Sean's house, a sense of foreboding overcomes me. It's too…quiet.

I park the truck by the curb and reach into the console for my knife and gun. I don't plan on using them as I intend to get my hands dirty. But just in case.

I slowly walk up the drive, carefully scanning my surroundings. The hair at the back of my neck stands on end, but it's too late.

"Hands in the air! Yer trespassin.'"

I'm blinded by a bright torch, but I know who this is.

"Good evenin', Constable," I quip, leisurely raising my hands in surrender. "Just out for a stroll, is it?"

"Quit runnin' yer smart mouth," he snarls, grabbing my

wrist with force and snapping a cuff onto it. He then proceeds to handcuff me.

Sean has called in the reinforcements. He must be scared as he knows I know…I know everything. It also means he's gone on the run.

Constable Shane Moore is here to slow me down.

However, when he flashes the torch toward my hands, I know he's going to do a lot more than slow me down.

"Is that blood? Ach, y've just made my job so much easier."

I don't have a chance to reply because he's shoving me in the back toward the concealed police car parked in the back garden.

"Yer just as shifty as yer dad," I spit, struggling against him as he forces me forward. "He made a career out of me. He knew I wasn't guilty, but that didn't stop him from throwin' me in prison while he reaped the benefits."

Shane has had enough of my cheek and uses his baton to wind me as he drives it into my stomach. I drop to my knees, hands cuffed behind me as I wheeze out an amused laugh.

"Is that the best y've got?"

Shane snarls and begins to beat me with his baton. I fend him off as best I can with my hands cuffed behind me, but it's not long before he's beating me senseless. I don't feel pain anymore. It's like my brain and body have shut off from it.

There is no way he's dragging me down to the police station because it doesn't end this way—Sean once again eluding me.

But when I hear a piercing boom, I know that won't happen again.

This is something that's changed. Sean can run, but he can't hide. I have the whole of Northern Ireland looking for him.

Shane realizes he's under attack, and like the coward that he is, takes cover behind his car. I roll onto my stomach, catching sight of who's saved me.

"Getawaytafuck." There is no way.

But as Cian and Ethan come running toward me, guns raised, it seems the impossible has happened.

Cian drops to his knees, attempting to help me, but when he sees I'm cuffed, he snarls angrily. "He beat ya when yer cuffed? Fucking dog."

Ethan is covering us, shooting at Shane as he ducks out from behind the car, letting off a few rounds. Cian is livid. I don't remember seeing him this worked up. With his gun raised, he walks toward Shane, not bothered that he could be shot dead.

"Cian!" I scream, rolling onto my side so I can stand. "Stop!"

But he doesn't.

He charges toward Shane, and when the night sky erupts into gunfire, my heart threatens to claw its way from my ribcage.

With hands still bound behind me, I run toward Cian, and as Shane stands, gun poised, ready to kill my best friend, I shoulder Cian to the ground, covering him with my body. Pops echo in the distance, hinting Ethan has our backs.

But there is no way this fucker, Shane, is going to get out of this unscathed.

Cian fights me, angered I would stop him. But his vengeance will blind him and result in his death.

"Cian, enough! I won't lose you too."

He continues to struggle. I have to make him see reason. And there is only one way.

"I'm sorry, mate. For everythin'. I've fucked up, so I did. I've fucked up a lot. But the one thing which I didn't fuck up was punchin' ye in the gob when we first met as kids 'cause I knew we'd be best mates for as long as we lived."

"We should have killed them when we had the chance, but yer pride..." he says, incensed I've allowed it to get to this.

"This has always been about pride, honor! That's all I have left," I reason, begging we work together because I don't want another enemy.

"That's all I have now too...Amber...she's dead."

My brain refuses to accept his words as truth. "Naw, it's not so."

Tears spill from his eyes, explaining his anger, justifying his vigilante act. He has nothing left to live for. "I came home...I thought she was asleep. She was on the bed—"

A sob spills from him, breaking me. I want to express how sorry I am for his loss. And there is only one way to do that.

Jumping up, I gesture with my chin toward Shane. Ethan is keeping him under control. "Cover me."

With a newfound purpose in life, Cian does as I order. We

run toward the police car, Cian and Ethan covering me as I charge for Shane. He springs up, gun trained on me, but I don't give him a chance to breathe as I headbutt him.

He staggers back, and there is no time to recover before I kick him in the stomach. He drops to his knees, wheezing for air. Ethan shoves him onto his back, keeping him pinned to the ground with one knee as he searches him for the keys to my cuffs.

When he finds them, he punches Shane in the nose, breaking it.

Cian reaches for Shane's gun, which lies feet away. I recognize the look in his eye. It's one which I've seen reflected in the mirror since I was five years old.

"Yer to blame," he snarls, eyeing Shane who lies on the ground, bleeding and wounded. "All of youse are."

Anyone who sided with Sean is the enemy, and they should be treated as such.

When Ethan uncuffs me, I reach for his gun and, without pause, walk toward Shane. He peers up, recognizing what this means for him.

"You can't kill a policeman," he says, shuffling backward on his elbows. "This will be the end. Once and for all. Y'll be locked up for the rest of yer lives."

"So be it then." Without hesitation, I shoot Shane between the eyes.

His badge means nothing to me. Nor do his threats.

The night sky is replaced with silence as no more blood will be spilled—for now. Ethan, Cian, and I stand over Shane's corpse, all three of us not feeling a thing.

"We're goin' to drag his arse into Sean's gaff," I instruct coolly. "And we're goin' to show his colleagues what a dirty pig he was."

The boys nod, understanding we need to move quickly. No doubt backup is coming soon.

Gripping his feet, I drag him toward the back door. Cian picks up a brick and smashes the window, where he climbs inside. Ethan and I wait for him to let us in.

"Ye held yer own, cub," I proudly say to Ethan.

"I learned from the best, brother," he replies, which touches me deeply. Even though I'm not his brother, he won't see me as anything but that.

The door opens, and Cian holds it open so I can drag Shane's cooling corpse inside.

I dump his body in the hallway, not caring where he falls. I need to attend to other pressing matters.

"We need to find proof he was workin' with Sean. I'm sure Sean has paperwork here to blackmail Shane. That's how he works."

We take off into a sprint toward Sean's office, and when inside, we quickly search drawers and filing cabinets for any incriminating evidence. I need something to make this look like a business deal gone wrong as there is no way we are taking the blame—again.

"Gotcha, you fucker," Cian curses in elation as he holds up a piece of paper.

What he holds is clear proof of Sean's and Shane's involvement in money laundering for years. Shane's signature is proof of it. But I know there is more, and I find it as I break into the bottom drawer of Sean's desk.

His journal.

I discovered Sean's love for journaling when it was revealed who he really was. So I knew he would have entries about Shane Moore.

I skim through the pages quickly, hoping it will contain what we need to reinforce Shane's involvement with Sean. And I find it.

The entry details how Shane exploited his power to help keep Sean hidden when I was behind bars. I always wondered how Sean remained so elusive. Now I know. He had the law on his side—no wonder he thinks he's untouchable.

I place the paper on Sean's desk, where the police will find it. But the journal, I conceal beneath Sean's diary. I can't stage the crime scene. It has to look like Sean and Shane had an argument that ended in Shane's death, forcing Sean to flee.

This will make hiding impossible for Sean as the police force won't stop until Shane's killer is caught. But we're going to get to him first.

Once everything is set, I can't help but look at Sean's

drawer, where more journals are stored. I hate him, but I want to understand him. I don't understand it myself, but maybe these journals will help. Collecting as many as I can carry, we race out the back door and flee into the dead of night.

Cian and Ethan speed away, and I follow soon after, headed for the castle.

Checking my phone, I sigh in relief when I don't have any missed calls or text messages. I hope that means everything is all right.

The grounds are quiet when I arrive so I drive straight to my home.

Parking my truck and reaching for Sean's journals, I tread with caution as I walk toward my front door. It's unlocked. Just as I'm about to call out, Babydoll appears, and just like that, I can breathe again.

She runs, wrapping her arms around me. Her cast is off early. She must have seen Dr. Shannon, insisting he take it off. My brave girl. "Thank God you're all right."

I kiss the top of her head, inhaling her comforting scent. "Where's Shay?"

"He's sleeping. I don't think he understands what's going on."

"I don't either," I confess, gently pulling out of our embrace. "You look knackered. Go sleep."

"I can't," she says, shaking her head. "What are we going to do?"

She only just realizes I'm holding the stack of journals.

"Sean has run, but I didn't expect anythin' less." When she works her bottom lip, I place the journals onto the kitchen bench. "It's goin' to be okay. We're goin' to find him."

"You don't know that." Her response reflects her fear. I wish I could make it go away.

But the only way I can do that is to find Sean.

"What happened?" she asks, watching me closely.

There will never be a right time to tell her what happened to Amber. When I proposed to Babydoll, it was a promise to never keep anything from her.

So, reaching out and cupping her cheek, I break her heart as gently as I can. "Amber, she didn't…she's dead. I'm so sorry, Cami."

She blinks once. "What? Dead? Wh-what do you mean she's dead?" Her voice raises in volume, hinting at her impending breakdown.

"I don't know the details," I explain, brushing my thumb across the apple of her cheek. "But I saw Cian. He and Ethan came to Sean's house as I was gettin' beaten by Constable Shane Moore."

"Oh my God," she gasps, tears welling. "Are you all right?"

When she tries to fuss, I grip her hands. "I'm fine. But the constable is not. I shot him. He's dead."

The realization of what I just shared hits her, and she pulls back, beginning to pace the room.

I give her the time and space she needs, as I know this is a lot to take in. But it always is. There is never a pause button option for us. We are always moving in fast forward.

"This is—" But she stops midsentence, clearly needing more time.

I really need to regroup with my men as time is of the essence. But I won't rush this. Babydoll always comes first.

"You killed a cop?" she questions, only wrapping her head around what I shared.

"Aye. But it's goin' to be okay. We've laid the evidence out for the peelers to find. They'll see he was dirty. That he was workin' with Sean. With Sean missing, they'll assume he killed the constable. They won't stop lookin' for him, which means he doesn't have many places left to hide.

"His time is comin', and it's comin' soon. We will find him, and he will get everythin' he deserves."

"But last time—"

"This isn't like last time," I assure her. "There is no sequel."

When her bottom lip trembles, I lower my mouth to hers and kiss her softly. I can't stand to see her cry.

"I promise ye, y'll be my wife," I whisper against her mouth. "Yer goin' to be the mum to my kids. We're goin' to live a normal, boring life. We're goin' to grow aul' together. And when this life ends for me, I'm goin' to look back and not regret a thing because I got to live it…with you."

She bursts into tears, wrapping her arms around me and

hugging me tight.

Everything I do, I do for her. I want her to know that.

We stay hugging for minutes, and when Babydoll's breathing becomes shallow, I assume she's almost asleep on her feet.

"Get some rest, Baby."

This time, she doesn't protest.

However, I don't want to be away from her, so I gently lead her to the couch. She lies down, her eyes at half-mast. Reaching for a blanket, I gently place it over her, and she's asleep within seconds.

Peering down at her, I smile, unbelieving she is mine.

My phone chimes, and when I reach for it, I see it's a text message from Ron.

We're out looking for him. There aren't many places left for him to hide.

I know this means Ron won't give up either. I could help him, but I don't want to leave Babydoll and Shay. I know that's selfish, but I won't lose either of them again.

I'm sure Alek has his own men looking out for Sean because this affects him too.

There is no way he will elude us again, which is why I decide to get to know the man who is my father better. I reach for the journals, but an envelope pushed aside on the bench catches my eye. Turning it over, I see the official stamp of the paternity testing company I used.

Slipping my finger under the seal, I open it and retrieve the sheet of paper. I don't take a moment to process what I'm about to read. Instead, I scan through the results and read what I already knew to be true.

Shay is my son. He is a Kelly. And I'm the only parent he'll know.

But when I look at the sleeping angel on my sofa, I realize that's not true. Cami knew who Shay was the first moment she met him. She will love and nurture him like he is her own. She already has.

Tucking the results away, I decide to show Shay them when he's older as this is who he is, and I want him to be proud of the fact. I want to be the father I never had. I *will* be.

With that thought, I reach for the stack of journals and bring them over to the sofa. I sit next to Cami, ensuring not to wake her. I run my fingers over the leather bindings, wondering why someone like Sean Kelly would write in a journal.

When I look down at the love of my life, I suddenly understand why.

Sean has no one to share his secrets with. My mother was probably the closest thing he knew of love, and look what he did to her. So, writing in these journals is Sean's only form of communication with "another."

Even sociopaths need a good gurn every now and again, it seems.

Opening the journal, I instantly clench my jaw when I see Sean's distinct handwriting. Memories of when I first saw it crash into me, and I inhale slowly, needing to calm down.

The entry is dated when I was ten years old, which surprises me. Why is he looking at these old passages?

Connor is at it again—treating me like some eejit. He believes his kingdom is impenetrable. But soon, he will see that it's not.

He's hard on Punky. I wonder if it's because he knows he isn't his wain?

I know Cara would be disgusted in us both.

I often wonder if maybe I should take Puck away from this? He loves and respects me. I know he wishes I was his dad. If only he knew the truth. That I really am his father. But I know nothing of being a dad. I would only destroy him.

But when I rule, I'd like it to be with my son.

That's not possible, though. Punky was born a leader, and I admire him for that.

I slam the journal shut, suddenly feeling uncomfortable reading a passage where Sean speaks so…fondly of me. Why is he reading these? Why is he digging up the past?

I've had enough reminiscing for the evening, so I carefully stand and decide to shower and catch a few hours' sleep.

I send Cian a text first, however. It simply says:

I'm sorry. I'm here. Always.

He won't want to see anyone. That's how Cian is. But I want him to know I'm here if he needs me. I don't know what happened to Amber, but no doubt, this was Liam's or Sean's doing. I only hope no one else loses their life to this never-ending war.

Ethan proved he can look after himself and those he loves. He doesn't need protection. He is the toughest, most courageous man on my side.

Closing the door to the bathroom softly, I strip out of my bloody clothes, the events of the past…ten years catching up to me. Running a hand down my face, I decide to shave first.

Lathering the shaving gel onto my face, I reach for my razor but stop when the door opens, and Babydoll appears. She looks like she's just woken up.

"Did I wake ya?"

She shakes her head, closing the door behind her.

She doesn't speak, and I wonder if something is wrong. But when she gestures for the razor, I understand what she wants. Shaving is just a façade for what she really seeks.

I offer it to her.

She slides between me and the sink, her front facing mine. My body's natural response to Babydoll is to shove her back against the wall and fuck her senseless. But I allow her this; this act of normalcy is what she needs.

I know the death of Amber hasn't sunk in.

She commences shaving me carefully, her tender eyes watching her strokes cautiously. I trust her completely and savor being tended to this way, but only with her.

"I'm the world's worst sister," she says softly, never breaking concentration. "I haven't spent any time with Eva since this entire ordeal started."

"She's safe with Ethan."

"Who would have thought my sister and your brother?"

Again, it touches me that Ethan is referred to as being my brother.

"We can't help who we love."

She nods, appearing pensive over what I shared.

"Is that why you were reading Sean's journals?"

Curiosity got the better of her, no surprise there.

"I don't know why I took them," I confess, trying to keep still as she shaves my cheek. She's careful around the scar. "I hate him, and there is no doubt he will die by my hand. But I don't understand him. I don't understand how greed could change a person the way it has him.

"Those journals, they were from when I was a child. I found them in his drawer. Why would he be lookin' at them? He has destroyed my life, but he's lookin' at journal entries from when I was a wain? Why? Why is he reminiscin'?

"It doesn't make any sense."

"You don't understand him because you could never be like

him," she says softly. "I know you see yourself as a monster, but you're not. You're nothing like him."

Even though I've never said it, Babydoll knows I'm afraid that I'm exactly like him. Truth be told, Sean has been the only father figure in my life. Connor was nothing like a father to me, but Sean was. He protected me, which to this day, I still don't understand why.

Was he trying to shape me into his puppet, knowing it would come to this one day?

Killing him without answers will eat away at me for the rest of my life.

"It's okay to feel bad," she lightly states as she finishes shaving me.

Reaching for a washcloth, she runs it under the warm water and gently wipes it over my face. The act is so tender, I instantly feel relaxed.

"I didn't want to accept it when Brody died, but even after everything he did, I still felt bad that he died. A part of me hated myself for it, but I think if we didn't express some sense of remorse for those whose lives we take, then we're just as much a monster as them.

"Someone wise once told me that it's okay to feel bad. That vulnerability makes you strong. It makes you human—my human. And that's what you are, Puck Kelly, you're my human. I love you. Whatever choice you make, I want you to know I'll stand by you—always."

When she finishes washing my face, she lays a soft kiss against my mouth, comforting me as I did to her when she came to terms with her father's death. I don't want to accept what she says because what does that make me?

Weak, that's what.

After everything Sean has done, I should be rejoicing in the fact that his days are numbered. But I'm not. I can't help but feel…sad. Not sad that he's dead, but rather, sorrowful that it's ended this way. I wish things were different.

I wish my ma never suffered the fate she did. I also wish I had the chance to tell Connor what a good man he really was. But there is one thing we can't control, that we can never get back, and that is time, which is why I wrap my fingers around the back of Babydoll's neck and deepen our kiss.

She moans into my mouth, melting into me and welcoming my touch. I love how receptive she is. She always wants me as much as I want her.

"I love you," I profess against her wet lips.

There is nothing left to say because now, actions will speak louder than words. And I want her loud.

Picking her up from under her thighs, I walk us toward the shower, our lips never missing a beat as I turn on the water. Once the temperature is right, I step under the spray, drenching us both.

Babydoll is still fully clothed, which makes this even hotter.

She rubs herself against my aching cock, the friction of her jeans straddling the line of pleasure and pain. I slam her back against the wall, the water cascading around us like a waterfall. It's here in the water where we are baptized, we are reborn.

"Fuck me," she pants, writhing against me, locking her legs around my back.

She desperately tugs at the hem of her T-shirt, and I help strip her as I almost tear the garment in half. I unsnap the front clip on her bra, and the moment her breasts are free, I bend down and take her pearled nipple into my mouth.

A guttural cry leaves her. I'm hardly gentle. I bite and suck, just the way I know she likes. With my mouth still working from breast to breast, I yank down her zip and slide my fingers down her soft, wet flesh and sink into her with ease.

I don't lower her jeans as I know the restraint is driving her crazy. I fuck her with my fingers; the tempo in sync with my mouth. I show her no mercy when she arches into my touch, begging me to touch her needy clit.

"I want you."

She tries to reach for my cock, but I quickly remove my fingers from her. Her eyes snap open when I let her go, and her feet hit the shower floor. Her confusion soon turns to arousal when I grip her arms and slam them overhead, securing them in one hand.

She works her bottom lip, watching me grip my cock and commence running my hand up and down my shaft.

"Where do ya want me?" I ask, almost coming by the

ravenous look on her face.

"I want you everywhere," she confesses, her eyes fixated on my hand. "I want you to come in me…on me."

I love her filthy mouth.

I'm so worked up that I decide to give in to her request—both of them.

With her hands still bound, I work my cock, never breaking eye contact with her. This moment is unguarded and raw, but neither of us is embarrassed or ashamed. I want her to see what she does to me because I'm seconds from coming.

Her jeans slip down her thighs as she rubs them together, and when I see her hairless pussy, a growl escapes me. Her chest rises and falls quickly, betraying her arousal. Water sticks to her ripe flesh, and the sight has me working my cock faster, desperate to come.

"You're so fucking hot," she almost purrs, jutting out her chest so her nipples brush my chest. "I'm ashamed to admit this, but when I play with myself, it's only you I think of."

Her dirty words have me racing toward the finish line.

"You get me so wet. And when we…"

"When we what?" I coax her to continue because I know what she says next will be the death of me.

"When that house was crumbling around us as we fucked liked animals…I liked it. I felt like I was being split into two. You were everywhere. I felt so full."

To know she enjoyed it too has my orgasm careening into

me like a freight train.

"I want you to fuck me like that again."

I can't stand it any longer and come with a loud, sated groan onto her stomach. Ribbons of white are washed away, but the sight of me on her skin gets me hard once again.

I let her go and watch as she slips her hand between her legs and returns the favor as she commences playing with her pussy.

Water cascades down her body, and I'm envious of every drop. She knows she's getting me hot because there is something almost taboo watching your lover touch themselves. She nibbles on her bottom lip to mute her whimpers, but I want that mouth. I also want that pussy.

She wants me to fuck her without restraint, so I will give her what she craves.

Dropping to my knees, I place my entire mouth over her cunt, twirling my tongue inside her as she continues fucking herself with her fingers. I work alongside her, licking and sucking, aiding her with my mouth and tongue.

"Oh, fuck," she curses, increasing the tempo of her strokes.

She circles her clit desperately while I mimic the action of what my cock will be doing in seconds with my tongue. In and out, I fuck her, moving my face from side to side. She said she enjoyed being filled full, and this right here, I am all over her, holding her prisoner with my mouth.

She reaches down and grips my long hair, riding my face as she removes her fingers, begging me to take over.

I suck over her clit while fucking her with my tongue. She doesn't hold back and fucks my face without apology. Just as she is about to come, I pull away.

"Punky—" she cries, but she won't have to beg.

Standing up, I turn her around and press her against the shower wall, where I slide into her pussy with ease. I don't allow her time to adjust to the sharp intrusion. Instead, I fuck her hard. I grip her hips and bounce her up and down on my cock hastily.

She splays her hands against the wall, arching her back as I wrap her long, wet hair around my fist and use it as reins as I slam into her over and over again. The slapping of flesh crashes into the rivulets of water, making this a haven for our carnal lust.

I'm far from gentle, but Babydoll takes what I give. Her supple arse is my weakness, so I spread a cheek wide and watch the way I slide in and out of her cunt. She hugs me tight, and I almost come when she clenches around me with a vise-like grip.

Her body is a conduit I want to possess every single day of my life, and when her engagement ring catches the light, I realize that my happily ever after is within reach. I haven't come this far to fail.

"I promise ye," I pant between thrusts. "It's only ever us, Baby. I would die for you."

"Me…too," she whimpers, her body quivering around me.

"Where you go, I go."

I will fight for my family—at whatever cost.

Leaning forward, like a fucking animal, I bite the side of her neck and don't let go as I continue fucking her, and as I hit her deep, her impassioned cries echo off the walls. But with Shay sleeping down the hall, I offer her my fist, which she bites down on as she comes with a muffled scream.

Her body convulses around me, spasming and sucking me deep, and just as she slumps forward, I wrap my arm around her waist, holding her up. I continue sinking into her, losing myself to this beautiful woman who will soon be my wife.

She is trembling, her fatigue clear, so I pull out and spin her around. Lifting her, I support her and do all the work as I lower her onto my cock. I hold her tight, helping her bounce up and down on me. She wraps her arms around my neck, tiny mewls slipping past her plump lips as I enter her hard and deeply— over and over.

Leaning down, I take her nipple into my mouth and slam her back against the wall. Her body is lax. She allows me to milk my pleasure from her as I continue savoring her parful body.

We lock eyes, and all I see is love reflected back at me. Even though this is far from lovemaking, this is how Cami and I love—love is messy; it leaves you breathless. It isn't a choice. It chooses *you*.

But is it worth it?

Fuck yes.

"I love you," she cries, slamming her mouth over mine.

We kiss like we're one another's life supply, and when she rocks against me in just the right way, I come so fucking hard, I almost blackout. We don't stop kissing. She swallows my pleasure, and I swallow hers.

We are one. Now and forever. And I wouldn't change a fucking thing.

FIFTEEN

PUNKY

A soft knock on the door jars me awake. My brain takes a moment to remember where I am.

Peering over at Babydoll's bare back, I smile, thankful she wasn't a dream. I think that every morning I wake.

When the knock sounds again, I quietly peel back the blanket on the sofa bed and cover Babydoll. Searching for some jeans, I slip into them. I also reach for my gun.

When I open the door and see a young woman I don't know standing in front of me, I don't know whether to be relieved or not. "Can I help ye?"

Her eyes nervously drift to the gun I'm holding. But until I know who she is, it's not going anywhere.

"I've wanted to call on ye for so long. To introduce myself," she adds quickly.

"Well, now's yer chance, love," I bluntly say, wishing she'd hurry up.

"My name is Julia…Julia Foster. Yer ma, Cara, she was my father's sister. I'm yer cousin."

I take a moment to process what she just shared because what the fuck? I know I have an uncle, one I haven't given any thought to since he had no issues living in the house my ma was slain in. Also, the fact that I burned his gaff to the ground would make any Christmas dinner uncomfortable.

I steered clear for a reason—the Fosters abandoned my ma when she needed them. She was her own woman, but they did wrong by her, and I'll never forgive them for it.

But here stands Julia Foster—my cousin.

"No offense, Julia, but why are ye here?"

She pales as this clearly isn't the family reunion she anticipated. "For as long as I can remember, our family has been full of secrets. My parents never told me what happened to Auntie Cara. Kids at school told me.

"How messed up is that?"

"You don't know the half of it."

"Our grandparents, they're gettin' on in age, and I know all they want is for all of us to be together as a family."

"Is that why ye're here?" I snicker, shaking my head. "Did the aul' doll send ye?"

Julia has taken offense it appears when she curls her lip.

"No one sent me," she reveals, flicking her blonde hair over her shoulder. "I'm here 'cause I thought if yer uncle can—"

But her sentence will forever remain unfinished.

"What? What uncle?" I question, every sense heightened.

Julia appears confused and clarifies, "Yer Uncle Sean."

Of course, she is confused. She has no fucking idea what's going on. None of them do. I never told my grandparents who Sean really is. Or that when I offered them protection, it was because Sean was hunting them.

I never thought he'd go after them because I'm sure he knows they mean nothing to me. Yes, I protected them because it was the right thing to do. But that doesn't mean I'm interested in rekindling something that was never there.

However, I have no idea what game he's playing because Julia hasn't mentioned that he's hurt them. Or that they're in danger.

This means he's waiting…but waiting for what?

"What's going on?" Babydoll sleepily asks from behind me.

Julia smiles, but it's strained.

"Cami, this is Julia. My cousin."

I move aside so Babydoll can stand by me. She's wearing my hoodie, which is about three sizes too big for her. Julia joins the dots to who she is to me.

"I'm sorry for comin' over unannounced. I'll leave ye be."

She goes to turn, but I reach out, snaring her wrist. When she peers down, I loosen my hold.

"Where's my uncle now?" I try my best to sound casual.

"He asked if he could stay with us, seein' as it's yer mum's birthday and all. He's lost everyone, and I think he's awful lonely. My dad said he always preferred him over yer da. Oh," she adds as an afterthought. "I'm sorry. That was rude of me to say."

"It is?" The question was never supposed to be spoken aloud, but my brain and mouth aren't connected right now because it's her birthday? Why don't I know this?

I don't know anything because the man who has the answers is holding them as ransom. But what I do know is…is that Sean wants me to find him.

"Yer right," I say, slipping into the role Julia wanted. "It would be nice to get the family together. If ya give me yer address, I can come by later. To celebrate my ma's birthday… like a family."

Her green eyes narrow, and she has every right to be suspicious, but it seems her need to play make-believe overrides good sense. "Really? Oh, Grandma is goin' to be so happy."

"How 'bout we keep this to ourselves?" I gently suggest. "I'd like to surprise them."

She nods eagerly, appearing to believe me as she rattles off her address and mobile number. Babydoll doesn't say a word, but she doesn't have to. I know what she's thinking. Sean is there for a reason. And the fact it's my mum's birthday is no coincidence either.

This is definitely a trap…one I'll be walking into willingly.

"All right, phone me when yer on the way," Julia says, smiling broadly.

She waves goodbye, and we watch in silence as she gets in her car and drives away.

"This is a trap," Babydoll says, her panic clear. "We need to call on everyone to surround that house so we can take Sean out. How do we even know she is who she claims to be? This could be another one of Sean's tricks."

I don't reply.

Instead, I pull her into my arms and spin her so her back is nestled against my front. "Have you thought about what month ye'd like us to marry in?"

"Puck," she says, trying to turn around. But I hold her tightly, kissing her temple.

"And what about the venue? If it's okay with you, I'd like to have it here. In the castle. Once it's finished, of course. I think Connor and my ma would have liked that."

"We need to talk to Ron and—"

"Cami, it's all right. It'll be all right."

"How?" She sighs, shaking her head. "Yer father is no doubt planning something horrible, and yer talking about our wedding. Why?"

"'Cause I need this," I explain, calmly staring into the clear morning sky. "I need this sense of normal because nothing about what we're walkin' into is. A new day means hope, and I hope come nightfall, y'll tell me what date yer goin' to be my wife. That's all I care about."

She sighs, leaning into me. "I'm sorry."

"Don't be." I kiss the top of her head before letting her go. "Let's get ready."

It's not even a question of her not coming. We are in this together. But I do need someone to look after Shay, and there is only one person who I trust.

We walk inside, and I'm surprised to see Shay sitting at the counter, eating a bowl of cereal. I've not told Cami about the paternity results. But she always knew, results or not. And I did too.

"Hi, mate," I say, not wanting to make a fuss. "Ya sleep all right?"

He nods, eating from his oversized bowl.

"Grand. My wee brother and sister and Cami's sister are goin' to come over and look after ye. Maybe they can take ya to the zoo? I'll ask them to bring some clothes over for ye too. And maybe some toys?"

I sound away in the head, but I have a lot of learning and catching up to do.

"Where's Mummy?"

I look at Cami, not sure how I'm supposed to tackle this. A part of me is relieved he doesn't know or didn't see what happened, but how am I meant to tell him his ma is dead?

I know what that does to a chile, and I hate that my son and I share this experience. I hate that our innocence was stolen.

But unlike my childhood, I'll never hide who Aoife was. Shay needs to know who his mother was because I won't have him chasing ghosts his entire life—like me.

However, Cami steps in because now is not the time to tell him the truth. "She's got something really important to do. But she's thinking of you and loves you. So much."

Not a lie as Aoife, God bless her soul, wherever she is, is most definitely hoping her son is safe.

I'll make sure of it, which is why I send Ethan a text. He replies a moment later. I knew I could count on him.

I leave Shay to finish his breakfast while I have a quick shower and dress in my best clothes. I'm knotting my navy tie when Babydoll enters. She's in a lovely green dress.

She watches closely but doesn't say a word. Instead, I notice she has something in her hand.

My face paints.

"One last time," she whispers, offering them to me. And she's right. It ends with Sean, as he is the reason I needed these paints to escape the demons trapped within my soul.

It's time to set them free.

My uncle's gaff is in the Republic.

I suppose he wanted to get as far away from the

neighborhood where his old house was, the house I burned to the ground.

Babydoll has been quiet. I know that's because she's nervous. Coming face to face with the man who kidnapped her must be playing with her emotions. As for me, I don't know how I'm going to stop myself from stabbing Sean in the jugular.

But he is here for a reason, and I would be lying if I didn't admit I was curious to know what that is.

I knock on the front door firmly as there is no point in drawing out the inevitable. Babydoll doesn't release my hand, and when the door opens, her grip only tightens.

"I'm so happy yer here." Julia opens the door wider, permitting us entry.

I never let go of Babydoll's hand because I still don't know what we're walking into. However, I haven't called for backup because I believe Julia is who she says she is. And when we walk into the living room and see my grandparents sitting on the couch, it seems my gut intuition was right.

Imogen comes to a shaky stand while Keegan remains seated. We hardly left things on the best of terms as I pretty much told my grandparents I never wanted to see them again.

"Puck," Imogen says, hobbling over to me. "It's good of ye to come."

She leans in for a hug which I loosely reciprocate.

"Hi, Camilla. Good to see ye again."

Cami nods but stays close to me. Being here is dredging up

memories she wishes to forget because the last time she saw my grandma was when she left with Rory. I don't believe in ghosts, but Rory sure as shit is one that continues to haunt me every single day.

A man with dark brown hair enters with a photo album, flicking through the pages, so he's yet to see me. But when he lifts those familiar blue eyes and notices he has company, he almost trips over the edge of the rug.

"Boys a dear," he gasps, shook to the core. "Yer the spit of yer ma."

I am?

An uncomfortable silence fills the room. But that soon turns to a deadly silence when a woman's joyful titter can be heard before she enters, and who she enters the room with rouses the devil inside me.

"Puck," Sean happily says, carrying a silver tray filled with nibbles. "It's good to see ye, lad."

I advance, ready to tear out his throat, but Babydoll pulls me back as she's still holding my hand.

Everyone is watching one another, a mixture of happiness, astonishment, and confusion filling the room. But Sean, Cami, and I are the only people who know what's really going on.

Sean places the tray onto the coffee table before stealing a cube of cheese and casually popping it into his mouth like we are having a fucking tea party. He is baiting me as he knows I won't act in haste until I know what his angle is.

But time is ticking.

"Hello, Puck. I'm yer aunt Siobhan. And this is yer uncle Charlie. We're so happy yer here."

I wish I could share the sentiment, but I can't take my eyes off Sean and the smug way he's eating that fucking piece of cheese.

Again, I spring forward, but Babydoll stops me. I know this is what Sean wants, but I want to rip his arrogant head from his shoulders.

"Thank you for inviting us into your home. I'm Camilla. Puck's fiancée."

Sean pauses from chewing as this is something he didn't know. "Ach, congratulations," he says, wiping his hands on a napkin. "It upsets me yer fathers can't be here to celebrate with us."

This fucker is going down, and going down now.

I don't get a chance to act, however, because Keegan stands. Even though he wronged my ma, I won't disrespect him.

"Congratulations," he says, and it surprises me to see he now needs a frame to walk. He was a tough aul' lad when we first met. My head still hurts from when he drove his shotgun into it. But to see him this frail, it does something to me I can't explain.

"Thank you," I reply, shaking his trembling hand as he extends it.

Imogen huddles into his side, her broad smile expressing

how happy she is that we're all together.

It's still fucking awkward, but something has shifted with Keegan's peace offering.

"I'm sorry," Charlie says. "I don't mean to stare, but ye look just like Cara."

Imogen sniffles, clutching at the small gold crucifix around her neck. Keegan averts his eyes, no doubt not wanting anyone to see his tears. Sean stands indifferent, but the spasm of his jaw, which one would miss if they weren't looking for a response, tells a different story.

When he looks at me…all he sees is my mum too…and what he did to her. No wonder he wants me dead.

"I wouldn't know," I reply. "Her memory is fadin'."

It takes all my willpower not to glare at Sean.

Charlie smiles, but it's bittersweet. "I thought as much, which is why—" He holds up the photo album. "I found some old family photos. Would ye like to see?"

Julia looks like she's about to burst into tears because this would be a first for her too.

"Sure, why not." Looking at family photos is not what I came here for, but Sean is where I want him.

So, I sit near Charlie as he sits on the couch. Babydoll sits beside me.

Imogen, Keegan, and Julia also sit on the opposite couch and recliner, eager to take a look as well. However, Sean chooses to stand. Auntie Siobhan ducks back into the kitchen to tend to whatever is in the oven.

"Yer ma was such a stubborn girl," Charlie says lightly as he opens the photo album. "She did what she wanted. When she got an idea in her head, no one could stop her."

A nostalgic chuckle leaves Imogen.

"Here is what I mean."

Charlie turns the photo album so I can see the first page, which has an aged photograph of a class picture. About twenty pupils are dressed immaculately as their parents clearly wanted this memory to be one they would look back on proudly.

I notice all the little girls are wearing dresses, all but one.

Her blue eyes dare the photographer to comment on her appearance, and of course, they didn't because my ma is the only wee girl wearing trousers. Back then, it would have been unheard of for a girl to wear trousers, but it seems my mum didn't give a fuck what anyone thought.

"Yer ma was awful stubborn, but she was also quare smart. Her nose was always in a book."

Charlie offers me the photo album, encouraging me to flick through the pages. I've never been offered this before, so now presented the opportunity, I take it.

Charlie commences sharing stories about my mum while I turn the pages of the album, gazing at each photograph, too afraid to blink. As my mum gets older, her personality shines through—she appears playful, a free spirit who wasn't afraid to try anything.

It's sensory overload, and my brain has a hard time connecting this person as my mum. I don't even see her as a person anymore. But being able to live her life through these photographs makes her real—makes what I'm fighting for real.

And when I peer up, locking eyes with Sean, he knows it. He knows I won't be beaten.

The photos suddenly lose their light, and I don't mean that they were taken in the wrong lighting. My mum's spark, it's gone. The carefree woman now seems plagued, like she carries the world on her shoulders…and I know why that is.

She became a Kelly.

Her spirit was crushed because like a bird, her wings were clipped, and she was tossed into a cage. No wonder she fell for Sean's bullshit. She was unhappy, a young woman caught up in a world she didn't understand.

And he provided her a haven, a light in the darkness. I know this because he did the same thing to me.

The last photograph stops my heart. It's of my ma, hands on her swollen belly as she smiles; a true smile. As this candid photo was taken mid-speech, it's safe to assume whatever she was whispering to her belly was a promise that it would be just her and me.

Her light returned, and it returned because of me. For once in my life, I brought light instead of darkness.

Babydoll places a reassuring hand on my thigh, reading my inner thoughts. This is all too much.

"No hard feelin's for burnin' down yer last gaff?" I say while Charlie snorts in laughter. "I don't know how ye managed to save these from the fire, but I'm awful glad ye did."

I offer him the album, but he shakes his head. "They belong with you. Yer ma would have wanted that."

Imogen bursts into tears. "Happy Birthday, Cara."

Charlie places his hand over my knuckles, the ones which spell my mum's name, and smiles. "Not one for tattoos myself, but this one, I like. Happy Birthday, wee sis."

Babydoll sniffs beside me.

The mood has mellowed, but this little trip down memory lane has not softened me. If this is Sean's way of waving a white flag, I'm about to use that flag to wipe his blood from my hands.

"Tea is almost ready," Siobhan says, blowing her nose on a tissue before heading into the kitchen.

"Uncle," I say between clenched teeth.

Charlie smiles, but when he realizes it's not him I'm addressing, he quickly stands and helps Siobhan.

"Can I have a word?"

Sean nods, but when he stays put, I gesture with my head that we're to speak outside.

He complies as it would look far more suspicious if he refused.

My family is none the wiser as to what is about to transpire as I lead my father outside. The moment I close the front door, I take a deep breath. I need to compose myself because if I don't,

I will kill Sean right here, right now.

"This is fucking pathetic, even for you," I say, turning around slowly to face him. "Ye think hidin' out here is goin' to keep ye safe?"

However, Sean's attention is not directed at me. It's at Cami.

She stands her ground, but I know he intimidates her, which is what he wants.

"Hey, arsehole," I holler, snapping my fingers. "Keep lookin' at her, and she'll be the last thing you ever see."

He simply smirks in response, hinting he doesn't take me seriously. I decide to show him how serious I am when I elbow him swiftly in the nose.

A pained grunt leaves him as he pinches his bloody nose with one hand while rummaging through his trouser pockets for a handkerchief.

Spilling his blood rouses the bloodlust, and I charge forward, only stopping from beating him to a pulp when he says, "Ye wouldn't want me to tell them what a whore yer mum really was, would ye? Tarnish their memory of her and break yer grandparents' fragile hearts."

And there he is; the vile animal I call father.

"What the fuck are we doin' here?"

Sean presses the handkerchief over his nose. "I thought ye wanted to know all 'bout yer past? About yer beloved ma whose name yer avenging. But where has that got ye? Yer throwin' yer life away for a ghost! A person ye don't even know!"

"Aye, I don't know her 'cause ye killed her, remember? So spare me the fucking theatrics. What do ye want?"

"Ye killed Liam then? And my friend, Shane Moore. Seems ye have a taste for it," he says, and if his nose wasn't still bleeding, I would elbow him again. "But I think before ye killed Liam, he told ye something which changed the course of everythin'."

I refuse to allow my interest to show because he is right. I still don't know who Liam was protecting.

"And I know what that somethin' is."

"Grand, how 'bout ye tell me so we can put an end to this? Yer not goin' to win. Tell me, and I promise not to hurt you… too badly."

Sean snickers, and it takes all my willpower not to break his neck. "You promised someone somethin', and if you don't deliver, I don't think he'll be a very happy man."

Sean knows about Alek, it seems.

I promised Alek my empire, that's why he's helped me, but if I don't deliver, he will kill me—a deal is a deal, and he made clear what happens when someone backs out of the deal. I can't offer him Northern Ireland in the state it's in. It would be like selling him a car that doesn't start. Or a house that needs major renovations.

I can't walk away from this.

"If I'm not there for the deal, then it doesn't go ahead, and we know what happens then. I'm my own collateral this time," Sean explains. "You kill me now, then y'll never know who's huntin' youse, and yer Russian will kill ya for backing out of a deal."

Alek and I shook hands. That means something in my world. I could walk away and give Alek everything, but what do I have to offer him? He wants the shipment as that is what will cement his power in a foreign country. And Sean is right. If I kill him, then I'll never know who the enemy is.

I make no mistake that Alek and I are friends. I would do the same if I were him and someone promised me something. This is business, his livelihood to feed his family. You don't fuck with a man's family.

"Yer anger just came back to bite you…again because it gave me an opportunity to strike. Y'll never learn, son."

Tipping my face to the heavens, I close my eyes and take a deep breath. I can't believe this arsehole isn't dead yet. For someone who has no friends, he sure as shit can manipulate many into doing his bidding. It makes me wonder just who this person is.

They hate me enough to do business with Sean. Whoever they are, I know I need to be careful.

"Why could ya not tell me this over the phone? Why come here?" I ask, finally looking at him.

But when I do, I see the reason. It's the reason he was reading over journals written a lifetime ago.

"You know yer goin' to lose, don't you? Yer here 'cause it's the only place ye feel close to her. Ye killed her, yet you really did love her. And in yer own fucked-up way, you love me…that's why I'm not dead yet."

And deep down, as much as I hate myself for it…that's the reason he's not dead either.

"This is yer way of makin' amends for the wrongs of yer past, is it? You knew how badly I wanted to know who she was…that's why we're here. Yer doin' this as some sort of peace offering?"

I want him to prove me wrong. I need him to be the monster I know he is because killing him will be so much easier. But showing me humanity…I can't deal with that.

"I've always wanted to rule with you, Puck. I've never made that a secret."

"You shut yer fucking mouth," I spit, unable to listen to this.

"But ye'd rather give it all away to a stranger because you hate me that much. I've done wrong, I know that, but I've also done some good."

"Good?" I scoff, shaking my head in disgust. "Are ye jokin' me? You were usin' my son for yer own personal gain!"

Sean removes the bloody handkerchief from his nose, allowing me to see the surprise on his face. "I was lookin' after my grandson," he amends, and I hate that I can't determine if he's lying or not. "Aoife had nothin'. I wouldn't let them starve."

"Bullshit! He was just another pawn for ye to use. You only know how to play dirty."

But he simply shrugs, refusing to argue and refusing to

fight. "Aye, fair play, but have ye forgotten who saved ye from Connor's fists? I fucked up, so I did, but I never forced anyone to do anythin' they didn't want to.

"Rory, Ethan, the men, they all made their choices. The Doyles made theirs. Every single person involved in this made a choice…as did yer ma. She chose to betray me when she promised never to. She knew the consequences involved. What would you do?

"She was takin' my son and goin' to destroy everythin' I worked so hard for. She used me to escape an unhappy marriage as I always knew, if given the choice…she would never choose me."

"She's not here to defend herself," I snarl, anger vibrating through me.

"But her family are here," Sean counters, revealing the true reason we're here. "You wouldn't believe me, but y'll believe them. I need ye to see who yer ma really was. She was all the things they said—stubborn, independent, and smart.

"She wasn't the angel you believe her to be. I never forced her or tricked her. She knew what she was doin', and she didn't care. She fucked her husband's brother because Cara did what she wanted. Y've heard it firsthand from her family.

"She wanted to get rid of ya. She knew Connor would find out the truth. But no matter her faults, I loved her as best I could."

This isn't the first time he's told me this. It's the only story he's stuck to this entire time. So is the claim that we are stronger ruling together. I'm the one who would rather cut out my heart than rule alongside my father.

Babydoll's calming voice in my ear is the voice of reason I need. "He's just playing mind games with you. Don't let him win."

He knows he can't win, so this is another angle he's playing. But he's right—my ma didn't do anything she didn't want to. At one time, she *wanted* to be with Sean, knowing what it would do to Connor. I always thought of her as the victim, but I see now, coming here and talking to the people who knew her best that Cara was never a victim.

She didn't deserve the fate which was delivered to her, but the choice she made came with consequences—ones which she knew about, yet she still acted.

She is fading, and all I hold onto now are memories that I want to believe are true. But the truth is, I don't know what to believe anymore. I wish I could remember more…but I can't. All I have to go on are the retellings, second-hand memories from people who Cara once knew.

"All right then, we will do this," I state, eyeing Sean. "But know, you won't leave with yer life intact. I'm keepin' *you* alive because *I* need you this time. Once this is done and I deliver what was promised, I *will* kill you."

Sean smirks but nods.

"How can I trust you? How do I know this isn't one of your

tricks?"

"Y've got an army to fight with you now, Puck. I don't stand a chance." Without Shane Moore on his side, Sean knows he has nowhere to hide. He's running out of friends awful fast, which is why he made a deal with whoever Liam was in cahoots with.

"Then why would ya agree to help me? Why not fight with whoever else I'm up against?"

Sean shrugs. "I fight for myself."

That's a load of shite. This other person is someone Sean clearly needs help overthrowing. They are also someone he doesn't trust. If he did, we wouldn't be having this conversation as I'd be dead. He made a deal with them because they trust him.

He no doubt sweet-talked them, and they now believe he's on their side. But the only side Sean is on is his own. He is making a deal with both of us because come the day of reckoning, whichever side wins, Sean will hope they show him mercy.

He has sorely misjudged me and my hatred toward him.

"You will not say a word to my mum's family about who you really are." I don't want to embarrass or tarnish my mum's memory with the truth. They've suffered enough.

Babydoll hasn't said a word, but that doesn't mean she doesn't have anything to say.

Sean makes a beeline for the door, but I reach out and grip his arm. "Where do you think yer goin'?"

"Inside to eat Siobhan's famous stew," he replies smartly.

I cluck my tongue. "Ye really didn't think I'd let ye out of my sight, did ya? Yer *my* prisoner now."

There is no way I'm risking Sean fleeing or have him conspiring behind my back. There's been enough of that. This ends—now.

After we ate Siobhan's stew—I can see why it's famous—we lit candles on a chocolate cake and sang "Happy Birthday" to my mum. It was the first time I ever sang to her. I didn't ask if this was something they did every year because it's not something I want to do again.

What Sean said has been playing on my mind.

I know it's all part of his games, but it's rubbed me the wrong way, and I think that's because I believe him. I don't want to, but I do agree with him—the choices we make are ours alone. Why did my mum choose to be with Sean?

Did she love him? I wanted to believe for so long that he conned her, just as he did to me. But tonight, talking to her family showed me that Cara was an intelligent, independent woman who made her own choices.

She didn't sound like the type of woman who did anything she didn't want, so that meant at one stage in her life, she wanted

Sean.

Cracking my neck from side to side, I secure the ropes around Sean's wrists tightly. I've not spoken a word to him because I've had enough for the night.

And when I come to a stand and face him, the smug grin he wears reveals he knows it. "Yer not goin' to gag me?" he quips. "Why stop now?"

"Shut up," I reply, nodding at Ron, who has offered to take the first shift.

Sean cannot be alone. He is my prisoner until that shipment arrives. Everything is a fucking mess. Nothing has been simple, but now, things seem impossible.

"Call out if he's any trouble," I instruct Ron.

I leave Sean bound and manned and walk toward my gaff where Cami is waiting. She was awful quiet on the way home, so I'm prepared for her to be anything but. I open the front door to see her sitting on the couch with Shay.

He's asleep, his head on her lap as she toys with his hair.

I close the door quietly and walk to the couch, but I don't sit. I look down at the two people who are my world. I want to ask Shay about Sean, but it'll have to wait until the morning.

Babydoll continues gently stroking Shay's hair. Something is clearly on her mind. "Why do we have to do this?" she questions softly. "We've finally got Sean. Why can't we just… deal with him? Why do you have to see this deal through?"

I understand her stance and if it was that simple, Sean would be in a shallow grave. "I made a promise to Alek," I explain. "I can't go back on my word. I don't want to. My feelin's haven't changed. I still plan on givin' Alek everythin' I promised him."

"But things have changed," she argues. "The deal was he was going to protect us. But now that we have Sean, who do we need protecting against?"

Sitting on the couch, I turn to look at her and Shay. "Liam was workin' with someone, and until I know who that is, we are yet again fightin' an unknown enemy—the most dangerous kind. Sean knows who that person is. Therefore, we need him.

"It literally could be anyone. We go to the port, and I don't know who to look for. If they get wind of us being there, the deal won't go ahead, and we're back to square one—constantly lookin' over our shoulders, waitin' for the enemy to strike.

"How can we trust that Sean hasn't made a deal to double-cross us? How do we know we're not walkin' into a trap?

"We don't know," I confess. "But we will be prepared for whatever comes our way. What I do know is that Sean is more valuable to us alive than he is dead. If he's lyin' or playin' us, we will be ready. Either way, his end is near."

Cami sniffs back her tears. She looks so tired.

"I'm sorry. For all of this. I wish I never involved ya in this mess."

"You didn't," she replies sadly. "My surname did."

She's right. Bearing the Kelly and Doyle name carry repercussions. Tomorrow, I'm about to face mine.

But for now, I embrace my family, a reminder of why I need to fight…and win.

SIXTEEN

PUNKY

I don't know what to expect, but that's nothing new. I've come to learn it's best not to walk into anything with expectations. It avoids disappointment this way. And I have a feeling once the meeting I called is over with, there will be much disappointment. And anger.

Ethan and Cian stand with me as we wait for our men to arrive at the factory.

Cian is hurting, and I don't know how to fix it. There isn't anything I can say or do because the love of his life is dead, and we don't know why. I asked Sean before I left if he had anything to do with Amber's murder.

He chose not to respond.

I can't wait for this to be over with, which is why I've asked my men to gather here at Kellys' Aluminum. It seemed fitting because this is where it started, so this is where it'll end.

The factory is filled with men, loyal men who I trust. *This is the army I needed, but it's the army I will give to Alek.* These familiar faces, I've known since I was a boy, but here I stand as their leader. A part of me is saddened that I can't lead them into battle.

But I've made my choice.

Once everyone is here, I stand silent. The silence mutes the whispers. I have their attention. Alek and Austin stand off to the side, showing me respect because this country isn't theirs—yet.

"Thank you for comin'," I commence, making eye contact with the men. "I called ye here because things are about to change."

Excited hollers pass between them, but they're soon to cease once I reveal why we're all here.

"Ye have been loyal to my family for years, and for that, I thank you. Connor thanks you. But it's time for change. I've been fightin' for freedom, mine and yers…and it's finally within reach."

The mood changes.

"Sean Kelly is now my prisoner," I disclose, watching the men's mouths fall open. "His regime is over. He singlehandedly ruined what we—what my father—worked so hard for."

Most know that Sean is my biological father, but I won't give that fucker the satisfaction of admitting that fact aloud.

"He's not dead because I need him for one final thing. The Doyles' shipment is still scheduled for arrival."

The men look at one another, confused. "But the Doyles are dead. You made sure of that," Ollie says, expressing what everyone is thinking.

"Aye, that I did, but someone is goin' to be there to make the deal, and I need to know who. That person is a threat to all of us. We haven't come this far; we haven't lost this much for some cunt to come and steal it from us."

The men clap loudly, whistling their approval as we've all lost so much in this war.

"And I promise ye this…I will find out who this person is, and I will kill them. Just as I killed every other fucker who wanted to double-cross me. And once they're dead and I take that haul for my own, I'll do to Sean what was done to my ma and to Connor."

My words rouse the crowd, and the static is almost electrifying. But that's soon to change.

"Once I avenge them, however…I'm out. This started the day my mum was slain. It ends the moment I kill her murderer."

"What are ye sayin', Puck?" Rogan Shea asks, eyes wide.

"I don't want this life. I never did. I can't do what Connor did…I don't want to. Which is why I made a deal with someone who does. I trust this man. His name is Aleksei Popov. Lord knows I should not trust him. But he is the ruler you want. Him, and Ethan—a true Kelly."

Ethan stands proudly beside me, but Cian is about to rip out my spleen.

I didn't tell him about Sean as I wanted to avoid this. I knew he'd act on impulse to kill him, and he's no use to me dead. I will deal with Cian later, however, because now, I have to face a factory full of angry Irish and Englishmen.

"Naw, we will not serve another!"

"This kingdom is yers!"

"A shift in power is the end of us all."

"You cannot trust Sean Kelly! This is a trap."

These are just a few grievances I hear because, at once, they all form into one big monotonous hum. The men argue and shout amongst themselves, infuriated at me and others.

I allow them to vent as I knew this decision would cause a riot, but this isn't a debate—this decision is done.

"Enough," I say calmly, but the men don't hear me. They've heard enough.

Usually, I would resort to violence, but I won't rule with fear. They respect me, and I wish for that to never change.

So I stand back, allowing them to squabble like aul' dolls.

The passion and loyalty they've shown Connor and me are why they're so upset. It's why they never accepted Sean or Brody Doyle. The throne was always mine…but I don't want it.

Patting Ethan on the back, I hand him the reins and make my way through the crowd because I was never one for goodbyes. I've done what I came here for—to tell the men of our last hurrah. The strident noise soon dims as the men watch me leave.

"Puck," Ollie says, gripping my forearm gently. "Don'tcha do this. Y've given us hope. Don't take it away. These men had nothin'. Y've given them somethin' to fight for."

"I appreciate that, Ollie, but I only have one fight left in me." I slap him on the shoulder and smile sadly.

He knows better than to argue with a Kelly.

I leave the men in the very capable hands of Aleksei Popov and Ethan. What they choose to do is their choice. Whether they stay or go will be up to them. But at least they have a choice.

As it was my choice to keep the truth from Cian, who stands by my truck, smoking a joint. I didn't even notice him leave.

I hate this friction between us. Fighting with him is just wrong.

"How could you not tell me?"

With a sigh, I stand near Cian and steal the joint from his fingers. "What would that achieve? We're almost at the end of this."

"He killed Amber!" he cries, pain and anger fueling his words. "And yer protectin' him? Tell me why we aren't over there now, torturing the shite out of him?"

"I need him."

"For fuck's sake, Punky! Have ye not learned anythin'? This cunt keeps fucking us over. This is another setup. Why can't you see that? If this were Cami—"

"I'm sorry, Cian. I really am," I say, blowing out a plume of smoke. "But if he dies…then all of this, every single death… it would have been for nothin'. I kill him now, and then there's some other fucker who I'll have to kill.

"And then when I kill him, someone else. It won't fucking end! We need one ruler, and that's not me."

"You selfish arsehole," he snarls. "This isn't just about you. You get to live yer happily ever after, but what about everyone else? We're expected to pick up the pieces, is that it? Sometimes, we have to sacrifice our happiness for what's right."

"And losin' ten years of my life wasn't enough?" I pose, tossing the joint onto the ground. "What more do youse want?"

"I want my best friend back," he replies, looking at me like nothing but a stranger. "The man who stood out in a crowd… not blended in. Go live yer happy life then. Turn yer back on the men who have sacrificed so much for you. For our fathers. I don't know who you are anymore."

He walks to his car, leaving me with an injury I never saw coming. I knew he wouldn't like my decision, but I thought he'd accept it, but it seems I was wrong. By gaining my freedom, I'll lose my best friend.

I'll lose the man I once was.

Jumping into my truck, I send Babydoll a message, making sure she and Shay are all right. She replies a moment later that they're fine.

I should get back, but I suddenly feel like I can't breathe. I need to drive.

Cian's words have pissed me off, and that's because a part of me agrees with him. Men have sacrificed their lives for me, and in a sense, it does look like I'm turning my back on them. But this life, it isn't one I would have ever chosen. For myself. For Cami. Or for Shay.

I know this decision is the sensible one to make. So why does it feel like a hole has been punched straight through my chest?

There is only one place that's calling my name, and it's the place where no one judges, and that's because the dead can't talk.

I park my truck and make my way through the cemetery.

The last time I was here, Ethan tried to kill me. How things have changed. Today, he stood tall, a true Kelly. Connor would be proud of him. I know I am.

Dropping to a squat, I look at Connor's grave, realizing I've come to see him willingly more often dead than when he was alive. I wish I could change that.

"Hello, aul' lad," I say aloud. "I'm sorry to be disturbin' ye, but I don't have anyone else to talk to. I've made a choice, one which has me wonderin' if maybe you wished ye could have made the same. But it was too late for you.

"Is that why ye let yer men stray? Had ye had enough? I fucking hated you. But now that I *am* you, I understand why you acted the way ye did. I have a son now, and I hate that our circumstances are the same.

"He too lost his mum. But I will do everythin' in my power to make sure he doesn't go down the road I did. I know you tried yer best. I know deep down, ye knew I wasn't yer son. Ye could have turned yer back on me, but ye didn't.

"Ye loved me as best you could. This world…it fucking takes and doesn't give back. I won't have that for my son. For the love of my life. I want them to be as far away from that as possible. And I thought that was what I wanted. But now…I don't know what I want.

"Sean has got into my head. Sayin' things about Mum. I don't know what to believe. What would you do? If you were given the choice, would you have left? Or wouldn't you change a thing? You died savin' me. Savin' yer kingdom.

"And I'm givin' it away. I'm torn between what's right and what I want. I want a future for Cami and Shay away from this. But will it be enough?

"The darkness, it's a part of me. It always has been. I fear by walkin' away, the demons will only lay dormant for a wee while. And when they rouse, they'll be hungry for so much more. Cami accepts me, and for that, I'm the luckiest man alive, but how can I marry her with hands covered in blood?

"Because that's all I'll have to offer her if I don't get out. If I live the life you did, I will end up in a hole in the ground, just like you did. Just how every single person involved in this fucking war has. I'm one of the last men standin'. But I don't know how long for.

"What would you do, Connor? What would you do…Dad?"

Tears well because I fucking miss this insufferable prick. Who would have thought?

My phone rings, interrupting this verbal onslaught with the dead. I really am losing my mind.

When I retrieve my mobile from my pocket and see it's Cami, I answer quickly. "Everythin' all right?"

"I—um, how long until you're home?" She is slightly panicked, which has me jumping up, kissing two fingers, and pressing them to Connor's gravestone before sprinting for my truck.

"I can be there in twenty minutes."

"Can you make it ten?"

"Why?" I ask, rummaging for my keys.

"Cian is here." I don't understand why that's a bad thing until she adds, "And he's about to kill Sean."

"Fuck." I hang up and almost tear the door from its hinges as I jump into my truck and speed out of the cemetery toward home.

I should have known Cian would do something like this. He is hurting, and the only way to stop that pain is to kill the person who inflicted a wound that will never heal. But he's gone against me when I explained why I need Sean alive.

He is forcing my hand, and when I get to my gaff and see his car parked out front, I wonder just how ugly this is going to get. I slam the door shut and run toward the castle. Cami is waiting outside for me, but she can't be here.

Kissing her forehead frantically, I gently order, "Please go back to our house. I don't want you to see whatever is about to happen."

She wants to argue, but she knows I wouldn't ask this of her if I wasn't afraid…for her.

"Okay. But remember, Cian lost Amber. What would you do if that were me?"

I don't realize she has something behind her back until she extends her hand toward me, offering me my face paints. She wants it to end and knows this face—the face Sean forced me to wear—is the only one who can do that.

Accepting the paints, I watch as she walks away. I don't know who I'll be when I see her again.

Opening the front door, I hear Cian screaming on the verge of hysteria. I wonder where Billy is as it was his turn to keep an eye on Sean. I'll deal with him later.

I keep my cool as I walk down the hallway and turn into the huge dining room. This place may be getting a facelift, but it seems regardless of the décor, blood and violence are entrenched into its foundations. It's been this way for generations, and I believe it will be this way long after I'm gone.

Cian's back is to me, but he knows I'm here. "Suppose yer here to stop me, seein' as ye want to live on the straight and narrow."

Sean looks to be in one piece—for now. He's still tied to the chair.

"This isn't the answer, Cian," I say, keeping my distance as I enter the room. "I know yer hurtin'."

"You don't know anythin'!" he screams, turning around to face me. A gun is in his hand. "This cunt took the only person who ever really loved me."

"That's not true," I calmly state. "I love you. We all do. I'm sorry about Amber. I know that means fuck all, but please don't do this."

"You choose him?"

"No, Cian, I choose you. Always."

But he's not convinced. "If that's true, then kill him. Slit his throat like he did to yer ma."

Sean watches me closely.

"And then what?" I pose because if Cian has a solution, I'm all ears. "We continue to live this vicious cycle where one by one, we all die?"

"We're all victims. In one way or another."

"No, we are not. I refuse to accept that," I amend firmly. "We're survivors. We've survived since we were kids. And I won't give up now. This life has taken so much from us. We both have a chance at freedom. I find out who Liam was workin' with, and I kill them.

"Someone wants this job…someone wants to make Belfast the place we remember. But you kill Sean now, and we're runnin' for the rest of our lives. I don't know about you, but I'm tired."

"How do you know this isn't another one of his tricks?" With a roar, Cian pistol-whips Sean in the temple.

Sean sways, but it's going to take a lot more than that.

"I don't know," I confess. "But I do know I need him there for this deal to go ahead. If he's lyin', then we have an army of men to protect us. But what if he's not? This is our chance to live a life we both deserve.

"I won't give in to temptation. Sean is *our* collateral this time. His fate will always end in his death. But not prematurely. Not when I have a chance at bein' free."

"And what if I don't want that?" Cian asks, his bloodshot eyes pleading I help him because he is so fucking lost. "What if I don't want to live some boring, normal life? I tried it on for size, and look where it got me. I'm back here, a gun in my hand.

"This life is in our blood, Puck. It was what we were born to do." He presses the gun to Sean's temple, sealing our fates forevermore.

"What do you want me to do?" I beg he sees reason. I haven't come this far to let it all go now.

"I want you to do the right thing. I want you to do what Punky would do. I know that man is still inside you, itchin' to break free. This cunt, he killed yer ma! He killed Connor! Remember them? Or are ya a whipped wee pussy now, forgettin' who we are? Forgettin' yer a fucking Kelly."

And just like that...the glimmer of light I held onto is

eclipsed by the darkness.

I tried. I really fucking tried to do the right thing.

But it seems everyone wants me to be someone else. I tried to do good…I tried to be the man Shay would be proud to call father. I tried to be the man Cami could proudly call her husband. I really fucking tried.

But as I look down at the face paints in my trembling hand, I nod slowly. "All right, Cian. If this is what you want."

"You do this, and yer runnin' for the rest of yer lives!" Sean cries, and it's the first time I've seen him show emotion, and that's because he knows his time has come. "Yer all dead! The enemy is closer than ya think. I know who they are. You need me!"

I ignore him because it's here, in the violence, where I thrive.

When I open the lid on the white face paint, memories of being locked away in that wardrobe crash into me, and I can't breathe.

"I want ya to be someone else. I want ya to pretend yer anywhere but here. Whatever ya see, whatever ya hear, I want ya to know it's not real because yer not really here."

Cara's voice is suddenly clearer than it's ever been, and as I dip my fingers into the paint and scoop out a glob, I close my eyes and transport myself back in time.

"Don't cry. I'll hide. I promise. A'll not make a sound."

"Good boy. Mummy loves ya. So much. Never forget it."

I don't need a mirror. I know each stroke by heart. I run circles over my cheeks, giving birth to the devil within. Once I'm done, the container drops to the floor with a thud. I then feed the darkness as I use a single finger to draw my black, sinister grin.

As his mother's mouth gets slit from ear to ear, Punky repeats the same action with his black face paint.

He runs the tip from the apple of his cheek to his mouth, where he draws lines across his lips, wishing to silence his screams, then repeats the action on the other side of his cheek. He now wears a grin as big as his ma's. With precise strokes, he draws slashes downward along the line he just drew, emphasizing his grin as something sinister, something grotesque.

I'm suddenly outside of my body, a voyeur given a front-row seat to the show.

I see Cara being tortured, beaten, and raped. I see it all.

Punky paints black around his eyes, not wanting to bear witness to his ma being defiled over and over again.

"I never wanted this for ya, Cara. But ya didn't listen."

Punky doesn't know what that means. But he knows his mother did something bad.

The man bends down and lifts Cara's head back by her hair, exposing her neck. Cara moans, her face barely recognizable. Her bloodshot eyes focus on the wardrobe door where she knows Punky is watching. She reaches out with a quivering arm, wanting to touch him, to tell him it'll be all right.

Cian is right. I am two people. Punky was born the day he watched his mum be slain by his dad, and right now, Punky is running the show.

Once I finish coloring my eyes black, I open them slowly. The first thing I see is Sean. He looks afraid.

He should be.

Cian stands off to the side, suddenly realizing what he asked me to do.

Inhaling, I tip my face to the ceiling, a smile spreading from cheek to cheek. I feel like I can breathe again.

"Father," I commence, returning my attention to him. "It seems I'm the only person who wants you alive."

"'Cause yer not a fucking idiot, that's why."

"Aren't I?" I question, walking toward him slowly. "All I could think about when locked up in that cell was killin' you. It was the only thing which kept me goin' because givin' up would mean ye'd won."

"Kill me now, and I promise ye, y'll forever be runnin'. Say goodbye to the normal life ye want for yer family. Isn't that why yer doin' this? Why y've done all of this? For them?"

He knows what to say. He knows how to manipulate me.

"Aye, they're all that matters to me. But that doesn't mean I can't have some fun. I may need you to ensure their safety and my freedom, but some parts aren't as vital as others."

Sean pales, knowing what this means for him. I'm going to torture him within an inch of his life, to the point that death would be a mercy.

I don't have much in the way of equipment, but I'm creative. There's some rope and a small hammer a tradesman must have left behind. I don't think he'll want it back once I'm finished.

Gathering both, I stand in front of Sean. "This is the face you created. Do ya like it? Mum told me to pretend to be someone else while you raped and killed her. She told me it wasn't real, but it was.

"It was really fucking real when you slit her throat with ease."

Sean's eyes follow the movement of the hammer as I gently bang the face into my open palm.

"You know why I did it," he says, hoping I see reason.

"Naw, I don't. Ya told me why, but that doesn't mean I understand or accept it."

Before he can say another word, I purse his cheeks between my fingers so his lips pop open. He doesn't fight me because he knows he won't win. Flipping the hammer, I force open Sean's mouth and place the claw of the hammer on his jaw.

Cian hisses, knowing what I plan on doing.

"I should slit yer mouth open, just as you did to her. But this will do."

With force, I jam the claw into his gum and pivot the hammer at an angle as I work it back and forth. When I feel his tooth wobble, I push down harder, laughing manically when blood trickles from Sean's mouth. The roots of the tooth are imbedded deep, but as I use a lot more strength, it dislodges, and with a squelch, it pops free.

Reaching into his mouth, I pull out the tooth.

Sean holds back his pained whimpers, but he looks to be on the cusp of passing out.

"Shall I put this under yer pillow for the tooth fairy?" I mock, holding the tooth between my thumb and pointer finger. "Y'll get at least five pounds for this big sucker."

The blood spilled only encourages me to continue.

I could break his kneecaps, but he needs to walk as I'm not carrying his sorry arse. So I decide to break his elbow instead.

He can't move as his wrists are still bound, but he's unable to hold the weight of his arm and it flops to the side limply. He flinches as the pain would be unbearable. He wants it to fall naturally, but he can't because he's bound…which gives me an idea.

Dropping the hammer, I pick up the rope and swing it high, securing it over a low-hanging rafter in the ceiling. I'm suddenly very pleased they've taken their time with the renovations.

Turning to Cian, I gesture he's to give me the knife he always carries. Only now do I realize he's turned a sickly shade of green.

"What's the matter, mate? Isn't this who you want me to be?"

Cian doesn't say a word as he gives me his blade.

Snatching the knife from his hand, I walk around Sean and

hack through the ropes at his wrists and ankles. Before he gets any ideas to flee, I stab him in the shoulder. It's a flesh wound as experience has taught me where to stab someone if I want to kill them—femoral artery, neck, heart.

This would merely tickle.

But as Sean sags forward, winded, I realize tickle is maybe underplaying it a wee bit.

Gripping him by the back of the neck, I walk him to where the end of the rope hangs and roughly yank his arms behind his back, not bothered that his elbow is broken and he has a knife sticking out of his shoulder.

Once his wrists are tied tight, I pick up the other end of the rope and smile. We lock eyes, and I'll give it to him, he doesn't beg. He simply stares at me as I pull down on the rope with all my strength, dislocating his shoulders as his arms hyperextend.

This position restricts airflow, and he wheezes, desperately gasping for air.

"This is how my mum would have felt, gaspin' for air as you brutalized her in every way possible."

The memory has me pulling down harder, and when I hear a snap, I know Sean's shoulder has popped free from the socket. He sags forward, strung up with no place to go. I loosen the tension, allowing him a moment of reprieve because I don't want him passing out yet.

Where's the fun in that?

He greedily gulps in air, and just when he thinks I'm done, I pull down on the rope again. This time, I hear a crack, followed by a guttural scream as his feet lift off the floor.

"Yeo!"

"Puck, that's enough," Cian says, covering his mouth, horrified.

"Naw, it's not enough. I'm just gettin' started."

Sean won't die if I continue yanking on this rope. He's bound to pass out from the pain, but I can wake him as I extract another tooth.

"Puck, please...stop," Sean pants, his chin drooped to his chest.

I laugh in response. "Quit bein' such a pussy. My mum endured a lot more than you have. Yer fucking pathetic. Cian, will ya do me a kindness and hold this rope for me?"

But Cian shakes his head. "He's had enough."

"It'll never be enough," I correct, mesmerized by the blood splatter on the floor. "This is what ya wanted, is it not? This is the person I need to be to be the ruler this country needs. I stop now and that's showin' mercy. Something I cannot do 'cause it will get me, get my family killed."

Cian lowers his eyes, ashamed. "I'm sorry I asked this of ya."

But I don't want his apologies, and that's because I like it... this side of me—I feel comfortable in this skin.

"Don't be sorry. I'm not. In fact—" I gesture with my head that Cian is to come take the rope, and it's not optional.

With a sigh, he walks over and takes hold of the rope. I crack my neck from side to side and stretch my fingers. Sean has flopped forward, his arms bent back at a grotesque angle. His eyes are closed shut, but I know he's not passed out yet.

"You should have killed me when ya had the chance," I state, walking toward him.

I grip his snarled hair and yank back his head so we're face to face. "Yer just as much a monster as I am," he pants.

"The apple doesn't fall far from the tree, aul' lad," I counter because if he is trying to evoke sympathy, he better try harder. "This is all I know. It's where I feel alive. I wanted a life away from this because I like the depravity, the control, too much, and I know if I continue down this road, I won't stop.

"I will want more. Like a druggie, I will become hooked to the taste and nothin', no one will matter. I will need to feed the monsters, and I know them well; they're ravenous. They will always, *always* want and need more.

"Sound familiar?" I pose while Sean clenches his jaw. "It should 'cause sooner or later, I'll turn into you."

And there it is—the truth I was so afraid to face. The reason I want, the reason I *need* to give this away. I don't want to turn out like my father—*fathers*. It's all I know, but I have a chance to break free. But as I let Sean go, only to slam my fist into his cheek, I wonder if I'll ever be free.

The thought that this is my future, that if I continue down this road, it may be me strung up like a Christmas ham, beaten to a pulp by my son, has me punching Sean over and over again.

Each time my fist connects with his flesh, I hope and pray that it will chip away at this anger festering within me. That I will be content with avenging my mum and living a normal life. But as Sean's blood coats my knuckles, I know that it won't.

This is who I am—a cold, calculated murderer who needs violence to survive.

However, three simple words collide with my rage, fighting for dominance—fighting for me.

"I love you."

No, I don't know what love is. Everything I touch turns to shite. It dies. And the same fate is headed for Shay and Cami if I don't push them away.

"Puck…I love you. You're good. You're a good man."

"No!" I cry, refusing to let those words win.

I continue slamming my fists into Sean—his face, his body, any part of him that is exposed, I will violate and destroy. It's what he taught me when he made me watch my mum be slain.

"You cunt! I fucking hate you! You fucking ruined my life! You ruined…me."

Sean is unconscious, but he's still breathing, which infuriates me further. I punch him in the face so hard, a tooth lodges free and somersaults to the floor.

I want more.

I raise my fist, ready to end this once and for all, but arms wrap around my middle, enclosing me in a heaven I don't deserve.

"Come back to me, Punky. Fight it. Don't be who he thinks you are because you're not. You're kind. Loyal. You are hope."

No longer am I battling Sean; I never was because the enemy is me. I'll never win this war because I need to overthrow myself first.

My breathing grows slower and follows Cami's as she takes the lead. Soon, we are in sync. Her front pressed to my back as she grounds me, as she drags me back from hell.

The room suddenly spins into focus because when I was punching Sean, I was in a blind rage. I was not in control of my actions, and when I turn around and see Cami is bleeding from her lip, I realize how far gone I really was.

"The fuck?"

But when she quickly wipes her bloody lip with the back of her hand, I know I'm the reason she's bleeding.

"Oh, fuck. I did that?" It's not a question because I know the answer. I hit the woman I love with every fiber of my soul. I hurt her, something I said I'd never do again.

Without thought, I drop to my knees before her, head bowed, begging for forgiveness. I don't deserve it, but I will spend every waking moment making it up to her.

"I'm sorry. I'm so fucking sorry. I'm worthless. Nothin' but a fucking arsehole. I'm exactly like the man I hate most in this world."

Something happens, and I'm powerless to stop it.

Tears begin to fall, washing away the face which has owned me since I was five years old.

With the gentlest of touches, Cami lifts my chin, but I recoil—I don't deserve her touch or her kindness. I never have. But she won't let me win. She will be my beacon in a weathering storm.

"You're nothing like him," she whispers, reaching into her pocket for a tissue.

She commences rubbing my cheek, cleansing my face of the demon which stains my skin.

"You fight to better the lives of everyone. That's all you've ever done. You've sacrificed your life, your happiness for all of us. You've been our strength, so now"—she gently wipes around my mouth—"let me be yours.

"I want you. The good. The bad. The ugly. I want it all because I want, I will always want you, Puck Kelly. Demons and all."

She pulls away, and I'm confused why as she's only cleaned half my face. One side is still slathered in paint, and that's the cheek she cups tenderly.

"You're split right down the middle. You wear two faces, regardless of if I clean it away. These scars are yours to carry forever. There has to be darkness for us to appreciate the light, and even though your darkness rules you, those glimmers of light are blinding.

"And that's enough. Your darkness may reign, but I know,

in the end, your light will win."

She lowers her lips and kisses me softly, granting me the greatest gift of all—her.

I lick away her blood, a primitive move like one does when they get a paper cut. Their first instinct is to put their thumb into their mouth. We are one—one blood, one body.

She coaxes me to stand, and when I do, I look at Cian, who sheepishly averts his gaze. But this isn't his fault. I don't blame him for wanting revenge. That's all I've sought for my entire life. But now I have something more.

A family.

Cian lets the rope go slowly, and Sean collapses onto his front. He's out cold. He's a mess, and I wish the sight made me happy, but it doesn't.

"I'll meet you inside." She knows I need time.

I kiss Cami on her forehead, still repulsed at myself for accidentally striking her in my rage.

When she leaves, I exhale deeply. "Can I nick a feg?"

Cian digs into his pocket and offers me the box and a lighter.

With bloodied fingers, I reach for them and go outside. I need fresh air; I need to feel it on my heated cheeks to remind me that I'm still alive.

My hands shake as I place the cigarette into my mouth, cupping it to light it. Once the nicotine hits my lungs, I sigh because it helps take the edge off. It's dusk, which has me wondering just how long I tortured Sean for.

I lost myself, and if it wasn't for Cami, I think I would be gone for good.

"Why is yer face painted like that?"

Shay's voice catches me off guard. I don't want him seeing me like this, so I quickly turn my back to him and butt out my smoke. But I should know that isn't a deterrent for him.

"A'll be inside in a minute. D'ya need anythin'?"

"Where's Mummy?"

I want to lie to him, to save him the pain I've experienced firsthand. But look where that got me.

"Is she dead?"

Exhaling deeply, I turn back around to face him. His inquisitive eyes search mine, and he doesn't seem bothered that half my face is painted like the Grim Reaper, and I'm slathered in blood.

"Why would ya think that?" I ask, worried he saw what Liam did.

"'Cause she told me that if she ever left me, it was 'cause she was in heaven, with the angels. But my angel on earth would look after me when she's gone. I think Cami is my angel."

My heart clenches at his innocence. "Aye, she's both of ours."

Shay nods, mulling over what I shared. "Am I gonna live with you now?"

"How would ye feel about that? Livin' with Cami and me?"

"What about Sean?"

I pale because if he knew where Sean was now and what I

did to him, his answer may change.

"Would ye like to live with him?"

Shay purses his lips as if contemplating both options. "He's a nice man. He made Mummy smile."

He did?

Shay's admission unsettles me because I never factored him into my revenge plans. By killing Sean, I'm taking away his grandfather, someone who Shay clearly likes. But Sean is nothing but poison, and I know sooner or later, he will infect my son.

"But I think I'd like to live with youse."

I know Shay and I have a lot of catching up to do, but this is progress.

He cocks his head, examining my face. I wonder what he sees. "I like yer face."

"Which side?" I ask, startled that he isn't afraid.

"Both sides. Yer half monster, half man."

Such a childlike way to explain things, but the description is perfect.

"I'm only a monster when I have to be," I explain, hoping he understands.

And what he says next proves he's far wiser than his young years.

"Yer a monster to keep the monsters away. Maybe one day I can paint my face too?"

Shaking my head, I drop to a squat in front of him. "Naw,

son, I wear this face so you don't have to. It's my job to keep the monsters away."

"But what's my job then?" he asks, working his bottom lip.

Shay needs to know where he'll fit in. He thinks if he has a job, he'll be an integral part of the family. He needs to know that he's safe, and that Cami and I will never send him away. Losing Aoife will change him forever, and he's afraid to love. I once was too.

Gripping the back of his neck lovingly, I smile. "I just want ye to be happy. That's it. I want ya to be happy for yer mum 'cause that's all she ever wanted for ya. Honor her by livin' the life she couldn't."

Tears well, but Shay sniffs them away. My courage, my stubbornness runs through his veins, and I couldn't be prouder. This is my son, a piece of me. I'll do everything to protect him—which is what makes the decision to kill Sean easier.

I may hate like he does. I may thrive in the bloodshed and violence like him, but when it comes to love and honor, we are worlds apart. I needed almost killing him to see that.

Cami and Shay are right—I'm half man, half monster, split right down the middle…and I will need both to help me survive this.

SEVENTEEN

Cami

Dawn is my favorite time of the day. A new day brings new hope, and after last night, that's all Punky and I have—hope that we get out of this alive.

I've seen Punky furious before, but last night was something else. For the first time ever—he scared me. I was terrified he was lost to me for good. He snapped, allowing me to see that he has this blinding rage inside him.

And I don't think it'll ever go away.

I thought once this was over, he could begin to heal, but too much has happened—I see that now. Sometimes, we don't heal; we just learn to deal with the demons trapped inside us.

Even if Punky wants out of this life, I don't think that he can. This is what he knows. This is who he is. And it's who I love.

Most would run for the hills, but I'm not most. We've come too far to give up now, which is why I'm nursing my second cup of coffee as I haven't been to bed.

Once Punky and Shay came home, Punky showered and went to sleep. He wouldn't even look at me, and I know that's because he's ashamed of what he did. If he had hit me on purpose, this day would go an entirely different way, but it's because of last night that I've done something which I hope will help Punky heal.

When I hear the freezer door open, followed by ice cubes being dropped into a glass, I quickly go inside. Punky is in the kitchen about to pour himself some vodka. He's obviously run out of whiskey. He pauses when we lock eyes.

At least he can look at me today.

"Yer lip," he says, clenching the bottle so hard I'm afraid it'll break. "Does it hurt?"

"I'm fin—"

He doesn't let me finish as he storms over, gripping my chin between his fingers. He gently turns my face from side to side so he can see the damage.

It hurts like a motherfucker because Punky can throw a mean punch, but it wasn't a direct hit as he struck me when I attempted to hold him back. My top lip is split open, but it looks a lot worse than it is. That doesn't make a difference to Punky, though.

All he sees is the bad in himself—never the good—which outweighs it.

"I want to cut off my fucking hands," he snarls, gently stroking over my cheek.

"Enough." I grip his hand in mine. "It was an accident, and I don't want to talk about it ever again. Okay?"

He shakes his head, his eyes still glued to my lip.

"Please. He's not worth it. He's already taken up too much of our lives."

I don't need to clarify who I speak of.

I refuse to allow him or anyone to ruin today because I have something special planned; something which I hope doesn't backfire. This is the reason I've not slept yet.

With so much death and misery surrounding us, we need this. This is the only thing I can do to help Punky understand how much I love him. That no matter how much blood he has on his hands, I will never leave his side.

This is forever…

"Today is about us."

Here goes nothing.

"Can you meet me at Kavanagh's at two o'clock?"

Instantly, a wave of panic overcomes him. "Yer goin' back there to stay?"

"No," I quickly reply as he's misunderstood. "Just meet me at two?"

"Cami—"

But I place my finger over his lips. "Stop arguing and do what you're told. For once."

I'm rewarded with a lopsided smirk before Punky wraps his arm around my waist and draws me into his chest. "I'd follow ya into hell if you asked me to."

Come nightfall, he just may regret his choice of words.

"I'll see you at two."

"Are you goin' to tell me what we're doin'?"

I shake my head with a grin. "It's a secret."

My sass soon crumbles, however, when Punky runs his thumb across my mouth. "I could make ya talk."

My heart launches into a deafening staccato, but I won't be distracted. I need to be strong and not give in to those piercing blue eyes, muscled bare chest, and luscious, full lips.

But he knows me better than I know myself, and a husky chuckle escapes him. "I think ye'd like that," he arrogantly states, gently slipping the tip of his thumb into my mouth.

He hungrily watches me, daring me to resist. I want him. I always want him. But I stamp down my desire and nip him with my teeth.

He hisses but doesn't remove his thumb.

"Savage," he teases, setting me on fire with that sultry look reserved only for me. "All right, Babydoll. Yer secret is safe. For now. A'll see you at two."

I wait for him to kiss me, but he simply removes his thumb, knowing that I'm totally hot for him. He just played me at my own game.

I go to turn, but he grips me by the throat and arches my head back. He smirks when he feels me swallow deeply beneath his grip. "I still plan on makin' ya talk…all night long."

My resolve is slipping, and just as I open my mouth, ready to spill all my secrets, he lets me go. I almost fall flat on my face but regain my footing and pride.

Punky saunters into the bathroom, knowing he's won this round. But little does he know, I've won the whole fucking game.

This was all my doing, and I'm still so nervous.

Taking what feels like the hundredth deep breath, I smooth out the invisible wrinkles in my white dress. It's a simple summer dress, but when I saw it in the store, I knew it was perfect. My feet are bare and I wear my hair loose.

The only piece of jewelry I wear is my necklace with Cara's rose brooch. I'll never forget it once belonged to her and the importance this brooch holds. The moment I stole it, I knew my life would be changed forevermore.

It seems fitting I wear it today.

"Are ya ready, love?" Aine asks, ducking her head into the bedroom. "He's been waitin' for twenty minutes."

Nodding at my reflection in the mirror, I take my last deep breath. I can do this. I *want* to do this.

Aine smiles, tears in her eyes, but these tears are filled with happiness for me because I finally found my happily ever after.

I follow her down the corridor, not paying any attention to the nosy guests because when I walk into the garden and see Punky, everything fades into the background, and all that exists is us; just like always. It's us versus the world.

He's as in tune to me as I am to him because when I'm a few feet away, he turns around. He looks beyond epic in ripped black jeans, a white button-up, and black combat boots. The sleeves are rolled up, exposing his taut forearms and tattoos.

Three buttons are undone, revealing an expanse of pure perfection. The light sprinkle of chest hair catches the sunlight, as does his tattoo. His nose ring and mussed hair just add to the bad-boy vibe, but Punky takes the term and makes it his own.

I know I'm staring, but I can't help it. He takes my breath away.

"You look beautiful," he says with nothing but love in his eyes.

"Thank you."

I know he's curious to why I asked him here, but when his attention drops to my ringless finger, that curiosity turns to dread. I applied some makeup, which has covered my busted lip, but no matter how much makeup I wear, Punky won't forget. And he believes I won't either.

But I won't let anything ruin today because today is the first day of the rest of our lives.

"Do you remember when you asked me what month I'd like for us to be married in?"

Punky nods, unsure and afraid.

"And you said you'd like for us to be married in the castle."

"Aye, I remember," he says, watching me closely. "What's goin' on, Cami?"

Taking a calming breath, I continue. "Well, what I should have replied was now."

Punky arches a brow, completely lost.

So, I clarify. "I know this isn't the castle, but this place is like my home. I used to pretend it was ours and that one day, you were going to walk up that driveway and tell me everything was going to be all right.

"You said to me a new day means hope, and you hoped that come nightfall, I would tell you what date I was going to be your wife. That date…it's now. I want to be your wife. No more waiting."

Punky is quiet, and I can see I've caught him off guard. His silence makes me nervous. Have I acted in haste?

Tomorrow we face the unknown, but that's not the reason I want to marry him. I've wanted to be his since the moment we met.

"Puck?" I coax when he continues staring at me, not saying a word. "We can wait—"

"No, we cannot," he finally speaks. "I want you. Always and forever. And I want you to be my wife."

Tears well. I'm unable to wipe my smile away.

"Let's do this then."

Aine stands in front of us, book in hand. Punky purses his lips, confused.

"I'm an officiant, lad," she explains, slipping on her silver-rimmed glasses. "Comes in handy for times such as this."

I can't help but laugh as Aine told me she got her license because there is something magical about Kavanagh's that has couples falling in love and wanting to get married. She said it was impossible to find a minister at the last minute, so she took matters into her own hands—who was she to stand in the way of love?

I think Aine is an old romantic at heart, but I dare not tell her that.

This idea of mine was sprung late last night, so it was a no-brainer who I wanted to marry us and where. There are no guests. Just two witnesses to make this official. But that's how I want it. When Shay is older, I will explain why, but I didn't think it was in good taste to have him at our wedding with his mom not even buried yet.

He's with Ethan, Hannah, and Eva, who have no idea about today. With everything going on and about to happen, getting married in the middle of it all may seem like a crazy idea, but Punky and I have never lived by the rules.

Crazy is where we thrive.

Aine opens her ceremonial book and clears her throat. "When I met Cami, she was broken. Like a caged bird, her wings were clipped."

Punky takes my hands into his, squeezing softly as we stand face to face.

"I thought if I opened her cage, she would eventually fly free, but lookin' at youse before me, I see she was waitin' for her mate to fly free with. The door was always open, but she chose to stay waitin', waitin' for you."

Punky's eyes soften because the analogy is perfect.

There was never another choice—it was always him.

"Marriage is a sacred vow we make to one another; a lifelong promise that no matter what, we choose that person. Always and forever. Do you, Puck Connor Kelly, take Camilla Doyle to be yer wife, always and forever?"

Punky takes a second to bask in this moment because it's absolutely perfect. But two simple words cement our perfection forever.

"I do."

A tear trickles down my cheek, one which Punky lovingly wipes away with his thumb.

"And do you, Camilla Doyle, take Puck Connor Kelly to be yer husband, always and forever?"

My heart is beating so fast. "I do."

Punky smiles, a true, genuine smile that lights up my entire world.

"Grand. Have ye got the rings?"

Punky's mouth pops open, as this is something he forgot about. But I've got it covered.

Reaching into my pocket, I produce two white gold wedding bands. They're simple, which is what I wanted. Their significance is priceless, however.

Nostalgia washes over Punky when he sees the two matching rings. I'm pleased he likes them as early this morning when he was still asleep, I paid a visit to the jeweler and bought them.

I hand them to Aine, who places them into her upturned palm. "A ring has no end, which displays yer lifelong commitment to each other. Puck, repeat after me."

She offers him my ring, which he accepts, and he recites the vow after Aine.

"I give you this ring as a symbol of my love. I give you everythin' I am. Now and forever. My heart and soul belong to you."

As he slips the ring onto my finger, I realize everything we endured has led us to this moment. And no matter what faces us, we will tackle it together.

When Aine asks me to do the same to Punky, I repeat the vows, my voice trembling because this day will be one I cherish and remember for the rest of my days. The ring is a perfect fit. He is mine. And I am his. Seeing him wear a wedding ring, *my* ring, does something to me which I never anticipated.

I feel whole; for the first time in my life, I'm complete.

"I now pronounce ye husband and wife. You may kiss—"

Aine doesn't even have a chance to finish her sentence because Puck swoops forward and slams his mouth to mine. I stand on tippy-toes, threading my arms around his nape as we seal our union with an affectionate kiss.

"Mine," he whispers against my lips, his possessive tone doing things to me, which turns my cheeks a bright red.

"Congratulations," Aine says, truly happy for me.

"Thank you. For everything." Aine and this place were a haven for me, and now, it's the place where I made my love for Punky official.

"I've prepared a little somethin' for youse." She gestures with her chin toward a picnic basket. "To the happy couple."

"Oh, Aine. It's too much. Thank you."

She smiles, and although she may have disliked Punky when she first met him because she thought he was the reason I was so sad all the time, she can now see that's not the case. I was sad because I was without him—without my other half.

"Thank you, Aine," he says with a polite nod. "This was grand."

"Yer welcome. But if ye break her heart, A'll break yer legs."

"Aine!" I scold playfully.

Punky chuckles. "I'd break my own legs, but y've got yerself a deal."

Linking my fingers through his, we collect the picnic basket, and Punky allows me to lead him as I know the grounds better than he does.

He doesn't ask where we're going. He follows as I lead him away from the property. I know the perfect place. The landscape gets a little rougher, and when we're enveloped in a green wonderland, I take a deep breath.

I used to come out here to think, which was often. It was the only place I felt like I could breathe. Guests never ventured out this far because there is no path and one could easily become lost. But that's the exact reason I would spend hours out here, happy to be lost to the silence.

But now, I'm happy to share the silence with my husband.

"It's beautiful out here," Punky says as we reach the lake.

Setting the basket down near my favorite towering tree, I open it and retrieve the red picnic blanket Aine packed for us. Spreading it out on the ground, I'm about to sit, but Punky picks me up and takes me to the ground with him.

Laughing, I straddle him as he gets comfortable against the trunk of the tree. We're inches apart, and I take a moment to admire the man I intend to spend the rest of my life with.

Running my fingers across his cheek, I appreciate how he's grown from when we first met. Punky has always had an edge, but now, he is a force to be reckoned with. I know tomorrow he will torture and kill whoever stands in his way, and I love him even more for it.

I know what that says about me, but it's who I fell in love with, and I don't want him to change.

"I love you," I say, stroking over his scar. "Husband."

A low growl escapes Punky. "Say it again."

"I love you, husband."

"And I love you, wife. Mrs. Puck Kelly. I can't get my head around it."

"Why?"

He places his hand over mine. "'Cause I don't deserve ye," he explains. "After everythin' I've done…it doesn't seem right that I deserve to be the happiest man alive."

"You do deserve it," I correct softly. "*We* deserve this. We deserve to be happy."

Punky senses I won't be swayed and nods.

He reaches for my left hand and rubs his thumb over my ring before drawing it to his lips and kissing over it softly. "When did ye do all this?"

"When you were sleeping."

He smiles broadly.

"I know you wanted to get married at the castle, probably with friends in attendance, but—"

He doesn't let me finish. "This was everythin' I could've ever hoped for and then some. All I care about is being yer husband. And you, my wife."

He lays a gentle kiss to the side of my throat, stirring the hunger within.

When my stomach rumbles, however, it seems I'll need to feed another hunger.

Punky laughs, rummaging through the picnic basket. He retrieves the bottle of champagne and two glasses. With me still propped on his lap, he aims the bottle away from us and pops open the cork. It goes careening into the sky.

The bubbly liquid spills over, but Punky quickly catches it into the glasses. Once they're full, he offers me one.

"To my parful wife, thank you for makin' today one of the best days of my life."

We clink glasses.

The French champagne is delicious, but when I see the array of food Aine packed, I swap the booze for the homemade onion and goat's cheese tarts.

Punky and I eat happily in silence, enjoying not only the food but our company as well. We haven't had a day when we've focused solely on us, so it's nice to get away—even for a few hours. I'm not sure when we'll have the opportunity again, so I try not to think about what tomorrow holds.

But Punky can read me like a book. "It's goin' to be all right. *We're* goin' to be all right."

I want to believe him, but history proves that a curveball is always around the corner.

With my appetite shot, I reach for my glass of champagne and toss it back quickly. I wish I could conceal my feelings better, but I can't hide anything from Punky.

"Let's go for a swim."

He stands, taking me with him as he walks us toward the lake's edge. I'm holding him tightly, never feeling safer than I do right now.

"I don't want to ruin yer pretty dress," he says, lowering my feet to the ground.

He doesn't hesitate and kicks off his socks and boots before unfastening the buttons on his shirt. When it parts and his smooth flesh is exposed, I forget to swallow. He slips it off while I stand motionless, ogling my very hot husband.

The sunlight illuminates him in a way that's almost godlike, and that's because he is—my own personal god.

He pauses from undoing his fly when he notices I'm still dressed. He stands before me with the top button of his jeans undone, revealing his defined V muscle and that soft trail of hair leading from his navel down into his pants.

My mouth waters because I know where it leads.

"See anythin' ya like then?" he teases, his muscled body taunting me as much as his words.

I'm like a kid in a candy store because I don't know where to start. Every part of him is delicious, and I want to taste it all.

Without thought, I slip my dress over my head and stand before Punky in my underwear and bra. It's nothing fancy, but the way those piercing blue eyes eat me up from head to toe, you'd think I was in expensive French lingerie.

Reaching behind me, I unhook my bra, but I hold the cups

to my breasts, keeping them concealed. Punky grins, a promise of things to come.

He takes off his jeans, allowing me to see his huge hard-on. I remove my hands, the bra falling to the grass. Now, we're both topless.

His cock jerks as he examines me slowly and instinctively, and I rub my thighs together because I am so turned on. When he hooks his thumbs in the waistband of his boxer briefs and lowers them a few inches, a whimper escapes me because the unseen is just as hot as seeing him naked.

He turns around and removes his underwear, gracing me with the sight of his glorious ass. It's firm and rounded, and I swear to God, every part of him looks to be carved from marble. His back is just as sexy as his front, and I watch as he enters the water, submerging himself fully.

It's sensory overload when he re-emerges, wet and oh-so fucking hot.

His biceps ripple as he runs his hands through his long hair. I am envious of every water drop clinging to his skin. I want to be each one, slipping and sliding through a muscled heaven. He beckons me to join him with a curl of his finger.

I am in so much trouble.

I relish in the mayhem and take off my underwear. The water is cool and invigorating as I dip my toes in. Punky watches me, skimming the water with his hands. How I wish those hands were all over me, in me.

"C'mere to me."

His smooth accent is like an electrical shock to my core, and I do as he commands.

The water isn't deep, so we're submerged to our waists. Punky reaches out and wraps an arm around me, drawing me toward him. We are inches apart, our lips a hair's breadth away.

"Yer shakin'," he says, rubbing his hand up and down my arm. "Are ye cold?"

"No," I reply, leaning into his touch.

"Then what's the matter?"

I wish I could forget that tomorrow has the potential to take all of this away. "I'm worried about tomorrow. I know we have the numbers on our side, but I can't help but feel a plot twist looms."

"Whatever happens, we have one another. Always. And forever." He links our left hands together, our rings united.

"Do you think we will win?"

"There's never a winner in war," he wisely says. "But come nightfall, we'll be free."

I don't know in what sense he means, and that's what scares me.

"Promise me you won't do anything stupid. No self-sacrifice bullshit."

He smirks. "Define stupid 'cause our standards may differ."

I playfully slap his chest. "I'm serious, Puck. Please don't do anything that will tear us apart. You have a tendency to put everyone's needs before your own. All I ask is that tomorrow, you put us first."

I know it's a big ask, and I'm being incredibly selfish, but I won't stand back and watch him sacrifice himself, which he has a tendency to do.

"I'll try my best," he confesses, which isn't promising. But it's honest. "My hope is that tomorrow, I'm able to say goodbye to the past. Northern Ireland will have a new leader, and you and I, we will have the world."

I understand this is his choice, but I still think it's the wrong one. This country runs through his blood and I don't think he will be able to give it up as easily as he thinks. Which leads us to another problem—the deal he made with the Russian drug lord was sealed in blood.

"But—"

"Enough talkin'," Punky says, leaning down to kiss over my throat.

It's a sweet distraction. "Don't you dare leave me," I warn, threading my fingers through his wet hair.

"I would never," he promises, laying a trail of kisses down my neck and over my chest. "I just made an honest woman out of ye."

A chuckle turns into a moan when he takes my nipple into his mouth, sucking gently. I arch back, granting him permission to devour me whole, and he does. His hands and mouth work in unison, touching and sucking to send me over the edge.

I grip his shaft and stroke him, the water a perfect lubricant as I jerk him off. I will never tire of him. I'll never have my fill because no matter how much he gives, I always want more.

We savor each other, taking our time to explore, but when Punky lifts me, supporting my weight as he suspends me over his cock, I know we're both impatient for more.

He rubs me over his cock, teasing me as he inches his head in and out of my sex. My greedy muscles beg for more.

"You want more, *wife*?"

"I want so much more, *husband*."

He grins, both of us appearing to cherish our new titles immensely.

"All right, Baby. Hold on tight."

I wrap my arms around his neck, shuddering as he enters me painfully slow. He controls the speed, which, to my surprise, is slow. Usually, we're caught up in a frantic sweaty mess, but this is different. Punky allows me to feel every hard inch of him, and when he hits the hilt, he doesn't move.

We stay locked, gazing into one another's eyes, vulnerable, our walls smashed down. Under the daylight, we have nowhere to hide. This is us—raw and unguarded.

"I love you," he states, melting my heart. "And I promise you, I'll always love you. I've loved ye from the first moment I saw ya. And I'll love you even after I take my last breath."

I don't want to think about anything so final, as I'm afraid there is a hidden meaning behind his promise. I don't have a chance to ask him, however, because he begins to move.

My legs and arms are locked around him, so I bounce on his cock as he thrusts into me. The pleasure I feel is beyond words. He is all over me, and I love it. I love him. The rhythm is slow, measured, unlike most times when he sinks into me hard and fast.

This is making love, I suppose. But each and every time we're together, nothing but love is shared between us.

He kisses me leisurely, his tongue and mouth devouring me whole. I bend to his touches, unable to stop myself from loving this man more than life itself. What we share is more than just love—it's innate.

He hits me so deep, a cry leaves me, but I arch into his thrusts, cherishing this moment of becoming one.

"My husband," I whimper, squeezing my eyes shut.

"My wife," he replies, sinking in and out of me.

My body is a live wire, and each time he strokes me, it drags me closer and closer to the finish line. I let go, giving myself to the man who owns me—mind, body, and soul.

Clenching my muscles around him, he pulls all the way out before slowly sinking back in. The intensity tips me over, and I come around his cock as he fucks me unhurriedly, milking every last tremor from me. I grow lax, but he doesn't give me a reprieve and continues driving into me.

He is in total control, and the more pliant I grow, the harder and faster his strokes become. I'm holding on tightly as the water splashes around us, and the moment he hits me hard, Punky comes with a low, sated growl.

He doesn't pull out, and I don't want him to.

When he's spent, he leans his forehead to my shoulder, gathering his breaths. I stay nestled in his arms, never wanting to leave this paradise.

But for us to return, we have to fight the demons which plague us. I only hope those demons don't win.

EIGHTEEN

PUNKY

I never thought I'd get here. I never thought the day would arrive. But as I walk toward the castle, I realize my freedom is within reach.

Yesterday was the first step.

Marrying Cami changed everything, and I didn't think it was possible, but we grew closer by saying a simple I do. It's more than just a piece of paper as some people say—it's a promise, one I don't intend on breaking.

Truth be told, I don't know what today holds. I wish I could say with certainty that I will survive today, but I can't. I have an army on my side, but when fighting against the unknown, you're at a disadvantage. Anything can happen.

The arsehole who is my father could put my mind at ease,

but of course, he won't.

One of Ron's men guards him, and when I see him slumped in the chair, I can't help but feel a sliver of disgust for what I did to him.

I took great pleasure in torturing him, and if it wasn't for Cami, I'm afraid of how far I would have gone. I wouldn't have killed him, but I would have come close.

He isn't bound because his arm is broken, amongst other things. But he won't escape. Something has shifted in him. I smell defeat.

"Let's go, aul' lad," I say, refusing to feel sorry for him because he looks utterly pathetic. The once-feared madman is no more.

He lifts his bloodshot eyes. "Aye, today's the day then."

I don't know exactly what that means, but I nod.

"Sure, whatever, let's go."

I don't offer him any assistance as he tries to stand. I simply fold my arms, expressing my annoyance that it's taking him so long to move.

He finally gets to his feet, taking his time to stay balanced. I don't have all day, however, so I grip his arm.

"Move yer arse, will ya not. I haven't got all day."

He leans onto me for support, and it takes all my willpower not to toss him to the floor. He doesn't deserve any help.

We start a slow shuffle as Sean can't stay upright for too long. I really did a number on him. I should be happy at the fact, but I'm not.

"Where is the big man who had big plans to overthrow them all? If only ye had yer journals to write in, I wonder what y'd say," I mock. "I don't know why y'd keep them. They're just collateral against ye."

Sean snickers. "They're also my legacy," he breathlessly states, leaning into me. "For the world to know who I was. History needs to be written, and what better way than by my own hand."

"Y'll be nothin' but a forgotten memory come nightfall," I reply, but I can't shake this ominous feeling that this is the end—for the both of us.

Sean doesn't reply as it appears too painful to breathe, let alone talk. I think I've broken a few ribs and maybe punctured a lung. But a dead man doesn't need these things. Sean is living on borrowed time.

A van waits for us out front, and I shove Sean inside when Cian opens the door.

"Should we tie him up?"

"No, he's not goin' anywhere."

Cian nods. With the state Sean is in, he wouldn't make it two steps without me putting a bullet in him first.

I buckle up Sean's seat belt. "Safety first," I quip, playfully smacking his cheek.

Once he's strapped in, I jump into the passenger seat while Cian takes the wheel. Our men wait for us by the curb, and as we exit the drive, our convoy follows.

Alek and Austin have said they're meeting us at the port in Dublin, as are Ethan's and Ollie's men.

I notice Cian peering at Sean in the rearview mirror every few seconds.

"What's the matter?"

Cian appears not to even realize he's been staring. "I just, why does this feel so easy? Why isn't he resistin'?"

I understand his concerns as I too can't shake the feeling that something lingers on the horizon. I don't know what, but I know Sean, and I know he has a plan up his sleeve. Which is why Cami isn't with me.

If we are to be ambushed en route, then there is no way Cami would be in this van with me. I've asked she meet me closer to Dublin. She's with Ron, so I know she'll be safe. Although she protested, insisting she wanted to ride with me, she knew this was the most sensible thing to do.

I don't plan on getting caught, so I *will* see her soon.

"Maybe 'cause he knows he's lost?" I offer to Cian, wishing to put his worries at ease.

Sean doesn't comment either way, which just adds to the mystery of what we're walking into.

Toying with the wedding band around my finger, I wonder just who I'm going to encounter. I hate to admit that I would have preferred it to be Liam as that would be easy. I could steal his haul, kill him and Sean, give Alek what I promised, and live happily ever after.

But the unknown troubles me.

Alek promised he has my back with whoever is waiting for me, and I know he won't betray me because I have something he wants. He is the reason I walk into this with confidence.

Shay is with Eva and Hannah. Alek's finest men are guarding them.

Exhaling, I just want this to be over with. But I know things have just begun.

Cian turns on the radio, needing to fill in the silence as much as me, it seems. We drive to the meeting point, barely speaking two words. But that doesn't mean we're not on the lookout. Every car that loiters a little too closely sets Cian and me into attack mode.

But we arrive at the petrol station unscathed.

Ron's van is parked up ahead, and I sigh in relief when we pull up beside it. Babydoll is inside. Her relief is also clear when she sees me. I don't want her anywhere near my father, so I nod at Cian.

"I'll see ya there."

Grabbing my backpack, I get out of the van and wait for one of our men to take my place. I won't leave Cian alone with Sean.

"You know what to do," I say as it's been discussed. At any sign of danger, they're to protect themselves, even if that means killing Sean.

I make my way to Ron's van, and the moment I approach the back door, Babydoll slides it open and throws herself into my arms. "Thank God you're okay."

I hug her back, inhaling her scent. "I made you a promise."

"Yes, you did."

I wish we could stay like this forever, but time is ticking, so I break our embrace, and we get into the back of Ron's white van. He doesn't waste a moment, and we head back onto the road. Cian is following close behind.

Babydoll huddles into my side, holding my hand. Seeing my ring on her finger is a powerful thing. I can't explain it, but I like it. It has me fighting harder for the future. Our future.

"Are you sure we can trust Alek?" she asks for the tenth time, and I reply the same way I have each and every time.

"I hope so."

We had a deal, and I know he's a man of his word. I also know he didn't get to the position he's in by passing opportunities by. If someone else offers him a better deal, I know he'll take it. That's business.

I haven't told Cami this as it'll only worry her.

We ride the rest of the trip in silence, but it speaks volumes as we all know the next few hours will change our lives forever.

When we arrive at the port, I push everything aside and focus on what's important. I can't be blindsided. I need to be wary of everything and everyone. Ron parks the van, and it does give me a sense of relief to see so many of our men here.

Alek's men flank us as he promised he would intervene if needed. But he didn't want to be involved in a war that wasn't his. I understand his reasoning—I wouldn't waste good men either.

Babydoll exhales heavily, wiping her palms onto her jeans. I want her to stay here, but I know that's out of the question, so I reach into my backpack and give her a gun.

"Shoot at anythin' that shoots at you."

She nods, holding the gun tightly. "I hope nothing shoots at me, but okay."

I hope that too.

We exit the van, and instinctively, I protect Cami with my body. I quickly examine our surroundings but don't see anyone yet. But that doesn't mean they're not watching.

Keeping her close, we casually walk toward the dock where the shipment should be arriving shortly. We've decided it's best to remain hidden to surprise the person or people meeting Sean. We are walking into this with complete blind faith.

It's busy, which was expected. That's why I need Sean alive. Any one of these people could be the enemy. So far, none of them look familiar. Police patrol the area as it's a breeding ground for illegal dealings.

Which has me thinking. I wonder why the peelers haven't announced Shane Moore's murder. No doubt, it will be swept under the rug. They don't want anyone knowing he was dirty. This world is full of corrupt arseholes.

None more corrupt than my father, however.

He and Cian catch up to us, but leave enough space between us that it doesn't rouse any suspicion. No one can know we're here together.

Each step we take puts me on higher alert. I continue studying our surroundings, desperate to see a familiar face in the crowd. The clock chimes on the hour, which is when the shipment should be arriving. There are a few boats and ships docked, but I don't see anything.

"This feels weird," Babydoll whispers into my ear, and I agree.

We're all geared up for a fight, but where's the enemy?

Have they been tipped off? Or has Sean been lying? Both are probable.

I make eye contact with Cian, who shakes his head. He too smells a rat. We've studied the dock and know the layout. There is no secret entry to speak of. All vessels port here so that means who we're looking for is here somewhere.

We just don't know where.

Sean does, though.

Just as I'm about to demand he tell us what the fuck is going on, a flash of something catches my eye. Turning quickly, I do a double take because the flash is someone I know.

"Oh my God," Cami gasps, hand covering her mouth. "That was Shay."

Without thought, she takes off into a sprint after him.

I gesture to Cian that he's not to take his eyes off Sean before chasing after Babydoll.

My heart is in my throat because this is a trap. I know it is. But it wasn't set by Sean. Alek's men were supposed to be watching Shay. Something is wrong.

Babydoll turns the corner, dodging shipping containers and running on pure adrenaline as she calls out to Shay. Her panic is clear.

My head is telling me to grab her and turn back, but my heart can't. I do that, and I know my son will pay the price. I won't allow him to be a victim of my vengeance. However, it's too late because both Cami and I stop dead in our tracks when we see Shay.

"Let him go," I order the woman who I do not know. She holds Shay tightly. He doesn't struggle.

Cami pales, hinting she knows who has my son. "It's *you?*" she gasps, shaking her head. "I can't believe I didn't guess it was you."

"Who are you?" I ask the woman who looks at me with nothing but pure hatred.

"We've not met, Puck Kelly, but I know you. Yer all I know."

Reaching for my gun, I train it on her, suggesting she stop with the theatrics and tell me who the fuck she is.

"My name is Annette."

"It's awful good of ye to tell me yer name, but if you don't tell me why yer holdin' my son, I'll shoot first and ask more questions later."

Shay doesn't miss my admission that I'm his father. I want to console him. But first, I need to save his life.

Cami shakes her head, tears welling. This is bad. Very bad. "She is Annette Doyle. She's Brody's wife."

"Widow," Annette corrects angrily. "I was also a mum, but you took that away from me when you killed my three kids."

And just like that, this comes full circle.

Liam was prepared to lay his life on the line for his mum because she was his ace up his sleeve—no one saw her coming. He knew she could blindside me and get revenge for the death of their family when he could not. I didn't even factor her into the equation, which is the most dangerous kind of enemy. None of us anticipated this, but she's a Doyle, someone her supplier trusts.

And just like that, the war between the Kellys and the Doyles is once more.

"The place is surrounded," I inform her, needing to bide my time. "Y'll not get away. Y'll end up like yer family. I'll make sure of it."

Her green eyes narrow, and I recognize what's reflected in them—revenge. She wants revenge on the man who destroyed her family, just like I do.

A cane echoing on the wooden planks offers me relief. We can't lose. We have Alek on our side.

Or, so I thought.

"Hello, Annette," Alek happily says as he rounds the corner.

Cian and Sean follow close behind, held at gunpoint by Austin.

Cami whimpers because she sees this for what it is. We have been played—not by Sean but by Alek. He's been in on this the entire time.

"Yer the supplier?" I ask him even though I know the answer.

"You got me," he replies with a smirk. "To be fair, I did tell you I had dealings with the Doyles."

"You fuck," I curse, shaking my head. "We had a deal."

This is my fault for trusting him.

"Yes, this is true, but I also had a deal with Annette. This is business. I'm sure you can appreciate that."

Tonguing my cheek, I take a moment to compose myself. "I'll appreciate yer mutilated corpse when I rip the head from yer shoulders."

Alek laughs loudly. "I'd like to see you try. You think I got to the position I'm in by siding with the weak? I need leaders. Strong men who aren't afraid."

"Afraid?" I scoff, training my gun on him. "I'm not afraid. Right now, I'm fucking pissed off I didn't kill you when I had the chance."

"Missed opportunities. That's all you seem to have."

Alek is right. I should have done this alone. I had enough manpower to win. But I *was* afraid. Not afraid of losing, but rather…I was afraid of winning. I was afraid of not living up to Connor. I would have rather given it away because that was the easy way out.

But look where that's got me.

"I'm here to watch who wants this"—he spreads his arms out wide—"more. That's the person I want to work with. Not someone ready to give it all away."

When Sean steps to the side, I expect Alek to reprimand him, but when he doesn't, I realize Annette's contract came with a clause. Cami and I watch as he hobbles over to Annette, and when he places a kiss on her cheek, I scoff, sickened.

She reaches into her handbag, giving him a gun.

"This is fucking incestuous. Can't you date outside yer social circle?" This isn't the time to be making jokes, but what the fuck?

"He's as much to blame as I am," I state, in case Annette has been blinded by "love."

Annette shoves Shay away, which is the opportunity I need. Cami knows it too. We just need to play it cool.

"He wasn't the one who used my husband's head as a football!" she screams, pointing her finger at me. "He wasn't the one who set Hugh on fire!"

The memory is a fond one, and I can't help but grin, which angers Annette further.

"He wasn't the one who killed my brother-in-law! He wasn't the one who slaughtered my Liam."

I suppose when listed that way, I can see why she would be angry, but they deserved it.

"Given the chance," I state, eyeing her coolly, "I'd do it again. In a heartbeat."

A scream leaves her as she comes charging for me. Sean grips her arm, however, stopping her. "Let's get this over with."

My interest is piqued as I want to know the real reason we're here.

"I can't have two kings," Alek reveals, looking at me. "I thought it was you, but you so easily gave up. You should have taken me up on my offer to sleep on it. But you're impulsive. You have a rotten temper."

Rolling my eyes, I reply, "I didn't realize this was a therapy session."

Alek chuckles. "Your father has made a deal on your behalf, to save your life."

"Let's hear it then."

Shay is standing off to the side. I need him closer.

Where the fuck are Ethan and the rest of my men? I suddenly realize they're not coming because I all but served Alek up on a silver platter when I introduced him as their new leader. They are looking for the enemy, and I vouched for this fucker when I said he could be trusted.

He's attacked us, Trojan horse style.

The only backup I have is myself. I won't put Cian and Cami in any more danger.

"He has bargained for your life, on the terms you leave here and never come back," Alek explains, detailing a deal I want no part in. "Very generous, if you ask me. But you can take your wife and child and leave.

"I will only offer this once."

"And what if I tell ya to go to hell?" I challenge, not backing down.

"Then I make you watch as I kill your family," he calmly replies. "You're a risk to me alive, and honestly, I'd rather you were dead. But a deal's a deal."

"Oh, you think yer funny?" I mock because what about our deal? Clearly, they mean nothing to him.

"Hilarious," he counters while Austin's lips twitch. "I think it's kismet—a Doyle and a Kelly uniting this country."

"And I think you shouldn't speak on matters ye have no idea about," I warn, my gun never wavering from him.

The more he speaks, the angrier I become. Not at him, but rather, myself. I was so worried about Sean betraying us, I didn't even see this arsehole for the snake that he is. If I get out of this alive, I will kill Ron Brady for introducing us.

"Shoot him," Cian says, but I don't know who he wants me to shoot first.

Alek knows I won't be shooting anyone. As long as Shay is here, I will bend to his demands, which is why I lower my gun.

"No, Cian, I can't," I sadly confess. "I wanted out. I got my wish, it seems. If ye can't beat 'em, join 'em, right?"

"Good choice, my friend."

"Shut yer fucking mouth," I snap at Alek, not interested in comradeship. "Fine, you win. Take it all. I don't want it."

Cami turns to look at me, horror reflected on her face. She wants me to fight, and I will—once she and Shay are safe.

"C'mere, Shay," I order gently because the moment I have him in my arms, it's game on.

He turns to look at Sean, who nods.

That, *that* breaks my heart more than any betrayal. My son looking at a monster for guidance instead of listening to me—his father. Sean must have brought him here, knowing that Shay will always be my weakness because Shay trusts him.

And that's the only reason he ever got involved in Shay's life; for a circumstance such as this. To manipulate and use him for his own personal gain.

That burns the fire brighter. I'm going to kill them all, including this fucking smug Russian bastard.

Shay doesn't run. My brave boy dares not show weakness. He looks at Cami, who drops to a squat, opening her arms. I breathe a sigh of relief because it's almost over…

Just not in the way I ever thought it would be.

"You killed my sons…so it only seems fair I kill yers." Those words echo loudly as the world suddenly moves in slow motion.

I watch through eyes that aren't mine as Annette steals the gun from Sean's hand, aims, and shoots. I don't understand what I'm seeing because when Shay collapses to the ground, unmoving, I'm surely stuck in a nightmare.

This can't be real.

But when Cami's guttural cries slam into me, I know this is very real—my son is…dead, dead because of me.

Annette stands motionless with the smoking gun in her hand. She appears stunned that she actually pulled the trigger. Cami almost falls over as she runs to where Shay lies in a crumpled heap. She drops to her knees and pulls him into her arms.

"No!" she screams over and over again, rocking my limp son. But the shot…it was a kill shot.

He's not dead. What kind of world would allow a child to die in such a manner?

But when everything collides into me in a whirlwind of delirium, I realize this world would. It has. This world has taken so much from me—it's time I took back.

I raise my gun, but Annette drops to the ground with a thud before I have a chance to fire. The loud boom confirms she's been shot, but shot by whom?

I desperately search who the shooter is, but it shouldn't come as a surprise when I see Babydoll's arm extended, gun never wavering from her grip. I don't have time to commend her, however, because we have company—and lots of it.

Thanks to the gunfire, we've drawn the attention of the police and also our men. Thank fuck—the cavalry has arrived.

"Run!" I order Babydoll, who picks up Shay and takes cover

behind a container.

Alek ducks between two containers, but it's not him I want. Not yet, anyway.

Sean can't run, thanks to his injuries, but as he scales down the ladder to an awaiting speedboat, I realize he intends to escape another way. But that's not happening.

Just as he starts the engine on the boat, I jump from the dock into the boat, not bothering to use the ladder. I tackle him hard, but he puts the boat into gear, and it speeds away. I slam his head into the dash, but he won't let go of the wheel as we sail away.

We continue fighting, but he won't give up.

When I punch him in ribs, the boat careens violently to the left. I lose my balance and almost topple overboard.

Searching for a weapon, I see it in the shape of a fire extinguisher. If Sean won't take his hands off the wheel, I will remove them for him. I turn around, ready to end this once and for all, but it seems Sean has the same idea.

The last thing I remember is a flash of silver, thanks to the hammer Sean struck me with, before everything turns to black.

And it's in the silence where I remain.

I wake with a start, thankful to wake from a nightmare that

robbed me of air. However, when I try to move and find that I can't because I'm bound to a chair, it's evident the nightmare was real.

That means…Shay.

My heart sinks, but I can deal with the pain later because right now, I need to deal with the arsehole who has me tied to this fucking chair.

"Yer like a fucking cat with nine lives," I spit, eyeing Sean angrily. "Do ya ever die?"

Sean sits opposite me, casually smoking a cigar. He has every right to be smug. He beat me. I still don't understand why he wouldn't just kill me when he had the chance.

"Go on then," I coax, daring him to finish it. "Y've won. Y've finally got yer kingdom. You couldn't do that with Liam or Brody Doyle, so y've settled for Annette Doyle instead. Have you no shame?"

I don't know why I bother because his actions have proved he only cares for one thing—power. He worked his way through everyone, using and abusing them, and once he was done with them, he discarded them like nothing but garbage.

Annette was an easy target. She's lost her entire lineage, thanks to me. Sean no doubt offered her the world. She allowed her revenge to blind her to who Sean really is.

As I sit here, tied to a chair, I can't help but think that this has come full circle. No matter how hard we fought, it was always going to come down to this—father versus son. I hoped

I would be the victor, but it seems I was mistaken.

Tugging at the ropes at my wrists, I feel they won't budge. We're at the factory, not the most discreet of locations, which gives me hope that maybe a miracle can still happen. I need to stall him and hope and pray Cami and Cian will find me in time.

"Why didn't you just kill me when you had the chance? There were multiple times you could. I can't get my head around it. Why go to all this trouble? You just wanted to fuck with me, is that it?"

Sean continues smoking, but something is different, something I didn't see coming. "I knew I'd lost," he reveals calmly. "So, I learned from you. I can see why everyone risks their life for you. Yer a leader. Yer hope."

A laugh bursts free. "Are you fucking serious? The time for bondin' has come and gone. Please kill me as I would rather die than listen to this nonsense."

"I was tryin' to save yer life," Sean states, continuing like he gives a fuck. "Annette had men comin'. I did it for your own good."

"My own good? Is that why I'm tied up? For my own good?"

I don't know what game he's playing, but I want out. And apparently, so does he.

"I needed to explain. That's why I brought ya here. I want to make a deal. Spare my life. Y'll never see me again. I can't beat you; I see that now. I always wanted to rule with ya, son. I've not made that a secret."

"Bullshit! This is another one of yer mind games."

"No, it's not. I thought I wanted this, and I did. But with you alive, I can't win. I don't want to win."

I don't want to believe him, but he's had ample opportunity to kill me or have me killed, yet here I am, still breathing. "You couldn't do it," I state, shaking my head in disgust. "When it got too hard, you realized it wasn't worth the hassle.

"Do you know how many people have died because of you! And now, suddenly, y've had a change of heart? No, I don't accept it. You wanted this, so take it. I fucking dare you. Kill me and take what so many have died for!"

This makes no sense.

Sean has Alek in his corner with Annette dead. This is what he wanted. So why isn't he gloating in victory?

"I can't kill you, Puck. Don'tcha see that? If I wanted ye dead, ye'd have been dead years ago. I thought ye'd eventually concede, but ya never did. Yer so fucking stubborn and I am so tired of fightin'. I protected you against Connor because I really do love you."

"Shut up," I snarl, shaking my head angrily.

I refuse to accept his words because they can't be true. But are they? Is that why he was reading over journals from the past? Is that why I'm still alive?

"With you alive, I can never be a leader. But the thing is, I can't kill you. So, what do I do? Everythin' I've done was because

I hoped we'd rule together. Think about it, Puck. I know I've not given you reason to trust me, but you know I speak the truth.

"All of this was because I wanted you by my side."

"Is that why my son is dead?" I challenge.

"I want you to really think about this for a minute. Every single person involved made a choice—yer ma, Connor, Ethan, Cami, Rory, everyone. I never forced anyone to do anythin' they didn't want to do."

"What about my choice?" I scream, angered he is still trying to make me believe he gives a fuck about me. But the more he speaks, the harder it is to deny the truth.

I *should* be dead. And the fact I'm not isn't because of luck. Sean has stuck to his claim of wanting to rule with me since I confronted him in this very factory. *I* was the one who refused. There once was a time I trusted him with my life.

He was the person I went to when Connor couldn't control his temper.

"You have every right to hate me. I killed yer ma and made ya watch. I am a monster."

I wait for something more, but there isn't anything else.

Sean has lied to me about many things, but he's never lied about wanting to rule alongside me. He's made that very clear. Has he kept me alive, hoping I would have a change of heart?

He comes to a stand, reaching into his pocket for a knife. I brace for death, but it doesn't come. Sean instead cuts the ropes binding me, granting me freedom.

This must be a trick, but when he stands in front of me, giving me a choice, I see this isn't a trick; this is him surrendering.

His claim that everyone made a choice is correct. No one was forced into doing anything they didn't want to. The brutal consequences were a result of their choices. And I hate that Sean is right.

"What do you want?" I ask, keeping my hands to myself—for now.

"I told ya. Let me leave with my life, and y'll never see me again."

"Are you thick? You double-crossed me—again. You made a deal with Annette! You lied to me—again. Shay is dead! You sacrificed yer own grandson for yer greed!"

But another fucking plot twist is about to be dropped.

"No, Punky, he's not dead."

Spinning, I see Babydoll and Cian enter the factory with Alek. Sean doesn't seem surprised to see them. What the fuck is going on? Did he call them?

Babydoll throws her arms around me, hugging me tight. "Shay is all right."

"How?" It's all I can vocalize right now.

"Sean."

Gently breaking our embrace, I put her out at arm's distance, begging her to explain. "He was wearing a bulletproof vest. Sean made sure of it."

"What?" I gasp, looking at Sean.

"It worked for me," he says with regret. "I knew Annette wouldn't let him live. I had to protect him. Grady knew what to do."

Sean *saved* him? No, I will not accept it.

"I don't get it. You grew a conscience 'cause you knew ye'd lost?"

"I can't explain it, just how you can't explain why you can't kill me."

"Did he make a deal with you?" I ask Alek, who stands off to the side. I can't wait to punch him in his fucking smug face.

"No, he didn't. Annette was the one who did."

This doesn't make sense. Sean had the opportunity to finally have it all. He could have gone behind my back and made a deal with Alek, but he didn't.

"Why was Shay there?"

"Because I needed Annette to think she'd won. This was the only way for you to assert yer control. The plan never changed. The players did, but in the end, y've showed the world who the real leader is. No one can win against you. No one will try.

"Not even me. Which is why I ask you to let me leave with my life. I saved yer son's life, in good faith, and now I hope y'll save mine."

Sean reaches into the small of his back and offers me his gun. Is this supposed to be the equivalent to a white flag?

So many lives have been lost, and now Sean has had a change of heart because he knows he can't win. This feels like a cop-out. All of this was for nothing.

"The choice is yours. Kill him, or let him go. What can you live with on your conscience for the rest of your life?" Alek questions with interest.

"This is a trick," I state, but Sean shakes his head. "Yer men are waitin' for yer command. Just like they were when blood was spilled on this very floor."

"I have no men," Sean confesses with sincerity. "Do you really think I'd be beggin' for my life if I did? They don't serve me. They never have. They serve you."

And he is right. No one is loyal to him any longer because no one wants to follow a fallen king.

I always expected the ending to be engulfed in gunfire and bloodshed. I think that's what we all expected. The obvious ending would be us fighting, me being near fatally wounded as I tried to protect my loved ones, only to triumph and kill the bad guys. It would be good versus evil.

But maybe this is the plot twist? Maybe there is no blood. Maybe there is only redemption.

For my entire life, I've sought answers. But some questions don't have any. They just are.

"What will ya do, Puck? I'm givin' you a choice, somethin' you were never given before. What will you choose?"

Looking at the gun in my hand, I know what I should do—I should let him go because if I kill him, I'll be an even bigger monster than he is. He is nothing, a pathetic shadow of who he strived to be.

That's what I should do…

Sean sighs, relieved I've chosen to spare him. But that's where he's wrong. This started with my mum, and it's time it ended with her. It's time I let her go.

"Goodbye, Ma."

Without remorse, I shoot Sean between the eyes, watching with no emotion as he drops to the ground with a hallowed thud. He's dead; he's dead for real this time. The gunshot echoes long after it rings out, filling the silence because it appears no one expected me to choose the way I did. But it's a choice I'll never regret.

Dropping to a squat, I dip three fingers in Sean's pooling blood and strike them down the center of my forehead. I did what I promised. I killed the three men who killed my ma.

Turning to look at Alek, I smirk wickedly.

He merely yawns in response.

Coming to a stand, I point the gun at him.

"I assume our deal is off then?" he says smartly.

"You assume correctly."

"Lucky I crossed my fingers when we made that deal then."

I have no idea what this Russian lunatic is going on about. Honestly, I don't care.

"I learned long ago that the first man to run into battle is usually the bravest. It takes a true leader to do that. I knew you had it in you, you just needed a little push. And I pushed you because I knew you didn't want to give it away.

"When I heard what you did to Brody, I organized this shipment with Liam, hoping, no, *knowing* we would meet. I knew Liam wouldn't be able to keep his mouth shut, wishing to brag about how he could fill his father's shoes.

"Plant the seeds and watch them grow," Alek wisely says. "Austin paid an 'accidental' visit to Ron, which put the idea in his head to connect us."

"And ye couldn't have just organized a meetin' with me? Why did you go to all this trouble?"

"You are noble, but the bloodlust, it runs through your veins. And that's the sort of man I want on my side. You just needed to see that."

"Hold up, yer tellin' me you set me up?" I ask, needing a minute.

"This was a test of strength and will. This was my test to see how far you'd go to protect the ones you love. I wanted to see how you'd act in war, and I'm impressed. Not only are you brave but you're also clever. And oh-so brutal. What you did to Liam…" Alek brings his thumb and forefinger together and kisses them before separating them again in a chef's kiss.

From the first moment we met, Alek was testing me.

"What do you run, a school for villains?"

Alek's laughter rumbles loudly. "I run a very successful business with men I can trust, and I trust you, Puck Kelly."

"Well, I sure as shite don't trust you," I counter because

we're not cool. He threw me under the bus, putting Shay's life at risk in hopes I would pass his wee test. "My son could have been killed."

"I wouldn't have allowed it. We saw Sean's only ally, Grady, give your son the vest. We knew he'd be protected."

"You knew Sean had surrendered, yet ya didn't say a word?" Alek had the power to save Sean, but he chose not to.

"That wasn't my choice to make. It was yours. You're far braver than me. I let my mother, who betrayed me as your father did to you, live. So even though this ending seems rather anticlimactic, it did end in bloodshed.

"Your father never saw you coming. He underestimated you. The greatest plot twist of all."

"Whose side are ya on?"

"My own," Alek replies. "I didn't know you. But I saw potential. I needed you to prove yourself. And you have. I want you to be the leader we both know you can be. I won't intervene, but I want to do business.

"In return, I promise you protection, and men you can trust."

"Why don't you do it?"

"Because I believe in honor. You are the rightful king of Belfast. No one else. This isn't my fight. It is yours."

I look at Cami because this decision affects her as much as me. I wanted out as I was afraid for her safety, but now, I have someone who is offering me a choice. I can do what Connor,

Sean, and Brody all failed to do—I can be a true leader. I can honor the Kelly name.

"But it seems you won't be satisfied until you have your war," Alek says, smirking.

I have no idea what he means until I hear car tires screech outside, followed by footsteps pounding on the concrete.

I glare at Alek, who raises his hands in mock surrender. "Don't look at me. They aren't my men."

Cian instantly reaches for his gun, armed and ready.

I stand in front of Cami, protecting her with my body. "I thought this was over?" she cries, her distress clear.

As I look at Sean's cooling corpse in the middle of the room, I realize things have just begun.

The factory erupts into gunfire as men who I recognize were loyal to Liam come streaming in. They're here to avenge their queen.

Sean did say Annette had men waiting in the wings, and it seems he was right. There are about twenty, hardly an army, but enough.

I frantically drag Cami behind a pallet stacked high with aluminum. Using it for cover, I poke my head around it and fire at anything that moves. I knew this would end with blood… and I am fucking happy for it.

This is the final fight because I *will* claim what is mine. But first, I need to kill every last association with the Doyles.

Cami stays behind me, holding my shirt as I fire at the

enemy. It's only Cian and me as Alek, it seems, *is* a man of his word and doesn't fight. This is my fight, he said. And the bastard is right.

He did all this, secretly rooting for me, hoping I would prove him right. I can see why he's one of the most powerful men in the world. The arsehole mind-fucked me and fucked me good.

"There are too many of them!" Cami cries, and she's right.

I wanted bloodshed. I wanted a big climax. And now that I've got it…I feel at home.

"Cian, cover me!"

Cami screams at me to stop, but Alek is right—the first man into battle is usually the hungriest for victory. This is my country, and I will protect it, even if I have to give my life.

I shoot at two fuckers, who drop to the ground with a thud, but three more take their place. Cian shoots at them, but they swarm us, and soon we are surrounded.

"Now would be a good time for that fucker to intervene," Cian shouts as we shoot anything that comes at us.

"Where's the fun in that?" I mock, shooting a cunt in the leg. "I'm sorry, Cian. You were right. I should have never given up. I thought I was doin' the right thing. I wanted to tell ya that…just in case we don't make it out of here alive."

"Don'tcha say that. We will. We haven't come this far to give up. We do this for our fathers. We do this for Amber."

We dive behind a stack of barrels, but we can't fight them all.

This is what I knew would happen. The enemy will never stop coming. There will always be someone who's ready to take their place, and that someone comes in the form of some ballbag who comes at me from the right, shooting me in the shoulder.

Cian shoots him dead before I can.

"Are ye all right?"

"Aye, just a scratch." Blood pours from the wound, but I ignore it because when I hear Cami scream, nothing else matters.

Jumping up, I desperately search for where she is. Some arsehole has her by the hair, dragging her toward the door. She's fighting him desperately, but she won't win.

She's been kidnapped once already. It won't happen again.

Cian covers me as I run and shoot at the man, and just as I raise my gun, ready to shoot, he drops to the ground with a thud. Cami's face is slathered in blood, and as she blinks in shock, I turn to see who shot the cunt.

"Yeo!" I scream when I see Ethan holding the smoking gun.

"Ya didn't think I'd let ya have all the fun," he quips, covering me as I make a run for Cami.

My men soon spill in, and it's on.

"Oh my God!" she cries, trying to look at my shoulder. "You've been shot."

"I'm fine," I assure her, checking her over for injuries. Thankfully, she's okay. "I made a promise to ya."

"Yes, you did. Now go kill those fuckers so we can go home."

"I love it when ya talk dirty." I deliver a frantic kiss to her lips, a promise of things to come because now…it's game on.

The factory is covered in a blanket of smoke, and as my boots slide in the spilled blood, I holler in exhilaration. Sean is dead, as are the remaining men who were loyal to the Doyles. All that's left is us.

The gunfire ceases, and the sight of pure carnality gets me fucking hard.

This is my home. The violence and bloodshed are a part of me, just as my painted face will forever be.

My men slap one another on the back because we've won this war for now, but there will be more—there will always be more. No matter if I want out, there isn't an out for me. And I don't want there to be.

Which is why, covered in blood, I walk to where Alek stands, smoking his cigar.

He has a way of being involved without even lifting a finger. But the difference between him and those before him is that he gives people a choice. If I choose to walk away, he would accept my choice.

But we both know that's not happening.

"Looks like you got your wish after all," he states calmly. "You got your war, and you won. But I never doubted you wouldn't. You—"

But I am done listening to him talk, and I make that clear when I punch him straight in the face.

"D'ya ever shut up?" I sigh, shaking out my fist because the fucker has a hard head. "Y've got yerself a deal. And this time, no crossin' yer fingers, ya hear?"

Alek smirks, cupping his bleeding nose. "Shall we shake on it?"

Extending my bloody palm, I look at Alek because the choice is his, and when he accepts the offering, I smirk. "Dead on."

The devil within adjusts his crown as he sits on his throne because finally…he has come home.

EPILOGUE

"**A**re ya sure a ten-year wedding anniversary gift is tin or aluminum?" Shay asks his uncle Ethan because this sounds like a load of shite.

"Aye," Ethan replies, quickly wrapping the small box with gold wrapping paper. "Its strength is supposed to symbolize the marriage that stood the test of time…or something naff like that. That's what Eva told me, anyway."

Shay snorts in laughter. "I'm pretty sure Dad is goin' to boke."

Ethan finishes wrapping the gift in total agreement with Shay. It's absolutely probable that Puck Kelly is going to call them out for being two big softies, but it's not every day you celebrate a milestone such as this.

In their world, being alive for ten years is a rarity, but Puck did what no one else could.

The moment he shook hands with Aleksei Popov, the world changed forevermore. He took control of Belfast and Dublin and returned them to their former glory. The fight for power was no more, as no one dared to challenge Punky.

They knew the consequences if they did.

Some have tried, but all have failed because the rightful king sits on the throne. He protects the people, as well as the countries, because he honors the fallen; and there are many.

Before Punky, Belfast was a mess. It was a mess Punky never wanted to clean up. But life has a funny way of steering you in the right direction, even when you veer off course. Punky thought he never had a choice, but the choice was always his.

He thought he wanted to walk away from this world, but the world wouldn't let him. It never gave up, even when he did.

Punky's army consists of loyal men and women who would never stray. He looks after them. And they look after him and his family. But most importantly, they look after the kingdom, which they all fight to protect.

Every king needs his queen, and Camilla Kelly has forever been Punky's queen. She sits by his throne, forever loyal, forever his Babydoll.

Shay has two brothers and one sister, and although his real mum, Aoife, was killed, Cami never once made him feel like anything but her own. He takes the role of big brother very seriously.

"Shay!" shrieks Maya, running toward him as he walks down the corridor.

He bends low to pick her up. "Bout ye, wee dote? Where's the fire?"

"Benjamin is being a dickhead. He stole my Barbie doll."

"Maya!" Shay scolds, attempting to hide his smile because hearing a five-year-old curse is fucking hilarious. "What did I tell ya about swearin'? Especially 'bout yer brother."

She pouts, knowing Shay doesn't stand a chance. She has him wrapped around her little finger. "Can ya come play outside with me?"

"Maybe later. I've got to see Da."

"Are ya gettin' the punks again?"

Shay's mouth falls open before he chuckles. "Who told ya I did that?"

Maya rolls her eyes. "No one told me. But I seen ya practicin' in the mirror."

"Practicin' what?"

Maya puts her fingers together, mimicking a gun, and lowers her voice. "Do ya feel lucky? Well, do ya, punk?"

Shay turns a blistering shade of red while Ethan covers his snort behind his hand. "I don't know what yer talkin' 'bout. Go play with yer brothers. And be nice."

He lowers her to the floor, where she takes off into a spirited skip. That wee doll is exactly like her mum.

Ethan doesn't say a word—for now. But that will change once they're out tonight meeting with their supplier. Ethan intends to ask Shay to see the *Dirty Harry* impression for himself.

Even though Punky is the king of this town, Ethan, Cian, and Shay are his right-hand men. Shay is sixteen years old, and although his father wishes he would wait, he knows the choice is Shay's to make.

Shay is the spit of his dad—in looks as well as character, so Punky knows there is no changing Shay's mind.

Shay and Ethan knock on Punky's office door before entering. Alek stands when they enter.

This aul' fucker is a handsome devil, but Shay's attention is instantly diverted to his daughter, Irina. She is beyond beautiful. But he doesn't stare for too long because he knows she will cut out his eyeballs. She scares him more than her Russian drug lord father.

"It's been a pleasure. As always." Alek stands, buttoning his jacket.

Irina kisses both of Punky's cheeks. "Thank you for offering me your home as a place to stay while I study abroad."

Her smooth Russian accent hits Shay low, but he remains composed as he knows Alek is watching and isn't afraid to castrate him for looking at his daughter.

"Maybe this isn't—"

"Papa," Irina interrupts, rolling her eyes.

She's the only person who could do either of those things to the infamous Aleksei Popov.

She doesn't address Shay as she passes him by, but she makes sure her arm skims his, a silent, flirty exchange for his eyes only. He's a goner.

Alek isn't as subtle, however. With Irina out of the room, he peers at Shay and states very calmly, "Don't even think about it."

Shay smirks, taking great pleasure in riling the aul' lad up. "Oh, I already have."

Alek smiles, but with so many teeth on display, it's fair to say Alek is anything but smiling on the inside.

Once he's gone, Cian, who sits on the couch, shakes his head. "Y'll give the poor bastard a heart attack."

Shay shrugs, untroubled.

"What do ya have there?" Punky has always had an air of authority about him, but he's simply grown into the man he was always destined to become.

He did what he promised—he avenged his mum, and by doing so, he not only saved himself, he saved his kingdom as well.

He buried his father in an unmarked grave because that's all he deserved. Even though Sean Kelly saved Punky in the end, that didn't change what he had done. Did he regret shooting his father in cold blood?

No, he did not.

Sean's death was Punky's rebirth. It came full circle. Cara's death wasn't in vain. None of the deaths were as the men honor the fallen every single day by fighting and keeping their memory alive.

"Happy anniversary," Ethan says, offering Punky the crudely-wrapped gift.

Punky accepts it with a slanted smile. "Thank you, Ethan. Ya wrapped it yerself, I see."

"Oh, shut the fuck up."

The room erupts into laughter.

There is no rivalry between them, which is why this works. No one is contending for power. Not like the two Kelly brothers before Punky's reign. Punky learned a lot from them and promised himself he would never follow in their shoes.

This is a new era. This is the Kellys' reign.

"Everythin' all right for tonight?" Punky asks, getting down to business.

They have a shipment of yokes coming in. He would usually be there, but tonight he has something special planned for his wife.

"Aye, all set. Don'tcha be worryin' 'bout a thing."

Things are good at the moment, but the men are never complacent, which is why Cian, Ethan, and Shay control their own paramilitary groups. Drugs, stolen weapons, and other illegal dealings will always be present.

Punky and his boys never claimed they were the good guys, and they're okay with that.

Shay excuses himself because there is one thing he wants to do before they leave. He leaves the castle and makes his way toward the stable yard building where he lives. It was where his father lived when he was Shay's age.

Like father like son…which is why when Shay enters his home, he walks into the bathroom and looks at the face paints on the sink. Punky is very open with his son, and he told him why he painted his face.

Shay remembers as a young boy, seeing his father slathered in war paint. He was terrified, but he was more intrigued by the absolute beauty of it. The face was so raw, and Shay believes that face still remains inside of his father.

He believes it's a part of him, that he's split right down the middle; part monster, part man.

Shay has seen it. He's seen his father kill and enjoy it. But he's also seen him nurture and protect. Puck Kelly is two people, and Shay loves them both.

He takes the white face paint and opens the container. He doesn't know what he's doing but works on instinct as he circles two fingers in the paint, feeling at one with the texture. He then rubs those two fingers across his cheek.

The moment the paint touches his skin, something inside him awakens, and he coolly paints his entire face. He looks in the mirror, exhilarated by what he sees. But when he opens the black face paint and works on memory, drawing what he saw on his father's face, that's when he really comes to life.

The container drops into the sink, circling around and around, and as Shay grips the counter, staring at his reflection, he suddenly understands why Punky painted his face—it allows him to be someone else.

His grin is wide, grotesque, and his eyes are as black as the night sky. He feels comfortable in this skin.

"A little less black around the eyes. It'll smudge otherwise."

Shay meets Punky's eyes in the mirror. He is embarrassed his father caught him, but Punky isn't angry. He knew the day would come.

Shay's mum was murdered like Punky's; he was bound to give birth to the same demons as his dad.

"I love you, son. Always remember that."

"I love you, too." Shay doesn't want to talk about why he felt compelled to do this, and Punky doesn't want to make a fuss, so he leaves his son to deal with his emotions because Punky knows this is something he needs to do all in good time.

Punky makes his way back to the castle, smiling when he sees his three wains playing tag with Hannah. She lives here too. They all do. This is as much their home as it is Punky's, and if he were being honest, nothing gives him more comfort than having his family all together.

When he walks up the staircase, headed for his bedroom, his body responds to her sweet perfume, just like it always does. Just like it did from the first moment they met.

He opens the door but pauses, needing a moment as

he watches Cami getting ready. She wears a long gold dress, hugging her delicate frame. But as he closes the door and leans up against it, she knows she'll have to change—as he's seconds away from ripping it off her.

"Don't even think about it," she teases, slipping in her diamond earring.

"Too late," Punky teases, pushing off the door.

He wraps his arms around his wife, pulling her back into his chest. "You look beautiful."

"Thank you. Dinner is at seven. Do you need a nap beforehand, old man?" she playfully says, looking over her shoulder.

"I intend on usin' the bed, but not for nappin.'"

Cami yelps as Punky tosses her over his shoulder and walks toward their bed. Before she can protest, he throws her onto the soft mattress.

"Punky, I just did my hair," she weakly protests because she wants this as much as he does. Her craving for him has only grown with age.

He lowers himself onto her, nudging her nose with his. They stare into one another's eyes, finally finding their happily ever after. It's not conventional, but it's theirs.

"Shay was paintin' his face."

Cami doesn't need Punky to explain the significance of that as she witnessed Punky's war paint firsthand.

"Well, he is your son," she says, running her fingers through his long hair.

Time has been kind to him as he still looks like her Punky, but like a fine wine, he only gets better with age.

"Whenever he wants to talk about it, we're here. That's all we can offer him. We can't push because, well, he is your son."

Punky grins, loving how she treats Shay like her own. She did that since he was a child. Their meeting was fate, and he never takes that for granted. Cami accepts Punky, knowing her husband is not what most would consider the good guy.

But to her, he's her guy, and she wouldn't change a thing. Besides, she isn't one to take a back seat. She never was. They built this empire together—the blood is on both of their hands. For what's a king without his queen?

"What's that in your pocket?" She giggles. "Or are you just really happy to see me?"

Punky laughs, reaching for Ethan's gift. "Happy anniversary from Ethan and Eva."

"My sister would not approve of a gift wrapped that way," she teases, accepting the small box.

Punky crawls off her, and they both lean against the headboard as she unwraps the present. She opens the box and is unable to contain her laughter.

"A pair of handcuffs. Well, I guess it goes with the tin and aluminum theme. I think they're meant more for you, however."

She passes them to Punky, but when those sultry blue eyes lock on hers, she makes a mental note to thank Ethan later...

much later.

"What about dinner?" she whispers as Punky coaxes her to lie on her back.

Securing her wrists above her head, Punky snaps the cuffs to the headboard and slides down her body. "I plan on eatin'… Babydoll. Happy anniversary."

As he buries his head between her legs, Cami squeezes her eyes shut, moaning in bliss. "Oh, happy days."

No matter that they are the king and queen of Belfast, no matter that they've done some deplorable things, behind closed doors, they're still just Babydoll and Punky. And their love will live on…always and forever.

The End…for now.

Subscribe to my Newsletter:

https://landing.mailerlite.com/webforms/landing/b4j1v6

Deliver Us From Evil Playlist:

https://spoti.fi/3wsgftp

ACKNOWLEDGEMENTS

My author family: Elle and Vi—I love you both very much.

My husband, Daniel. Love you. Always. Forever. Thanks for putting up with my craziness.

My ever-supporting parents. You guys are the best. I am who I am because of you. I love you. RIP Papa. Gone but never forgotten. You're in my heart. Always.

My agent, Kimberly Brower from Brower Literary & Management. Thank you for your patience and thank you for being an amazing human being.

My editor, Jenny Sims. What can I say other than I LOVE YOU! Thank you for everything. You go above and beyond for me.

My Irish Queens—Shauna McDonnell and Aimee Walker, your advice was priceless. Thank you so much for allowing me to pick your brains.

My proofreaders—Aimee Walker and Rumi Khan, you are amazing!

Michelle Lancaster—you took this story and created an image which is utter perfection. Your vision and talent are absolutely mind-blowing, and I feel so blessed to have worked with you. Your photos SLAY! Actually, YOU slay!! That makeup was FANTASTIC!! I love your face! #mytribe

Lochie Carey—dude, like wtf?! You are incredible! You are

my Punky. Thank you for bringing him to life. I adore you.

Lauren Rosa—this cover was born because of your suggestion. I thank you so much for always being there for me.

Sommer Stein, you NAILED this cover! Thank you for being so patient and making the process so fun. I'm sorry for annoying you constantly.

My publicist—Danielle Sanchez from Wildfire Marketing Solutions. Thank you for all your help.

A special shout-out to: Bombay Sapphire Gin, Ashlee O'Brien, Conor King, Cheri Grand Anderman, Louise, Nasha Lama, Gel Ytayz, Jessica—PeaceLoveBooks.

To the endless blogs that have supported me since day one—You guys rock my world.

My bookstagrammers—Your creativity astounds me. The effort you go to is just amazing. Thank you for the posts, the teasers, the support, the messages, the love, the EVERYTHING! I see what you do, and I am so, so thankful.

My ARC TEAM—You guys are THE BEST! Thanks for all the support.

My reader group—sending you all a big kiss.

Samantha and Amelia—I love you both so very much.

To my family in Holland and Italy, and abroad. Sending you guys much love and kisses.

Papa, Zio Nello, Zio Frank, Zia Rosetta, and Zia Giuseppina—you are in our hearts. Always.

My fur babies—mamma loves you so much! Dacca, I know

you're hanging with Jaggy, Dina, Ninja, and Papa.

To anyone I have missed, I'm sorry. It wasn't intentional!

Last but certainly not least, I want to thank YOU! Thank you for welcoming me into your hearts and homes. My readers are the BEST readers in this entire universe! Love you all!

ABOUT THE AUTHOR

Monica James spent her youth devouring the works of Anne Rice, William Shakespeare, and Emily Dickinson.

When she is not writing, Monica is busy running her own business, but she always finds a balance between the two. She enjoys writing honest, heartfelt, and turbulent stories, hoping to leave an imprint on her readers. She draws her inspiration from life.

She is a bestselling author in the U.S.A., Australia, Canada, France, Germany, Israel, and The U.K.

Monica James resides in Melbourne, Australia, with her wonderful family, and menagerie of animals. She is slightly obsessed with cats, chucks, and lip gloss, and secretly wishes she was a ninja on the weekends.

CONNECT WITH
MONICA JAMES

Facebook: facebook.com/authormonicajames

Twitter: twitter.com/monicajames81

Goodreads: goodreads.com/MonicaJames

Instagram: instagram.com/authormonicajames

Website: authormonicajames.com

Pinterest: pinterest.com/monicajames81

BookBub: bookbub.com/authors/monica-james

Amazon: https://amzn.to/2EWZSyS

Join my Reader Group: http://bit.ly/2nUaRyi

www.ingramcontent.com/pod-product-compliance
Lightning Source LLC
Chambersburg PA
CBHW070203120726
47909CB00001B/237